A Case of INFATUATION

By W.S. Gager

Oak Tree Press
Taylorville, Illinois

Oak Tree Press books may be purchased for educational, business or sales promotional purposes. Contact Publisher for quantity discounts.

First Edition, June 2009

978-1-892343-58-1

LCCN 2009930202

For J.S., N.S., and A.S. for always giving me
space and car time to write.

For T.G. and M.M. and especially for E.J. for always
pushing me into action.

Prologue

He had to kill them tonight.

These FBI agents thought they were safe, that nothing could touch them in this All American City. He studied the nearly dark house, watching for movement from his rented sedan. Only two small pockets of light were visible. One illuminated the second floor and another in the back of the ground floor.

He assumed they were nightlights, which made him laugh. Two tough FBI agents used nightlights so they didn't fall. Maybe they were scared of the dark. He'd show them what dark was. For the past hour, he'd been watching for an opportunity to settle an old score. Now that it was nearing midnight, it was time.

Luck was with him, when he spotted them sipping their champagne before they recognized him. Missing his four-star dinner would be a small price to pay for his revenge. His orders were to maintain a low profile and train the men in secrecy for their mission but he couldn't resist taking out an old nemesis. This execution would be worth it for the break in protocol. He was a master assassin. He would be in and out and no one would know. Maybe no one would find the bodies until after his mission was over.

Since following them home an hour ago, he watched the movements within the middle-class home. Now the house was dark, except for the nightlights for the scaredy-cat Federal officials.

Pulling his SIG Sauer from his pocket, he twisted on the silencer. He automatically dropped the magazine into his palm to see the full fifteen rounds were ready, then snapped it back into place. He'd only need two, but he always traveled with a full clip and a spare.

Sticking the gun into his waistband and the extra clip in his jacket pocket, he patted both to make sure they were secure.

He opened the car door and climbed out, scanning the neighborhood for witnesses. The lack of movement and noise increased his confidence. Not even a dog's bark broke the night. He wiped a line of sweat that broke over his forehead as the hot, humid air hit him after the air conditioned comfort of the car. His eyes continually scanned the street but he forced his gait to be casual as if he was out for walk a without a care in the world, his gloved hands hidden in his pocket. As he approached the porch, he took a last look up and down before he slid into the shadows, then moved beside the front door. The porch ran across the front with a white-rail fence that created deep shadows hiding his movements. *So stupid for law enforcement officers to have an entry shrouded in shadows.* The darkness hid his form as he crouched pulling the three slim picks from his pants' pocket. He manipulated them in the lock mechanism, then eased open the door. *So easy,* as he slipped inside. *Stupid infidels. They took no precautions.* He mounted the stairs to his left using the light from the second floor to guide his steps, mentally thanking them for making his job that much easier. He would like to take his time to torture this arrogant enemy but his men needed more drilling. The training was in its final refinements before they could move forward.

A noise stopped him in mid-step. It was like a firecracker in the silent home. He had gotten overconfident. The creaking step under his foot reminded him to continue with caution. He paused, listening. Overhead, he heard the springs of the mattress groan. His breath exhaled slowly as he realized no one heard the step creak. He rounded the turn in the stairs quickly. The glow was getting brighter. He stopped and peered around, making sure of the layout before proceeding. Nothing moved. He eased forward on the balls of his feet toward the light leaking out from the nearly closed door. Three other doors surrounded the landing. The first was open and dark. He froze as the bed springs groaned again. He smirked and hoped he was catching them coupling. He liked the thought of them dying just before orgasm. The excitement of watching them reach their peak before the kill gave him a hard-on that would add even more pleasure to his unexpected job.

He moved along the wall past another dark open door and smelled fresh aftershave and a damp interior. Realizing it was a bathroom, he moved forward with another groan of the bed springs. Smiling, he anticipated the moment of glory. He leaned into the room and stopped when he saw a white foot and long toenails uncovered at the end of the bed. His imagination supplied details of the woman on top. He rushed in gun out, bracing for the shot. In shock he realized that the man was all alone and facing him. He squeezed off a shot, aiming for the forehead.

He walked around the bed to ensure death. The sight of such pale naked flesh well on its way to roundness in the middle repulsed him. He pulled the covers up to the dead-man's chin turning the face away from the door. Where was the woman? The same squeak that paralyzed him earlier answered his question. He hurried for the stairs. After jumping to the landing, he saw the red of her dress near the front door. He squeezed off two shots as she pulled on the knob he had forgotten to lock when he entered.

He swore as the female agent slipped out the door. He took the remaining steps in two leaps before he heard a thump. He rushed forward to finish the job, but his aim was still perfect. She was bleeding out on the porch. She ruined his plans to keep the assassination undetected. His luck still held and no one was on the street. He couldn't take a chance on having someone see him move the body inside. He slipped toward the back of the house into the kitchen and spied a wallet and purse on the counter. He grabbed them on impulse. He barely noted the lack of a nightlight as he slipped out the back door into the dark. Cursing his clumsiness for not making sure they were both in bed for the night, he circled around the house. He slid into his car, setting the gun on his seat. A porch light was coming on next door as he eased away from the curb.

Chapter 1

The moment Patrenka Peterson walked into the newsroom on three-inch strapless stilettos, I was drooling and hard. I don't know if it was the delicate point of her nose and the chin set off by the aristocratic cheek bones or the sultry way she assessed the newsroom looking for a victim. I wanted to jump up and volunteer. Pain from her would be pure pleasure. The instant attraction should have warned me to stay clear of this babe. She was trouble with a capital T, but I couldn't look away.

Her finely-toned legs made me want to run to a gym and pump some iron before approaching. I had paused to stretch out my stiff back muscles after being hunched over the keyboard writing up a murder-suicide for the next morning's edition, when she entered.

No other woman created such a visceral reaction in me. Women seldom were on my radar unless they had information I needed. After ten years of seeing dead bodies and writing about families ripped apart by blood and violence, I thought I was immune to all that emotional crap. I was a loner and I enjoyed my solitude.

I didn't know why she walked into my newsroom. I knew I had to meet her. Lifting my six-foot frame from my chair in a trance, I hit my hip on the edge of the desk. She hadn't moved her stance from inside the doorway as if she were a model waiting for a photographer to take her picture. Her sharp glance assessed the room and missed nothing amid the bustling cubicles and fledgling reporters, each on a mission to a Pulitzer, at least in their own minds.

As I moved closer, I noticed her black hair had highlights of auburn in what could only be termed as an Elvira haircut off an old Halloween beer poster. My libido kicked in with a force and uncontrollability I hadn't felt since the wet dreams of puberty. A stream of sweat cascaded down my back in the air conditioned newsroom that I hadn't realized was hot minutes before.

She took my breath away. I'm trying to describe unique facets of a whole and the whole worked. Individually each feature was a rough cut, but together it was a diamond of the first quality. We would be a striking couple with my sandy-red hair and boy-next-door good looks.

"Can I help you?" I stuttered, after my race across the newsroom, moisture beading on my forehead at the exertion, my tongue dry and useless in my mouth.

"I'm here to see the city editor for an interview." My breath rushed out in disappointment. I had fantasized about her gratitude. I saw myself as the Superman helping with her escape from a jealous boyfriend or so I dreamed on my short hike to her side. Instead, she was one of hundreds of would-be reporters looking to take the newspaper's coveted internship for non-traditional journalism students.

"Sure, I can help you with that," I mimicked like a perky administrative assistant. "Can I tell him your name?"

"Patrenka Peterson."

Patrenka. What an exotic and unforgettable name especially in her sultry, slightly-accented voice. It went perfectly with the visual package. I wanted to continue to catalogue her assets, but knew I was being transparent in my admiration. I motioned for her to follow me as I navigated the labyrinth of cubicles to a ring of desks at its core, known as the city editors. My world had been shaken but no one else seemed to notice as we filed by.

"Ken, Patrenka Peterson is here about the internship," I said, reveling in letting her name roll off my tongue.

Ken looked at me oddly. Maybe it was my giddiness or my chauffeuring anyone across the newsroom who wasn't involved in my current story. I wasn't a team player nor did I socialize with other employees.

"Thanks, Mitch," he said, standing to shake her hand. He grabbed a yellow pad and motioned her ahead to a small glass-walled conference room that would allow them privacy for the interview. Before she walked away, I was given the gift of her smile, which I believe I returned in a sheepish fashion, another oddity in my behavior that I was unwilling to challenge or explain. I put my observation skills to the test, memorizing her graceful gait, starting at her heels, up to the black, calf-length pants hugging her legs until they disappeared under an oversized flowing shirt of fuchsia.

I was still standing at the inner circle when an assistant city editor noticed my presence and asked: "What's up?"

"Nothing," I replied tersely, returning to my cubicle. I again sat at my seat and wrote up the latest crime in the city, easily flowing back into prose. Although, I must admit, without the concentration I'd had only moments ago.

After a half hour, my stomach grumbled. I decided to check my regular haunts for third-shift officers on their dinner break and get some dinner myself. I rose from my chair putting on my black leather jacket over my collared shirt, my only concession to the newspaper's dress code for reporters. Ken blocked the exit from my small cubicle.

"Mitch, I want you to take Patrenka with you on your rounds tonight and see how she does." With that he was gone. No arguments, no refusals possible.

My anger was instant. I always worked alone. That was my rule. I didn't play well with the other reporters. Ken and the other suits in power acknowledged my gifts and allowed me perks few others attained. I didn't blend with the other staff. I came and went at all hours and never punched a time clock. That was the way I liked it. Crime was a never ending occupation in this West Michigan city of 800,000 people. My alarm clock was the police scanner that woke me when dispatchers squawked excitedly, signaling something was up. I never questioned my intuition when it came to a big story. My instincts hummed twenty-four, seven and led me off to many crime scenes, especially during the early morning hours when few others were on the streets.

I liked to think of myself as the man of mystery, who swooped down, wrote a riveting story and disappeared into the night until the next great piece of crime prose. Ask anybody, Mitch Malone didn't work with anyone and certainly didn't acquire strays. My not yelling profusely at being stuck with a partner was uncharacteristic.

Maybe my yearning for the five-foot-ten beauty overshadowed my desire for solitude. I drank in her exotic scent of jasmine combined with something earthy and musky. I was searing and tongue-tied again. I tried to bring my body back under my command, but my clever witticisms were gone. My anger melted; my mind went blank. Any other time I would have objected. How could I work? The cops would shut down if I had a shadow. But I hadn't uttered a peep. I nodded, stuffed a notebook into my back pocket and motioned for Patrenka to follow me.

My anger returned with the stifling air as we stepped outside. The September sun had set but the heat and humidity hadn't abated. I didn't need my coat but it was part of my uniform. I was always prepared for the elements. The coat contained extra pens, business cards and other odds and ends. I followed my normal route to Donna's Doughnuts a half-block away.

"Hiya Mitch," the waitress said as I slid into a booth. Patrenka flowed into the seat across from me and we locked our eyes.

"Can I get you something?" The waitress glanced at each of us. Silence. We didn't acknowledge her presence so intent on our mutual intimidation roles. "I'll start you with some coffee, then you let me know if you want to order." She disappeared.

I often brought interviewees here to make them feel more comfortable than in the glaring lights and stale air of the newsroom. The folksy coffee shop filled with cinnamon sweet smells offered a homey anonymity conducive to secrets and tonight I wanted to unwrap the package across from me.

Unfortunately, this parcel had a stubborn bow. I used an old newspaperman's trick of staring at her to make her uncomfortable, daring her to fill the void with words, but she only stared back. She accepted the coffee from the waitress with the hint of a smile and nod, but she never lost contact with my eyes. If anything, she challenged me with a look that said, "I know this ploy and I refuse. You first." So I did.

"Listen. I have to take you with me, but I don't have to like it." I paused for effect. "I don't do interns. They impede my style. Cops won't talk with someone they don't trust and that would be you."

She nodded slightly. Good! I was making headway with her.

"These are my rules. Maybe, if you're lucky, I'll ask you for some of your observations for the story. This is a one shot deal. To-night only. Got it?"

Another small nod of her head. I wasn't sure she was giving in, but she did understand my directions. She was no green kid, anxious to spill her life story and glean my trade secrets. She was a tough nut and she knew it. I knew it.

I decided to forgo dinner, as well as my usual haunts. I grabbed a jelly doughnut from under the Plexiglas dome on my way out and nodded to the waitress who filled my cup. I ran a tab. She gave me a single bill at the end of the month, which I submitted for expenses — my only expenses. No one knew when I ate or with whom. It added to my air of mystery or so I thought.

I turned to Patrenka as if it was an after thought. "Let's go."

I froze as I watched her flow out of the booth and stop. I took a deep breath to get myself under control and turned on my heel, nearly running out of the diner.

We hiked up the block to the main police station under the shadow of the street lights casting a gray shadow on the day. The station was at the top of a large hill. I wasn't sure if it was there be-cause the property was cheap or someone thought crimes would be solved faster if the cops were on top of the city. The climb to the sta-tion on foot was enough to get any heart rate up, but I was nearly running. I wanted her to fall behind and ask me to slow down be-cause of her high heels. She didn't. Instead she lengthened her stride. I increased my pace. I'm not sure if I was punishing her or me. My chest burned when we arrived, but I refused to gasp for breath. She looked ready to run a marathon. I looked for a tell-tale sheen of exer-tion on her face but only saw smooth olive skin and piercing green eyes.

I entered first and didn't hold open the door. The desk sergeant guarding the inner sanctum nodded as I waved. He gave me a quiz-zical look in Patrenka's direction, but let us both pass without com-ment. He buzzed us through a chipped metal door that read: "Authorized Personnel Only." His attention returned to the angry patron in front of him ranting about a parking ticket.

The hall we entered had yellowed from the age when the haze of smoke lingering in the air was the norm and not a long forgotten stain on the walls and ceiling tiles. I shuffled more slowly now toward the detective's bureau not expecting much in the harsh florescent light. The murder-suicide case I covered earlier was closed and the detectives would be working on older cases without much enthusiasm. I was tired from the fast past and trying to knock the women of mystery off her heels. She'd kept up and never missed a beat or even looked like she was trying, which didn't improve my humor much.

I turned to her and said. "Keep quiet and follow my lead."

As we entered there was an electricity in the air I could feel from my years on the beat. Something was up and it was big.

Chapter 2

I couldn't wait to get on the trail of a big case and give my brain some exercise. I hadn't had a case worthy of my interest in several days. I was on edge. This was a DRT, short for someone "dead right there." I wondered if it was another murder-suicide which seemed to be plaguing the city in the ninety-percent humidity that made the thick air hard to breathe. Maybe it was gang violence with teens looking for action in the idle nights that had their hormonal tempers flaring. I could feel the adrenaline pulsing. Maybe it wasn't adrenaline but something baser, more erotic as I smelled a perfume that I wanted to associate with tangled sheets and sweat of a different kind. While my body wanted to further this fantasy, having my exotic intern along wouldn't help me get the story. Because of her shadow, I would get crap for details and no access to the crime scene. I cast a side-long glance at Patrenka, hoping I could ditch her.

She raised one eyebrow and tilted her head in my direction. Her message was clear. "I feel it too and don't you dare."

Captain Horace Finkbinder was a large mixed race man who hadn't achieved his position through affirmative action, but through dogged police work and solving crimes. He gave instructions to one of the detectives I knew well. I hoped to intercept the detective, but he neatly buzzed around us and out the door.

"What's up?" I asked the captain.

"No comment," came the short, gravelly reply.

"Captain. I'm going to find out. Let's cut to the chase." This was our standard tap dance. He couldn't tell me straight out. I always had to work for information. Nothing fun or friendly about it, it just was. He tolerated me, but preferred I never enter the building. I was part of the media and that made me pond scum in his book.

The captain was old school. No reporters, period.

Other officers recognized my value. Part of what made me good at gathering the facts was a kinship with the boys in blue. I was allowed to see things other reporters weren't. I had a knack, if you will, of looking at a crime scene and seeing the minute details others missed. I never chased down a criminal, but many a crime in this fair city was solved because I pointed an officer in the right direction.

After ten years, I knew what to print and when to hold back. The officers trusted me and when they said it was off the record, I kept if off the record. I got the story right. Cops gave me the facts knowing they would be correct when they came out, something the television media couldn't do in their haste to exploit in Technicolor. When an officer might have been unduly harsh during an arrest, I was called to write the first story.

I never fudged the truth. If a police officer made a mistake, they wouldn't be mollycoddled, but there was a human element in my stories, I was told. I tried to be fair to everyone. I didn't canonize or demonize the victims or criminals. I gave them the facts, like Joe Friday used to say on *Dragnet*. My readers decided what happened, what the motivation was. Take for instance, a case of alleged police brutality. It wasn't as simple as a cop taking a few extra swings at a suspect's head after he was cuffed and pinned to the ground. It was complicated by the frustration of chasing a kid who was out in the dark hours of the morning trying to hijack a car to get his bones in a gang, or score some fast bucks to feed his habit. The frustration came from the cop who didn't want to admit they may be a little out of shape. The fear they may have met their match and their blood could be washing down the sidewalk instead of the suspect's trickling from his forehead.

I had my inside sources, but the captain was never one of them.

At that moment another detective hustled in, cinching his tie and pulling on his sports jacket. "Whadda we got?" he asked the captain.

"Don't know yet," the captain responded, knowing I was listening as well. "Third and Division. DRT."

I knew that was all I was going to get out of him. I turned and fled, forgetting Patrenka on my heels. I was on a story and from the looks of it, an even bigger one than I thought, if they were calling in other shifts to help.

I went out the side entrance labeled "Police Personnel Only" and into the employee lot. I fished a set of car keys out of my pocket and unlocked a five-year-old black Jeep Cherokee — my mode of transportation when I needed it. I always parked at the police station. It was safe and it saved me parking fees at my downtown apartment. The newspaper, police station and my apartment were within a five block radius.

I debated briefly whether to unlock the passenger door or not. I didn't need a stray but I yearned for her scent. I was curious. I didn't want her to know my secrets but I wanted her. I always worked alone, but I was willing to take on a partner for the oldest dance. I hit the unlock button without looking her way.

I started the engine and put it into gear, barely giving Patrenka time to click the seatbelt across her midsection. I pulled out of the lot onto Michigan Avenue, made a quick left turn onto Division under a yellow light that blurred to orange as I made the turn. If I hustled, I knew I could make most of the lights in the midnight-hour traffic when they were still programmed to ease traffic out of the downtown and to the suburbs.

After five minutes of driving with an intensity that usually scared passengers silly, I pulled in behind a stationary black and white. Its red and blue flashing lights creating macabre shadows on the mature trees lining the urban street.

I was the man of mystery and hated to call attention to my reporter status. Bystanders always wanted me to tell them what was happening, too cheap to wait for the newspaper. However, a reporter's perks came in handy at times like this. I slapped the "PRESS" placard from under my seat onto the dash to prevent parking tickets. It worked enough to make it useful. I only used it when I absolutely had to. As I exited, I pulled the narrow notebook, the pen caught in its revolving spin of the binding, from my back pocket.

Patrenka slid in step behind, but I wasn't sure if she felt the pull of the big story or excited to be with me. I was on adrenaline that only comes from knowing that this wasn't an ordinary crime. It was something big. I preferred covering stories from the beginning. That's the way I worked. No lame follow-up phone calls for me. I interviewed my sources in person. No one scooped Mitch Malone on crime in Grand River.

I gauged the scene, looking for details for my story as we maneuvered around the police car blocking the street. I nodded to the patrolman keeping gawkers out and shot a glance at Patrenka. She matched me step for step by the tell-tale click of her heels on the sidewalk behind me. More police cars and flashing strobe lights were a block down the street. The distance from the initial car to the scene reinforced my adrenaline rush. The further away the blockade, the bigger the story.

The block was two-story homes with large front porches and wide wood siding. Windows protruded from the second story in a mish-mash of variations on the same theme to create a homey neighborhood that had seen better days. Occupants were now mostly seniors trying to keep their biggest investment until their dying breath. Their grown children had moved to the suburbs to raise their children on bigger lots and larger houses. It wasn't a bad neighborhood yet, but it bordered some gang-ridden territory. I wondered if some of the violence had leaked out of the military zone they called the hood a couple blocks down.

I increased my pace, anxious to begin the work of gathering more details. The police were still securing the scene and I knew we were at the early stages of the investigation. We were nearly to the center of activity, when I stopped.

A woman's hand jutted off the front porch. The rest of the body was concealed behind the white railing. The long fingers were as smooth and well manicured like a hand model on a photo shoot. It didn't fit the neighborhood. My instincts went into overdrive telling me this was an even bigger story. I pulled a small digital camera from my leather coat pocket and snapped some shots. Reporters and cameras weren't supposed to mix. The digital photos easily shot in low-light without a flash helped me later to vividly describe a crime scene. Most reporters couldn't be bothered to take photos, but I was different. The photos rarely graced the printed page but were invaluable to me during the writing phase. I also used them to create follow-up articles giving rehashed information a fresh spin.

Detective Dennis Flaherty came out the front door and caught me replacing the camera in my pocket. Frowning he approached, stepping wide of the visible hand and grimacing.

"No photos." His voice was stern but the Irish detective knew I wouldn't print anything that would hurt a police case.

"Whatcha got, Dennis?"

"Who's the skirt?" he asked, nodding to my appendage whose skin glowed in the morbid scene of strobe lights.

I shrugged nonchalantly. "An intern I'm stuck with for the night. Nothing big." I gave him a look that said give me a minute.

I turned to Patrenka. "Why don't you make yourself useful and interview the neighbors? See if you can get some info on the kind of people who lived here."

Her eyes flashed and I saw a glimmer of her temper. She shrugged, smiled flirtatiously at the detective and left. No stomping, no voiced recriminations. Nothing. I had to admire that.

I turned back to Dennis. "So what do we have?"

"Follow me," he said. Dennis and I had worked dozens of cases over the years and knew each other's limitations. His mission was to solve crimes. I had pointed him in the right direction on a couple high-profile cases that resulted in his latest rank advancement. We'd developed an easy banter and helped each other through the years. We were friends as much as two people on opposite sides of the fence could be.

I followed him up the porch steps and got a good look at the woman's body attached to the hand hanging off the porch. Boy, what a looker! Perfect blonde locks I doubted were natural, but as close as you could get out of a professional's bottle. Her scarlet cocktail dress with a plunging V neckline screamed class too. For a minute I mentally pictured it on Patrenka and told myself to get a grip.

The woman was lying on her side. As I walked around, I caught a whiff of bile and rancid meat that unconsciously tightened my abdomen. I showed no reaction to the smell of blood and failing bodily functions assailing my nostrils. I saw the crimson spread congealing on the porch from a large wound in her back but didn't feel the emptiness it represented. I was used to death from too many crime scenes and the senseless violence in the big city. The loss of a woman's life didn't register except for the details I needed for my story. The mark of a true professional.

We stepped around the body. Dennis pulled a pair of latex gloves on and opened the door.

"We're dusting now," was all he said. I didn't need any other warning not to touch anything.

We entered a foyer lit by a tarnished chandelier, five flame-shaped bulbs emitting a glow through years of dust. Stairs went up along the left wall and the living room opened to the right. The entry continued down a hall, but Dennis took the stairs.

I was intrigued. Most crime is usually on one floor. Not that it's portrayed that way in the movies. The step creaked underfoot and I wondered how many teenagers in earlier days had skipped this step when sneaking in late at night.

After a dozen steps, the stairs turned to the right and rose for another half dozen before opening on a landing with five doors.

I did a quick inventory; three bedrooms and a bath and, if I had to guess, a linen closet was behind the only closed door.

More officers were in the first bedroom to the right, which I surmised was the master bedroom. Officers were milling around, dusting doorknobs and counters. Others opened dresser drawers and closets. Dennis entered and I followed.

I felt like I walked into Ward and June Cleaver's bedroom. I wanted to apologize for a frilly, pink-rose-print bedspread with a white eyelet dust ruffle. The room seethed romance, which didn't fit with the dead siren on the porch. You never knew who was kinky and who wasn't. I'd learned that a long time ago. It was the quiet ones who had the fetishes, not the ones in leather.

A bedside lamp cast a warm glow to the room that felt comfortable despite the humidity. When I stepped closer to the bed, I saw the half-inch-diameter hole in the dead man's forehead covered neatly by his brown hair. Had the woman not been lying in a pool of blood on the porch, this guy could have been sleeping.

His suit jacket, slacks, white shirt and tie had been draped over the arm of a flowered arm chair in the corner. A pair of diamond stud earrings graced the top of the dresser along with a walnut jewelry box, small lamp and a photo of a happy couple. Packing boxes had been tossed in another corner. The closet door was open and about half full with several pairs of heels lined up along one end. Clothes hung limply on a handful of hangers, boxes stacked along one end.

It looked tidy, but not lived in yet. The unpacking was only partially done.

Was this a professional hit? Somebody moved by the Witness Protection Program? Unlike movies you rarely saw a single shot to the forehead. Gunshots were messy business and this was too neat. I leaned in to get a better look and Dennis hauled me back to let the crime scene technicians do their job. A small red ring outlined the hole in his forehead visible at the edge of his hair line. The blood spatter was masked by the print of the bedspread. This was neat. The body on the porch was a messy murder. I now understood the cops' edginess. This was not going to be easy to solve. Someone had gone to a lot of trouble to be discreet upstairs and downstairs must have been a rushed job. Had the assailant been interrupted?

I started imagining possible scenarios and discarding them. Doing a slow turn, I pulled my camera out and started taking shots, when I spotted the captain's head as he climbed the stairs.

Not having time to give Dennis a heads up, I took a step back behind the door. I knew the moment the captain's frame filled the door because Dennis stiffened to a full, but wary, attention.

"Captain," Dennis said, nodding in his direction, pretending to consult his notes while looking for me surreptitiously. He let out his breath slowly as he spotted me behind the door. Working with the police was always a tap dance. Knowing when to step forward, when to retreat and when to circle the wagons was an art I had learned long ago. This was definitely time to retreat, but I wanted a photo of the dresser and of the happy couple. I needed to move the door forward an inch or two to allow me to take the photo without being seen by officers in the room. I put my forefinger on the doorknob and eased it forward.

"What do you have?" the captain rasped.

"Not much, sir. You need to take a look at this," Dennis steered him toward the bed to ease my getaway.

I pulled out the digital camera and snapped a couple of shots of the dresser in front of me from hip level. I didn't have much time and didn't want to get caught. I had to leave and quickly.

"The body doesn't appear to have been moved. We are waiting for the medical examiner and the crime scene techs to finish. I suspect we'll find the bullet exited out the back into the pillow or mattress along with all blood flow. Death would have been nearly instantaneous."

My mind absorbed the details and categorized them until I could note them. I was out the door scurrying down the stairs. The captain wouldn't take long to be briefed.

I couldn't be caught inside or it would be Dennis's neck and I would lose a valuable source. At some crime scenes, the rules were more relaxed, but this captain was by the book and that meant no media, period.

When I drew abreast of the front door, I couldn't help but mourn the loss of life. The attractive, happy woman from the photo had been cut down in the prime of her life. I mentally noted the description for my story. I bet she knew the danger and was running away. As I turned to take a photo of the stairs, a size fourteen, black wingtip made the turn from the second floor. The rest of the captain's body would soon be visible.

I hurried, around the body, off the porch and out of sight behind some hastily constructed partitions erected to block the gawkers' view of the crime scene.

I let my breath out slowly as I slipped between two parked cars on the street, believing I escaped detection, only to realize I had picked up a shadow.

Patrenka slid up beside me. She must have been watching for me. I assumed she had been waiting behind the partition. Again, my assumption about her was wrong.

"How many bodies?" Her voice shook with the words.

I turned, surprised to see her eyes shining with unshed tears or so I imagined. I surmised it was her first view of death and she was taking it hard – a rookie mistake. I should make her the butt of a joke; instead my heart softened at her naïveté. What was wrong with me? Where was the Ice Man who hated a shadow? Where was the cynic that questioned everyone's motivation? Gone. At least when it came to the enigma beside me.

"Two," I replied.

"The baby?"

Chapter 3

"Baby?" I questioned numbly. I didn't see any baby. Could it have been in a different room? I didn't see any baby pictures, toys, or nursery. I ran through my quick trip on the second story.

"The neighbor lady said they only moved in a week ago and they had the cutest little toddler. She said the woman, Ashley—" and she paused and I knew we were both remembering the hand from the porch.

I watched the mask slip back onto her face and the professionalism resume. I was impressed for a second time in less than an hour with the command she had on her emotions. I schooled my features so my admiration didn't show. I didn't want her to use it against me because I was going to dump her back on the news editor as fast as I could. I was on a case. I was a professional. I was never bothered by emotion. Just the facts.

I looked back over at the scene, willing myself to observe details for my story and not for my fantasies. The captain's frame filled the doorway and I followed his eyes down to stare at the body even though I couldn't see it anymore because of the screen. I watched him stiffen as he regarded "Ashley."

I could have sworn I saw a little crack in his armor. I mentally filed it away for future reference, if I ever needed something. This was the only weakness I had ever seen. Cracks were not allowed in the men in blue.

Cracks were not allowed in seasoned reporters either. I had work to do.

I watched as Dennis joined the captain and they conversed for a few moments. The captain was giving him his marching orders before briefing the police chief and developing the standard flat release that wouldn't tell anyone anything.

As the captain disappeared, I again approached the house and slid in front of the barrier. The uniformed officers were trying to keep the growing crowd of gawkers back and since I was behind them, they didn't even notice when I slipped up the stairs.

"I can't help you," Dennis said officially.

"I know. Just answer me this. How many bodies?"

Dennis looked at me shrewdly. "Why?"

"Dennis, please."

"Two."

I let my breath out slowly and looked around. It was easy to spot Patrenka's fuchsia shirt that had so caught my eye earlier but it wasn't a peep show. I needed information. I motioned her to join us.

Dennis started to retreat but I detained him by touching his arm. "It's important."

Dennis was smart. He knew I wouldn't waste his time. I hoped he was right. It hit me. I trusted her. I didn't even know her and I trusted her . . . her what? Her instincts, her skill? I didn't have time to figure it out as she approached.

"Patrenka, this is Detective Dennis Flaherty. Please tell us both what you discovered from the neighbor."

"Edith Kowlowski said the couple had a baby, a toddler, a small child," Patrenka said without referring to the pad she clutched in her hand. "Ashley was protective of the baby and the woman didn't get a good look at the child. Mrs. Kowlowski talked to Ashley over the back fence yesterday afternoon while the child played." Patrenka's voice trailed off. Dennis turned his thickset frame and rushed back into the house.

We waited and watched through the window as the detective conversed with two other officers animatedly and they split off in three directions. We could see them moving and turning on more lights as their search encompassed every nook and cranny. They were searching for the baby. Would they find it? Would it be alive?

We shifted uneasily from foot to foot, waiting impatiently for news. I looked at Patrenka. That was a mistake. Her eyes mirrored my pain. Pain that I didn't even know was there. How did she do that? Why did I feel pain? This was a murder scene. Nothing more. I never felt pain or emotion before. I know that seems cold, but it was the way I worked. Now I was antsy, disturbing the evening dew on the small patch of grass.

Dennis reappeared on the porch carrying a clear evidence bag containing a Teddy bear, big red plaid bow around his neck. It wasn't a large bear, just big enough for a two year old to easily clutch to his chest in a fierce hug. The picture in my mind came unbidden and with too much emotion. I was cracking. I didn't know why.

Through supreme force, I pulled it together and demanded: "Well?" before Dennis even reached us. He looked at me for a second like I had grown two heads. Maybe I had.

Dennis glanced at Patrenka and she moved him to speak by tilting her head forward in question.

"Nothing. No kid, just this bear found in the kitchen and a small box of clothes. No other kid paraphernalia was obvious. We don't know where the kid is now. We found infant baby clothes with their tags still on in a bedroom closet." Dennis stopped abruptly and ran his ungloved hand through his thinning red hair, realizing he was rambling with reporters. He took a deep breath and put his hand in his pocket, the rubber gloves forgotten in the hasty search.

"There was a small box of toys and a few clothes in the kitchen underneath a desk area by the table alcove. It didn't look like they had unpacked the child's stuff yet."

We all looked at the house, deep in our own thoughts, our own terrors, concern for the child we couldn't find. I was about to suggest an Amber Alert when the voice I was sure was going to be haunting my dreams for years to come spoke.

"The baby's still there."

She said it so matter of fact, you had to believe her. Maybe it was gypsy blood running through her veins or the second sight, as popular culture called it. Maybe she was an angel from that TV show from the eighties and had been sent by a higher authority. Now that was really a wild idea. I had given up on God a long time ago. But maybe God still talked to Patrenka.

Whatever it was, I believed her, unquestioningly. Looking at Dennis, I was sure he did too. Two hardened, seasoned professionals trusting a voice they had never heard until an hour before. Odd. Maybe we didn't want to think about anything happening to a small child. Adults had died and that was bad enough, but children . . . I didn't want to finish the sentence.

"May I?" she asked.

"What are you, a physic?" Dennis demanded.

She didn't answer, but moved around him. We followed her like the whipped dogs we were, right on her heels. Patrenka averted her eyes from Ashley still laid out on the porch, but now mercifully covered with a tarp, except for the hand.

As if in a trance, Patrenka went up the stairs without stopping or looking anywhere else. It looked like an officer was going to stop her and then spied Dennis who shook his head.

The officers were still frantically searching, but losing steam and hope. They were looking in places that could never hope to hold a living child.

Each time they opened a drawer or cupboard their eyes mirrored trepidation instead of hope, despair instead of relief.

Something nagged in my mind. Something I had seen earlier but hadn't put together in my rush to get out undiscovered. What was it? It was there, I had to bring it back. I retraced my steps to the bedroom and stood where I had been before. I turned in a slow 360 trying to figure out what had happened.

Why was he in bed and the woman fully clothed as if she had been out for the evening? Was he waiting for her to join him? Was the woman not the main target? I couldn't think of her as Ashley. Typically the victims I saw only had names after the main story had ran and all the relatives were notified.

Then it hit me. What if the woman was coming up the stairs and had seen the gunman? She must have retreated and then I heard it. The squeaky stair. Had she almost made a clean escape when the intruder caught her, before she made it out?

I went to the stairs and tested every one on my way down bouncing a little to see which one I had heard. She wouldn't have known which one creaked yet in their new home. I was only a step from the bottom when I found it. It was loud and the gunman would have heard it in the quiet after the shot.

I retraced my steps up the stairs slowly. When I made the turn I would be able to see most of the bedroom, if the door had been open.

Dennis came out on the landing from the child's room and watched me, questions lurking behind his eyes, but he let me continue. I couldn't meet his eyes, unsure what I was thinking myself. As I lowered my eyes, the bear was still clutched in his hand inside the plastic covering. I motioned for the bear.

Dennis tossed it cleanly. I again retraced my steps to the bottom and came up holding the bag as if it were a child and not evidence in a grisly death. I looked down to make sure of my footing. I bent down and picked up a Cheerio, a little crushed on one end. Was that because it had been stepped on? I looked up. I was about to make the corner. I could have seen the killer shooting the man in the bed. The killer must have had a silencer because no one reported hearing any shots, only seeing the body lying on the porch.

I felt possessed. Did I have gypsy blood in me too? I can't explain it. I was Ashley, frantic to save myself and my child, knowing my husband was gone. I wouldn't have run with the child. I would have hid the child. I looked around. The fake white stucco yielded no clues on the outside wall. The other wall was a garish green wood paneling that had been added later maybe when the coat closet was installed under the stairs below.

I was deep in thought when I heard, "Mitch."

I looked at Dennis and then looked behind me. The medical examiner had arrived and was bringing up the gurney. I flattened myself against the inside stair wall to give them room and felt the wall behind me give.

"What the . . ." I said flailing my arms, trying to get my feet under me.

Dennis grabbed my arm to help steady me.

"Why do I let you into these scenes?" he said harshly under his breath.

I turned to see what had caused my unbalance and Dennis followed my gaze. A three-by-three-foot section popped open from the wall on one end along a seam between pieces. It matched the adjoining panel to perfection and was nearly impossible to notice unless you knew it was there. It released on a spring that held it closed. My weight against it had popped it open.

We looked at each other with hope for the first time.

Chapter 4

I started to reach for the door that had opened an inch.

"Wait." Dennis said, grabbing my arm, shouting back over his shoulder and up the stairs. "Bob, George, get down here."

Bob Sever, an evidence tech on the graveyard shift, approached followed by a tall, thin guy with a large camera hanging around his neck. I assumed he was George until he was followed by a half dozen other crime scene professionals curious about the excitement. As they crowded in to view the storage area, I was pushed further down the stairs and against the rough stucco. My temperature started to rise as the officers asked what we had and each examined the door.

"Excuse you," I said, forgetting I was the guest at the crime scene as I pushed one crime scene technician away. He turned and frowned at me, but I slid in front of him and squeezed myself up a stair. My way was blocked by Dennis as he put on another pair of gloves.

"I found the cubbyhole. I want to see what's inside," I declared trying to pacify his annoyed look. "You wouldn't even have known about the kid if it hadn't been for my reporting skills."

I was sure he was going to point out that it was my intern who had the skills when the fingerprint technician moved back up to the landing and the crime scene photographer snapped a couple final shots saying: "I'm set. Are you ready to open it?"

Dennis turned and pulled the door open by the edge. Leaning over his shoulder I peered into the darkness but was unable to see much. I felt the press of the others on my back.

Dennis snapped on his Mag flashlight and the silence was followed by a collective exhale. The beam illuminated a rather large space with the angelic face of a sleeping child curled into a ball, a thumb stuck firmly in its mouth. A Detroit Tigers cap atop a tousled head seemed out of place with the rest of the body zipped into a fuzzy royal blue pajamas complete with feet.

I looked up to give Dennis a smug grin when my eyes widened to see Patrenka. She was glancing into the cubby from above as officers moved out of her way to let her peer in. Her face was luminous. A smile rose as her features relaxed with relief. She was beautiful and I wanted her but was frozen to the step. She gave a slight nod, which I returned.

"I say we wake the child and find out what he knows," one uniformed officer said.

"Let him sleep until we get the bodies out. Best he doesn't see his parents and get scared," another offered.

I gulped as Patrenka eyes hardened as she turned to the officers. I had been distracted by heaven above in fuchsia; now my mind went from wet dream back to reporter. What did the child see? Would it be able to tell them anything? Could it talk?

Dennis shut the door and motioned the group down the stairs and into the living room. He pulled his cell off his hip and hit a preprogrammed number.

"Captain, we have a situation. There was a child. Yes, alive. We think the mother came up the stairs and may have seen the shooter and hid the child before being discovered."

Dennis looked at me with that "I got away with something" twinkle in his blue eyes. The captain would burst a blood vessel if he knew I had found the child, creating the scenario Dennis gave.

Dennis went back to full concentration on the conversation. "Yes, sir. I believe so. But we have to hurry. We need to finish processing the scene. We can't wait for much longer or the media will be all over this.

"Yes, the child could be a witness and therefore in danger. This wasn't a crime of passion. I have an idea, sir, but you are not going to like it." Dennis rushed on not giving the captain time to say nay or yea. "Mitch from the *Journal* is here along with a woman intern. We could use them and a civilian vehicle. We could contain it."

Dennis looked at me and I nodded, then he turned back to his phone conversation.

"I hadn't thought about it beyond that," I heard.

"I could take the child for the night until you decide how to handle it," said the husky voice of my dreams.

"The woman has agreed. We could provide some protection. Yes, I agree, it would be better, the fewer people that know the better. Yes, sir."

Dennis dispatched an officer up the stairs to see when the body would be leaving. He peered quickly through the curtains and grimaced as the news vans started pulling in and setting up their garish lights. "Damned monsters are already here," Dennis said than added, "Present company excluded, of course."

I knew he was talking about the TV media. The cell on my hip had vibrated a couple times but I had been ignoring it, my general concession to wearing it at all. The only one with the number was my editor and I didn't have anything for him yet.

"You can care for the child until we know what we have?" Dennis asked scrutinizing Patrenka.

"Yes sir. Mitch could provide transportation out of here and no one would suspect. I could hide the child under a large jacket."

My head came up quickly as my mouth fell open. It was a great idea and I would get a chance to question the child. It would be a great human interest piece on the child, after he was out of danger. I wanted to kiss Patrenka for her quick thinking. She would make a hell of a journalist under my tutelage.

Dennis pulled on his chin thinking, his eyes on the ceiling. "That's a good idea. We won't have to wait for a vehicle." Dennis smiled at Patrenka, his Irish eyes twinkling in admiration.

"The plan is while the body goes out the front, the baby and Ms. . ."

"Peterson," she said.

"Yea, Ms. Peterson goes out the back where Sam Spade here is waiting in his dark paneled van," he said pointing to me.

"That would be a Jeep," I corrected, but it didn't really matter. I had the gist of it.

The uniformed officer came back and had a hurried conversation with Dennis who then returned his focus to us.

"The medical examiner will be wrapped up in about five minutes. Give me your coat, Mitch. The idea is to get the kid out without waking. I'm sure hoping he's a heavy sleeper because his squalls will ruin any hope we have of hiding his existence."

I slid out of my leather jacket. To my chagrin Dennis grabbed it from me and helped Patrenka into it. His hands lingered on her shoulders and jealousy rose like bile in my throat. I noticed how her willowy form disappeared into the too large coat as it caressed her shoulders. How I would trade anything to be my coat right now. I snarled: "Let's get this show on the road."

"Yes, you'd better get going, Mitch," Dennis chided as he escorted Patrenka from the room. I couldn't believe he understood my irritated attitude. I'd never before given any emotion away until Patrenka had sauntered into my newsroom. Unwilling to give that any more thought, I headed out the front door to the porch, noting that only a pool of blood remained of the child's mother.

"Hey Mitch, what's going on in there?" a reporter from the ABC affiliate yelled from behind an officer. Jerked out of my funk, I knew I had to throw the news hounds off the chase.

"You can't keep me away," I yelled back toward the house. "The public has a right to know what is going on." To emphasize my disgruntlement, I kicked at the dirt and stomped my way down the street through the crowd barely constrained behind the yellow police tape.

I jumped in my car, removed the press sign and gunned the engine in an appearance of frustration. I maneuvered around the road block at the end of the street and kept going for a couple of blocks. I went to the next street over and down it before cutting back to the alley so my passenger door would be closest to the house. The patrol car blocking the alley moved forward to allow me to enter, and then reversed back into place.

I had barely braked when a dark form materialized. My passenger door opened silently on well-oiled hinges. Patrenka was helped in, carrying the silent bundle. The back door opened and a box was added to the seat there.

The interior remained dark. I had short circuited the light right after I bought the car a couple of years ago. Because I worked the graveyard shift it was easier and safer to keep the inside dim at crime scenes so no one would know if I was in the car or not. It was perfect now for removing the only witness to a grisly crime.

I pulled out of the alley and away from the scene. I concentrated on my driving for several blocks making sure I wasn't tailed. I watched Patrenka shift in the seat to get comfortable, letting the armrest help her support the deadweight of the sleeping child. The child hid most of her body filling the Jeep's cavity to the dash.

Satisfied we had made a clean getaway, I asked: "Where to?"

Patrenka looked at me with deer-in-the-headlight eyes. What I wouldn't give to know how her mind worked. For now I could only guess. I pulled to a stop at a red light. "Where are you planning on taking care of him? Do you have an apartment or house?"

In reply, she opened my coat and again I wanted to be my coat, feeling the warmth of her skin next to me. The glow from the streetlights we past under caught the iridescence in her shirt that pulled under the weight of my jacket lower than before. A horn sounded behind me jerking me back. I pulled through the intersection. I tried to contain my glances to the sleeping child but it slipped to where it nestled against her bosom. I felt my libido kick in, picturing my head in place of the child's.

I watched as she hugged the child tighter to her, surprised by her intensity of feeling for a child she was holding for the first time.

"I'm glad 'e never woke," she replied in her slow drawl.

We stopped at another traffic light even though we were the only car in view. I looked again at the child. The Detroit Tigers cap was still perched on his head. "Detroit's a nice choice of teams. They'll be making a comeback," I said to no one in particular.

"The hat never fell off. Odd to be wearing it to bed," was Patrenka's response, but still no destination was forthcoming.

After another ten minutes of circling blocks, I was tired of driving. I had a deadline. I did another loop past the newspaper and police station hoping she would realize we needed a place to go. I was frustrated. I pulled off to the side of the street. What did she want me to do? Get a location by wavelength or ESP? I was tired of driving aimlessly. "Where am I going?"

Patrenka shook her head from side to side, dropping it down to look at the child, her hair falling and covering the features on her face.

"What? What does that mean?" I slammed my hand down on the steering wheel in frustration. Silence filled the car and I thought she would never utter another word. I started to put the car into gear and take her to the police station

"I got into town today. I don't have a place to stay. I wanted to keep the child safe."

I brought my arm to the wheel and lowered my head in frustration. She didn't have a place. I needed to get back to the paper and get my story done. I couldn't drop her at the rescue mission, not at this hour and not with a child who could be in danger.

"Mitch," I felt a hand touch my arm. I turned and looked at her. Big mistake. Her eyes compelled me, softly, hypnotizing me. "This child has been found in a house where two people were brutally killed. Don't make her stay at a police station where she could become a target."

As if all my will had left my body, I straightened, putting the car into reverse. I pulled out of the parking spot. I made a quick decision and jerked on the wheel, turning quickly down a one-way street and pulling into the parking garage below my building.

"In a previous life, my building had been the Y," I said trying to make conversation as I circled around toward the elevator. "The building sat empty for a couple of years before an enterprising developer had capitalized on the resurgence in the downtown. I grabbed up a two-bedroom relatively early in the process. I got a steal before they caught on. I suspected the developer needed some quick cash. What do you think of staying here until we find out what the cops want to do with the child?" I talked to keep myself from strangling my companion. Watching me murder Patrenka was probably not a good thing for the young witness.

My condo came with parking for an additional monthly fee that I never took advantage of with my free parking at the police station. When I had groceries, almost never, or something to unload, I pulled in to the designated visitor spots for short periods and returned the car to the police lot afterward. It had worked so far.

I pulled into a visitor space now, knowing I wouldn't be staying long with my deadline looming and who would complain in the dead of night. Without another word, Patrenka waited for me to open her door and assist her out. We walked in silence to the elevators. The doors opened immediately. We took a step forward in unison and I punched in three. The doors closed suffocating us in the hot stale air. It was a relief when the doors opened onto a short hallway in either direction.

I left the elevator quickly, letting her follow. I'd briefly thought about letting her guess which of the ten units were mine. Then another thought came to me. Had I made my bed that morning? My bed, could I get Patrenka into it? I stepped out and then motioned her to the right, my hand cupping her back to guide her. We walked by four doors before arriving at mine. The hallway was silent, but blessedly cool.

As I fitted the key in the lock, I realized I'd never had a visitor before. No one stopped by unannounced and I didn't know my neighbors. I opened the door and then stepped away to allow her to enter. I followed and flipped a switch that bathed the living room in soft light from two lamps flanking my brown leather sofa. The area had an industrial feel with high, open ceilings, visible pipes and real wood floors that could have been a basketball or racquetball court in another life.

I had a luxury corner apartment that boasted windows on two walls instead of one. It was an odd feeling leading Patrenka and her bundle into my abode. I quickly glanced around taking inventory. Only a few dirty coffee cups on the kitchen counter and newspapers scattered around my black leather recliner. Other than that, basically clean looking, not taking into account dust. The newspapers would have to be forgiven; I was a journalist after all.

I watched Patrenka for a reaction to my place but saw none. She went right to my bedroom like she had visited before. She laid the small child down in the center of my unmade, California king-size bed, pulling the sheet and blanket up over the child and then tucking them in securely on each side.

I leaned against the door waiting for her to finish. Patrenka flexed her hands, opened them and repeated the process to restore circulation. I felt like a jackass for not offering to carry the child who would have gotten heavy on the walk from the SUV.

I recalled my mother's attempt to instill manners and gentlemanly behavior in me during my youth. My anger at myself for not offering assistance ebbed as my backbone stiffened and other emotions took over. Patrenka could have asked for help, but I knew from my reporter instincts that it wasn't in her nature.

We left the bedroom and entered the living room. The cell on my hip vibrated again. I looked at the readout and shrugged my shoulders. I opened it and said, "Malone here."

"Where the hell have you been? I've been calling you for the past two hours. The early deadline is in less than an hour. Where is your copy?"

"I'm on my way back as we speak. Got a great story." I watched Patrenka take off my jacket, lay it on my recliner and survey the room.

"You'd better." The line went dead.

"Yea, thanks to you, too." I closed the phone returning it to my hip. "I gotta go. You gonna be alright here on your own?"

She nodded. Not much of a talker was an understatement.

Chapter 5

I liked being the man of mystery at the newspaper, if only in my own mind. I didn't bother anyone and no one bothered me. I wrote my stories and wrote them well and when I was done, I was on my own. No questions asked. No one to answer to. Patrenka Peterson had me beat in spades on the mystery angle. The only time she had talked with any animation was when she had asked about the kid.

That in itself spoke volumes about her. If anyone would have told me a woman and a child would be staying with me for any amount of time, I would have bet big money against it. Now within the scope of a few hours, my solitary life was gone.

The irony made me chuckle to myself as I walked into the newsroom. Ken Clark, who was coming in with a steaming cup of coffee in a Styrofoam cup, looked at me strangely. "Whatcha got?" the graying potbellied editor asked, sipping the hot brew.

I wanted to say, wait until you read it, but ignored the impulse, which put another smile on my usually stoic face. Ken looked at me again, an eyebrow rose in question. As we made our way through the maze of cubicles I said: "Double murder."

"Any details?"

"Not much yet. Cops are keeping a tight lid on things. Media wasn't allowed close. I'm hoping for a couple of confirming phone calls before deadline to firm up some conjecture on my part."

"Such as?" asked the editor.

"Could be a contract killing. Seems the couple, who I need to confirm was husband and wife, had only moved in within the last week."

"Any chance it was murder/suicide?"

"No. The man took one to the forehead. The woman was found with a hole in her back as she tried to leave. No weapon left at the scene."

"Any photos?" I paused. My photos were mostly for my use and rarely printed. I thought of the photo I had taken when I walked up. The hand protruding from off the top of the porch would make a powerful graphic. I shook my head. For the first time, I held back.

"No."

"Right. Editorial meeting in fifteen minutes. Like to see what you have in ten." With that I knew I was dismissed and better get to work.

After seating myself at the computer, I pulled the camera from my pocket. I attached the computer photo cord to the camera starting the download process. While the computer sucked out the photos, I opened a file and named it "Malone/murder/8/15/07." It was the system I used to name all my files for reference when I needed to do updates or turn the files over to the reporter who covered the courthouse beat. I started typing . . .

> A graceful, long-fingered hand adorned with red nail polish protruding off the front porch alerted neighbors to a grizzly scene at a southeast side home where two people were found shot to death.
>
> A neighbor notified police when she noticed the woman as she returned from work Friday night. Police said a man was also found dead in the home.
>
> Neighbors said the couple only recently moved into the home in the two hundred block of Third Street. The woman appeared to be shot while leaving. Police haven't released any details or suspects in the case.
>
> Both were pronounced dead at the scene, police sources said.
>
> Neighbor Edith Kowlowski said a married couple had

moved into the two-story home only days before. She didn't hear any shots.

Police have not released the identity of either victim pending notification of relatives.

Neighbors said the couple was friendly.

The computer beeped signaling the camera download was complete. Switching from word processing to the photo program, I opened the first file. The hand with the bright red nail polish spotlighted by the porch light contrasted with the white railing and dark surroundings. It looked like a still life painting with graying shadows outlining a bowl of garish fruit. The digital image was award-winning material, but I was hesitant to use it. I didn't have time to examine my motives. I closed it and moved the file to my thumb drive I carried in my pocket. I didn't trust the newspaper's computer system and always saved a copy for my files.

I sent the first paragraphs of my story to Ken to present at the editorial meeting where the editors would decide which stories would be on the front page and which elsewhere. I knew the story would make front page news. Most people didn't realize that most major newspapers printed their afternoon editions in the wee hours of the morning to be delivered in the early afternoon in outlying areas. The local edition wouldn't be done until after most businessmen arrived at their job although all the news would be gathered earlier.

I was surprised to see other editors and reporters arrive and glanced at my watch realizing it was later than I thought. I looked up and out the bank of windows along one wall. The gray of night was being replaced the orange hue of upcoming sunrise along the horizon.

With a few minutes of breathing space, I picked up the phone and punched in Dennis' cell number; I drummed my fingers on the desk waiting for him to answer.

"Flaherty here," boomed the voice irritably.

"Mitch, here. How goes things?"

"I'm in the middle of an investigation, dear. Can I call you back, later?" he said sweetly.

"If you must, honey," I replied. "But I'm on a deadline and there is the kid to consider."

I clicked off knowing I had made my point and turned back to the screen to continue pounding out the few details I knew, while waiting for Dennis. I watched the editorial meeting behind the same glass-walled conference room where Patrenka had been interviewed. I polished the story, hit "save" and glanced up at the wall clock above the conference room door. The meeting was breaking up and Ken would demand my copy . It was going to be tight if Dennis didn't call back quickly.

My phone vibrated.

"Mitch Malone."

"Sorry, honey," Dennis said. I was surprised, he even sounded apologetic. "Tonight I got a really bad one and everyone is trying to keep a tight lid on it," he said in code that meant he still couldn't talk.

"I'm running out of time."

"I know dear, I promised, but I can't help it."

"Ya, ya. This is what I got," I told him reading him my story. "Any additions?"

"No, that is even more than they want. Make sure you drive carefully going through the downtown area," he said.

"Got it. Unnamed police sources close to the chief, right?"

"Yes. Where are the kids?" Dennis had two of them but I knew this wasn't about them.

"My place with Patrenka. The kid never woke up at all, so no information there. I want to finish here and return."

"Yes, I need to meet you there, say an hour or so," he said.

"I should be done by then."

"Good, see you then."

The line went dead. I played with the story a little more and sent it to the editing queue.

I looked up to see Ken coming toward me. "Great lead. Will be running it top 1A," he said about the front page.

"I don't have much more. They have a tight lid on it. I would like to get back to the cop shop and see what else I can get. Maybe the later city editions can be updated."

"Great. Let me do a quick read before you head out."

I walked out of the newsroom to the employee lounge, stuck a handful of change into the slot, then grabbed a steaming Styrofoam cup. Ouch! The hot liquid jolted my stomach reminding me it needed more than caffeine. I hadn't eaten a meal all day and the sugar from the coffee shop doughnut was long out of my system. I made a mental note to pick up something on my way back to my apartment. When I returned to the newsroom, Ken motioned me over.

"This all you got?"

"Yes. I'm lucky to get that. None of the news shows will know much beyond what they could see through a long-range lens. Our paper will be the source for the early morning news shows. Bet on it."

"Okay, but get something more for the local editions."

"Will do," I said thinking about the child nestled against Patrenka's bosom. I bolted out the door stopping only to grab my jacket, but my news story was the last thing on my mind. Instead I had thoughts of two perfect mounds shrouded under layers of fuchsia.

Chapter 6

Wendy's late night drive thru past the police station was my preferred fast food joint. I picked up three bags of food and drinks and headed to my apartment, again parking in the visitor space. I juggled my dinner as I slammed the door shut, crossed to the elevator bank and punched the call button with my elbow. As I waited, a car pulled in the garage. I noticed the long dark shadows and the emptiness of the garage, my mind flashing to the shadows in my photo of the hand. I winched and moved back into the shadows near the stairs, just beyond the lighted elevator doors.

I couldn't tell you what had my nerves on edge. Maybe I had never inserted myself in a story before or the fact that a professional killer was looking for the small child in my apartment. Whatever it was, I was being careful.

I smelled hot fries and my stomach grumbled. I sank back further. I wasn't invisible in the dimness, but I wasn't obvious either. No one had emerged from the car. The elevator beeped its arrival. I debated on holding my spot or sprinting to the elevator when I heard a car door open followed by a familiar whistle, if you could call that off-key blowing music. Unlike most people who whistled when happy and carefree, Dennis whistled under stress.

My breath whooshed from my lungs as I stepped into the elevator and pressed the door open button waiting for Dennis to catch up.

"Dinner? Great!" he said spotting the bags.

"It's the least the little woman could do for her hard working man," I replied in a breathy whisper, smooching my lips at the end.

"Knock it off, will ya? If I get caught feeding you information, I'm back to wearing a uniform and that would be the best case scenario. I was only supposed to have you transport the kid to Social Services, not let you set up house." The elevator doors closed.

"Then I guess I can't feed you. How long until we turn the child over to social services?"

"We should have already, but because the kid is a potential witness, we can hold off. It's a question of whether we want to put other children in a foster care home in danger. At least that was the captain's take on sanctioning your removal of the child."

"Who knows about the kid?" I asked.

"Me and the captain, two other detectives and any crime scene techs in the house at the time. We're hoping it will stay under wraps, but the Grand River Police Department rarely keeps a secret for long. Unless someone else notifies Social Services, they won't know about the child."

"Any more information on the couple?"

"No. It's like they don't exist. Their IDs were fake and good ones. We're checking with the feds about the witness protection program, but haven't gotten anywhere yet. Definitely a contract hit for the man. We don't know if the woman and child also were targets or in the wrong place at the wrong time. We're running down some leads from neighbors, but basically we're at a dead end for now."

We lapsed into quiet as the bell dinged my floor and the elevator doors slid open. Dennis exited first and turned toward my door. Surprised, I asked: "How do you know where I live?"

"I've always known. I ran your plate once early on and scoped the place out right after I made detective. Just wanted to be sure I knew who I was working with before I got in too deep."

"Oh." I handed a bag to Dennis before unlocking my door, not sure if I should be offended or not. I wondered if all my secrecy had not been a secret at all.

When I walked in, I smelled Patrenka, a smell I would always associate with her. I looked around, but couldn't see her.

I headed for my bedroom. As I crossed the threshold, Patrenka was lying next to the kid, asleep. The child had curled into her. They looked like a match made in heaven, mother and child. I wanted to join only Patrenka on the bed and spoon with her, drinking in her scent and unwrapping her erogenous zones. I thought about moving the kid to the other bedroom and locking me and my intern in together. Dennis could question the kid, and I would interrogate my babe.

I took a step toward the bed and stopped abruptly, Dennis nearly crashing into my backside. What had happened to me? Hardened reporter. Woman proof. Loner. I had to get this obsession out of my system. This had to be purely sexual. I needed a quickie and then I'd go back to being asexual and uninvolved again.

As if she knew my hormones were screaming for satisfaction, Patrenka's body remained still but her green eyes popped open like in those horror films when the pretty-faced hero checks to see if the villain is dead, only to be locked in a fight for his life.

I was drowning in a sea green of her eyes and I didn't want to come up for a breath. I wanted to dive deeper and found myself being pulled to the bed when a squeal erupted from what had been the cherubic face rounded into Patrenka. Maybe the child sensed the tension, or had incredibly bad timing. He had to wake up sometime. The kid had the good timing to sleep through the murders or he wouldn't be here now. I reached the end of the bed and realized I still clutched the bags from Wendy's, albeit a little crushed.

"Hungry?" I asked wanting to add, "for me?" but kept silent. Patrenka nodded.

Patrenka started to rise but was grabbed in what only could have been described as a death grip by the child whose intensity and pitch increased, struggling to recognize something in an unfamiliar world.

"No problem," I said, walking around to the other side of the bed to get away from the wailing. I set the bags of fast food and myself on the end of bed. To my dismay, Dennis sat on the other side closest to Patrenka, opening the bag I'd given him. Patrenka patted the child on the back and muttered soothing words I couldn't distinguish. The child quieted but looked around wide-eyed ready to squeal at a moment's notice.

I opened the bags and passed out burgers and fries. My rumpled bed linens became the tablecloth as the wrappers became plates for our fast food haut cuisine. The beverages remained bagged to avoid tainting my mattress with root beer and Coke smells.

I started to raise my burger to my lips, but my hunger disappeared. I was mesmerized by Patrenka offering a French fry to the child. The tears still streamed down the red cheeks but the little body quivered and took a deep breath. The kid grabbed the fast food staple like it was manna from heaven and started eating it loudly and quickly.

"Must be hungry," I mused as Patrenka invited the tot to help himself to the fries she put on a napkin in front of him.

Patrenka picked at her burger. She pulled off a piece of bun and ate in small bites. In contrast Dennis wolfed his burger down and was looking for more. He eyed mine but I finally managed a bite.

The kid made quick work of Patrenka's fries. Patrenka broke off part of her burger and gave that to him. He started eating but was much more uneasy with the bigger piece. As if sensing his discomfort, Patrenka again stopped her eating and broke it into smaller pieces and set them in front of him. He dug in.

"Good appetite," Dennis observed.

We all stared at the child wondering what he had seen, wondering how to ask.

"Mommy?" the child asked looking up after finishing off all the burger pieces.

The eyes that fastened on me were large and trusting. I knew I wasn't the one to tell him anything. The kid reached up and pulled the Tigers cap off his head and looked at it and set it aside.

"Mommy!" came the voice again this time more high pitched. I glanced at Patrenka and then Dennis. Each was as lost as I was. What could you say to a child? How can you make them understand? How can you tell such a small child that his world crashed?

Patrenka reached out and smoothed the hair on his head down where the cap had mussed it. The child instinctively curved into her touch.

How do you question a child about something so horrible you knew it would haunt their dreams for years?

My phone buzzed on my hip and I knew it was my editors looking for an update.

"Mommy," the voice said again in the single-mindedness of youth, but looked at my phone.

"Did mommy have a phone?" I asked, not answering mine.

His head went up and down in an affirmative.

I looked at Dennis and he seemed puzzled. I watched as Dennis slipped off the bed and onto his knees to be at eye-level with the boy.

"Where was mommy's phone?"

The boy seemed innocent and younger with the puzzled look on his face.

"Potty," came the boy's reply after what seemed like an eternity where we sat silent, but hopeful.

Dennis and I looked at each other in bafflement. Patrenka understood perfectly. She reached over and grabbed him under the arms, setting him on his feet and walked to my bathroom. After a few moments we heard a flush, the water running and the door opened.

The child walked out. "All done," he announced proudly.

"Great job," Dennis said.

Patrenka followed more slowly but motioned us over when the kid climbed back on the bed.

"What?" I asked.

"She. I mean, he is a she."

"What?" Dennis asked.

"The child is a girl."

Chapter 7

"Are you sure?" I asked stunned.

"Very." Patrenka added.

My brain was kicking into high gear. Why had we assumed it was a boy? I knew the answer immediately. The clothes. The baseball cap. The one-piece pajamas were royal blue. Who puts a baseball cap on a girl?

When we looked back, the child was laying on the bed seemingly ready to go back to sleep. Dennis walked back over and slid to his knees on the floor bringing his face to eye level again. "What do you remember last?"

The child looked at Dennis and then at each of us. Then she laid on the bed, put her thumb in her mouth and closed her eyes.

I knew we would get nothing more tonight. And that we three would need more professional help in getting answers out of this child who was running from the world. I could only hope her sleep wouldn't be marred by nightmares.

Patrenka grabbed the food wrappers off the bed and stuffed them into one of the bags. She nestled the blanket over the child and gently brushed her cheek with her lips. I felt jealous of the intimate gesture.

We melted back into the living room and sat.

"What do we do now?" I voiced in frustration.

"I don't know," Dennis responded. "I was hoping for a name or something so we could place the child with a relative."

"Me, too. Any more on the parents who were killed?"

"No. We believe they were Mark and Ashley Jones, but they don't have any history anywhere, nor did we find a purse or wallet. Other than the neighbor knowing the woman's name was Ashley, we don't have any clues. The house was rented by a Mr. and Mrs. Jones. Not very original. There weren't any forms of identification in the house. There wasn't even a phone hooked up."

Patrenka nodded. "She used Mrs. Kowlowski's phone to call the telephone company and make arrangements. They were supposed to come on Monday."

We gaped at Patrenka.

"Anything else you care to add?" Dennis said.

She shook her head as if that sentence exhausted her.

"Why would she use a neighbor's phone if she had a cell? Maybe the child doesn't know." I looked at Patrenka who didn't meet my gaze. No one had any answers. An uncomfortable silence filled the void.

"I've got to get back to the station. The uniforms should have their reports done from canvassing more of the neighbors. Maybe they will have gotten something more from Mrs. Kowlowski." Dennis stood and headed for the door.

"I've got to get back and finish my story for the morning edition." I rose and followed.

We both bolted from the apartment before Patrenka could wonder why we were leaving her with the child.

In the elevator, I asked. "Anything else I can print?"

"No. I wish there were. This is the strangest case. Usually you don't know the murderer but to not know who the victims are, that's strange. I keep thinking we're missing something, but what, I don't have a clue," he said rubbing his hand along the back of his neck.

"There was nothing for identification?"

"Not even a utility bill."

"Are you running their prints?"

"Yes, but we haven't had any hits yet."

We were both deep in thought when the doors slid open on the first floor parking level. We nodded to each other and went to our respective vehicles.

I intended to head straight to the newspaper office, but I didn't have anything more to add to my story. By habit more than anything, I pulled into the police station and headed to the detective bureau.

My luck must have been in high gear because as I entered, a detective said. "We got a hit. The prints came back from Detroit Police Department, Ashley Knowles. Arrested in 1987 for possession of marijuana when she was sixteen."

The detective didn't even look up from his screen after reciting the information. I peeked at the screen to get the spelling of her last name and anything else quickly. The screen flashed and he was pulling up a history from the Secretary of State's office for driver's license information in Virginia.

He started reading again. "Seems Ashley Knowles became Ashley Jones three years ago when she married Mark D. Jones. Wonder if that could be the vic. . ."

"Malone, who let you into the department?"

I turned at the threatening tone of the captain. "I was looking for more information on the double murder. Whatcha ya got?"

"No comment. Hit the road."

"Captain, let me help. If I print a partial bio, then others might come forward with more information."

I could see the captain mulling over my suggestion. I knew if they were using driving records for identification, they were seriously hurting for information. Dental records would be useless unless they knew where to look. Police used media to get leads all the time, maybe even to flush out the dentist.

"Okay, Malone, but you can only print what I give you. Agreed?" I nodded my head and held up my right hand as I pulled my notebook and pen from my back pocket.

"Shoot."

"The police are asking for anyone who saw any unusual activity in the Third Street neighborhood to contact our department or Silent Observer. The victims of a double homicide have not been identified. If anyone has any information on the occupants of 223 Third Street, contact the police."

"Can I run a photo? Might help people to know what they looked like?"

I could see the captain contemplate the pros and cons. The captain was nothing if he wasn't methodic.

"Flaherty, any personal photos we could release to the media?"

I looked over my shoulder to see Dennis walking through the door, his eyes narrowing when he saw me with the captain.

"Don't know. Want me to check?"

"See if there isn't something Malone could use." The captain turned to dismiss me after throwing me a rather large bone, but I wasn't done with my questions.

"What about how they were killed?"

It was the captain's turn to look over his shoulder at me and steal his eyes and clench his teeth.

"Shot," I said, answering my own question daring him to contradict me. He took a step away and I followed. A good reporter never gives up easily even in the face of rejection.

"How, where, what type of gun?" I pressed.

"Don't you already have all the answers?"

"Was it a contract killing?"

The captain whirled around and was in my face. "What makes you say that?"

"Two people, no identification and you haven't said anything about a domestic dispute." I stood my ground. "Contract killing would make big headlines."

The captain rolled his eyes in a plea for mercy and patience with bumbling reporters, but it distracted him from asking me more questions about how I got my information.

"No comment." The interview was over. "Captain, can I quote you or attribute to anonymous sources within the police department?"

He stopped and turned. "Do what you do for other information that comes from my department," was the snide reply.

"Gotcha, unnamed sources," I cockily parroted as I scribbled.

I knew he was angry for having to say anonymous because of the many times he had hauled me over the coals for my unnamed sources wanting to know who the leak was. He also knew his secret was safe because I never revealed the names, although I think he could guess.

I had all I was going to get and time was ticking. It was nearing dawn as I walked down the hill from the station to the paper. I stopped by the coffee shop and got a large java to go. Sipping it gingerly, I headed to my cubicle trying to erase the memory of Patrenka in my bed.

I couldn't believe that not even twelve hours had gone by and so much had changed. It all started when Patrenka sucker-punched me from the doorway. What was Patrenka? Reporter-wanna-be? Gypsy? Clairvoyant? Psychic? Soul nurturer?

Was I reading too much into her? What was it about her that captivated my thinking, my libido? I only had to close my eyes and call up the picture of her in fuchsia standing in the doorway or lying on my bed with the child's head nestled to her breast. Each made me uncharacteristically hot, hard and frustrated. She didn't act much like a reporter. She didn't even ask to help write the story or if she was getting a byline. Reporters were glory hounds when it came to bylines.

"Mitch, what do you have?" Ken's voice brought me out of my reverie.

"A few more details, not much, but I do have a photo of the couple. I'll plug in the new stuff and send the picture to comp."

"Let's see the photo." He waited while I opened it from my flash drive. The digital replica of the photo from the bedroom dresser opened on my screen. I sent the photo on its way to the photo department who would do their best to make my photo of a photo clear and legible with the magic of digital editing. As Ken walked away, I returned to my screen and opened the Internet browser.

I Googled "Mark D. Jones." I found 100,000 entries. Refining my search adding Michigan netted a Mark D. Jones, who was associated with the federal Bureau of Alcohol, Tobacco and Firearms along with dozens of others. Interesting. Next was Ashley Jones with 151,000 entries including an actress, an athlete and college students on honor rolls. Even narrowing my search by adding Michigan to the criteria found 18,000 entries. Who would have figured there would be more Ashleys than Marks? I tried using Mark and Ashley Jones but there was nothing. I tried again using Ashley's maiden name of Knowles. Another plethora of names and no way to know which was the key.

Out of curiosity, I put Patrenka in for a search. I read in fascination. I should have known. Patrenka was the name for a beautiful Arabian horse known for her high spirit and lovely lines. Maybe my

Patrenka was incarnated into a human. When had she become my Patrenka? I had to snap out of this obsession. I had a story to finish and I already was pushing my deadline.

I opened the file I started earlier on the murder and added what I knew and sent it to the editing queue with a minute to spare and looked up to see Ken staring at me. I smiled sheepishly. I dropped my gaze back to my computer screen, deciding I was done for the night, err day. I shut it off.

It was after seven in the morning and the sun had already awakened the city as I stepped out of the newspaper's employee entrance onto a narrow alley. As I hit the sidewalk I felt the temperature spike with heat. It was going to be another hot one and the sun was only half up. I worked nights, mostly. Usually if it was a quiet night I would be done much earlier. I was bushed and needed sleep. But I wasn't rushing out for the shut eye. I was rushing back to the sleeping forms in my bed and — who knew — I might get lucky.

Not wanting to follow that train of thought much farther, I put my hands in my coat pocket, thankful there was a breeze that ruffled my hair. I automatically headed up the hill toward the police station. I decided against grabbing my car. I entered Donna's and breathed in the smell of fresh doughnuts. I picked up a dozen and a couple of pint bottles of chocolate milk — the breakfast of champions for me and my house guests. Not the best, I realized but the grocery store would require more time and energy I didn't have.

I carried my purchases the three blocks to my apartment and entered by a side door using my key. I took the stairs figuring I needed to work off some of my nervous energy and giddiness as my hope for pleasure increased.

I jangled the keys I pulled from my pocket in a merry jingle to match my mood and skipped up the three flights in rhythm. I punched open the fire door in my eagerness and stopped, getting struck by the backlash of the door trying to close. A Herman Munster of a man was bent over my door knob trying to get inside.

Chapter 8

"Can I help you?" I asked trying to gauge the man's height from hips that were higher than the knob he was trying to open.

The man straightened and looked at the interruption. My mind again flashed to *The Munsters* TV show and its lead character, Herman. The lack of emotion on his face surprised me into inaction. Herman bent at the waist, turned as if in a football stance then headed straight for me. I swallowed and braced for impact as an elbow hit my side. I fell against the wall with the intruder never breaking stride to the exit. I struggled to regain my feet and only succeeded in sliding down the wall to the floor. I sat and mentally told myself to breath in, then out. I thought weakly about asking if anyone got the number of that truck. I put my hands down to push myself up, surprised to realize one hand still held the bag with the milk and doughnuts. Using my free hand, I staggered up. I peeked into the bag hoping the doughnuts would still be edible. I needed a fix and doughnuts were my only option.

It took two tries to get my key into the lock and get it open. I tried to calm my racing pulse but mental action was required to breathe. I moved to the living room window to see if I could find the stranger on the street below. Not seeing him, I went to the bedroom to see if my guests were hurt. As I rushed in, all I could think about was the man with a shot to his head in another bed tonight. Patrenka's eyes opened in surprise at my quick entrance, but the child continued to sleep. I walked to the window and peered down.

Herman exited the door I had entered only moments before. A dark sedan pulled to the curb and he entered casually. I waited for the car to squeal from the curb, but it didn't.

It sat there.

Realizing I was still holding a dozen doughnuts and chocolate milk. I glanced around and saw Patrenka watching me silently. I set the bag on the top of the nearby dresser unwilling to break eye contact. I pulled out my cell and hit Dennis's number hoping he would answer.

"Flaherty here," I let out a breath in relief.

"It's Mitch. Some guy was trying to get into the apartment when I got home. He's still sitting out front in a dark sedan."

"Dark sedan, eh? I'll check it out. Got a plate number?"

"No. I can see the car from my window but not the plate. I don't want to leave."

"Hang on a sec."

I could hear him talking to a couple other guys for a second.

"Got a description of the guy?

"Huge, tall. Herman Munsterish height. Broad shoulders."

"Anything else? Distinguishing features, besides the height?"

"No. I didn't get a look at his face. He was bent over the door when I came home. I asked him what he was doing and he chucked me into the wall and was gone before I could do anything."

"For a man who is always hounding me for details you didn't get many. Hang on."

I could hear the phone placed on the desk. I looked down and saw a patrol car pull up behind the sedan and turn on its red and blue overhead flashing lights.

The officer got out and approached the side of the car. About the time he was even with the passenger door, the car pulled out and sped into traffic, disappearing around the next corner.

After about thirty seconds, Dennis was back. "They got away," he said.

"Yeah, I saw. What about a plate?"

"Rental. We'll check further but don't expect much. Probably used a fake name."

"Do I need to be worried here? Do you think they will return?"

"Don't know. Let me get back to you. Stay on your toes."

Great! I didn't have a weapon and I had a defenseless woman and child here. Two people had already been killed for some unknown reason and the only survivor was here.

"What happened?" Patrenka asked. She spoke in a low melodic voice.

"I don't know. You heard what I told him. Did you see or hear anything?"

She shook her head.

How had they known anyone was here? Was it related to the homicides? Or someone trying to break in?

It had to be related. Any thief would have left immediately, not waited in a car. Puzzling. Another unknown to add to the equation. Too many unknowns and I needed some answers.

"Is there anyone you need to call or let know where you are?"

She again shook her head.

"Do you ever answer any questions verbally?" I said in frustration.

She looked at me like I was an alien. I tried again.

"Will you be able to stay here for at least today and maybe tomorrow? What about your internship?"

This time she nodded her head to affirm staying but added nothing about the internship.

I thought I was closed-mouth but she was really something.

My cell phone rang.

"I need you to get out now. Don't tell me where. Go," and then the voice I knew so well as my inside source was gone.

"Come on," I said. "We have to get out of here, now."

I pulled out a suitcase and threw in some clothes, sweats and stuff I thought we would need. I grabbed the box of stuff that had come with the child and dumped that in as well. We had yet to touch the food. I grabbed the bag of milk and doughnuts too. Within five minutes I was closing the door and locking it. Patrenka was carrying the child pulling the Tigers cap low on her head. I had the suitcase and food. I also slung my laptop over my shoulder as an afterthought.

"Crap." I muttered angrily and Patrenka looked at me curiously. I had left my car at the police lot. Nothing to do about it now. Probably better we didn't use it. It was weird but the cloak and dagger hero stuff was appealing to me in a macho, man about town way.

We exited through the back basement entrance, away from my apartment and the paper and headed three blocks to the Marriott by the convention center. I was huffing and puffing from my loads but Patrenka seemed like she was carrying a feather. As we entered the circular drive, I dropped the suitcase and lifted my arm signaling to a yellow taxi. Lady luck smiled on us as we sank into the back seat of a cab as it pulled away for the curb.

Chapter 9

"Potty," came the small voice that I had hoped had fallen into dreamland. My misgivings must have been written all over my face as Patrenka rose from the other double bed and helped the child to the bathroom.

I was sitting in an uncomfortable arm chair in a Best Western in suburbia land. We were adjacent to a mall. I had done some quick thinking when we jumped in the cab. I didn't want to be too far from the action but wanted to be hidden. I figured most people would never think of looking for us by a mall filled with people and vacationing families. We would hide in plain sight. Patrenka was her usual silent self during the short taxi drive. I checked in as Mr. and Mrs. Smith from Toledo paying cash for the fifty dollar a night room. The hotel marketed itself as a family retreat complete with large pool, several water slides, and a wading pool for smaller kids. I had heard a couple of female reporters talking about taking a long weekend there to beat the winter blues. This was September so it wasn't too busy with most families having started a new school year.

The child awakened in our hurry but surprisingly hadn't put up any fuss. The kid ate three doughnuts leaving a trail of powdered sugar around her mouth and down her pajamas. Patrenka used a wet washcloth to wash her down but wasn't having much success with the sugar trapped in the fuzzy cloth. I was surprised how many doughnuts a small child can consume. I thought after eating, she would be ready for a nap but I wasn't having much luck lately.

The thought of a nap drove me to test out the bed as they used the bathroom. I reclined grabbing the extra pillow for behind my head.

As the pair exited the bathroom, the little girl picked up her pace and jumped on the bed opposite mine giggling in delight. I didn't have the right or the inclination to scold her although her joy seemed loud in the silence of our thoughts. Patrenka opened the suitcase and went through pulling out a few toys but little to change into.

"I'm going to go to the mall and pick up a few clothes for the child. Target should be open," Patrenka said slinging her purse over her shoulder as she exited.

I stared at the empty door closing with a click. She was as fast as she was quiet.

I watched the kid bounce and was wondering how I had gotten myself into such a mess. I covered stories. I had never immersed myself into one before. I idly watched the antics of the child. I needed a name. I couldn't think of her as Child A. I was deep in thought when a cry shattered my musings.

Crocodile tears rolled down her cheeks, which were rosy. I looked down at her. I had no idea what to do. Why was she crying? Then it hit me. She wasn't on the bed anymore. She had either slid or fallen. She was on her butt between the double beds. I felt like an idiot. I now knew why kids weren't supposed to jump on beds. I stood, still not sure what to do. I took a hesitant step in her direction and stopped. The crying intensified. I looked around for Patrenka. She hadn't returned. Should I continue toward her? Was I making her more upset? I had no idea and my frantic glance around the room told me what I already knew. There was no one there to help me.

I knew I had to see what was wrong. I took another step toward her. I crouched low and looked her over closely from head to toe but didn't want to touch her for fear I would touch the spot that was injured. The tears continued to roll down her cheeks but the volume control seemed to be lowering. I guess I was doing something right, but I didn't know what.

After my perusal, it seemed she was getting frustrated with me as I tried to figure out what to do. Sucking her thumb for comfort, she stared at me with big, damp eyes and lashes that stuck together with the moisture in a jagged outline around her eyes making her look like a life-sized Kewpie doll. She lifted her other arm and pointed her bent elbow in my direction.

"You hurt there?" I pointed. She nodded. "It will be all right." With all she had been through, she accepted that explanation. I was surprised and immensely relieved that she didn't ask for mommy. She took a deep breath and while she didn't smile, she didn't look sad anymore either. She stared back at me with those big trusting eyes. I had to look away. I was getting choked up and I didn't know why. It was barely a booboo. My knees started to ache from squatting. I stood and shook each leg. The child stood and I watched her shake each of her legs as she got up, just like I had.

The next thing I knew, she was next to me, standing on the bed looking me in the eye. I was spooked and my knees buckled, dropping me to the bed. As she climbed into my lap resting her cheek on my chest, I panicked. I felt her little heart beating. Bravely, I moved an arm around her and patted her back as I had seen Patrenka do.

We stayed like that for a few minutes. I was hugging a child and the child wasn't running away screaming. I wasn't sure when I had acquired my child phobia but this child was breaking it down, gesture by gesture, hug for hug. This kid. I didn't even have a name. I needed a name. I needed to quit feeling, and get some information. That was what I was good at, getting information. I needed a name.

"Hey, Sport," I said leaning back so I could look her in the face. "My name is Mitch." I said pointing at myself. "What's your name?"

"Joey," she replied. Great. I got a name.

"Joey what?" I tried again.

"Joey Smith," the child responded then leaned back against my chest.

"Okay, Joey Smith." But it wasn't okay. There we sat. Joey in my lap. I didn't know what to do. I didn't want to move Joey, nor admit I felt comforted by the warmth she gave. Little by little I settled back on the bed. Finally I was lying on the pillows I arranged earlier and was only going to rest my eyes for a moment. It was the last thing I remembered.

I awoke to the melodic sound of my cell ringing.

"Malone here," I answered trying to remember where I was and glancing around sleepily. The room was quiet and empty which didn't seem right, but the reason escaped me.

"You okay?" I recognized the voice.

"Yea, what's up?" I said glancing around the room remembering what had happened. I was beginning to panic because Joey who had been asleep beside me was nowhere to be seen. Patrenka wasn't there either and I didn't know if she'd returned or not.

"The Feds. They've taken over the investigation and are asking all kinds of questions, but not the right ones. The child hasn't come up at all. Everything alright on your end?"

"Yeah, fine," I lied.

"Well, hang tight. I'll get back to you," Dennis said.

"Wait. What about work? I'm supposed to show up in a few hours and make my rounds. I'm supposed to ferret out the story, not be the story."

"Yeah, yeah, right. Can you leave them? It'd be suspicious if you didn't make a pain of yourself. That'd be good. See what you can get. I've been removed."

With that the conversation ended.

Chapter 10

With the phone hanging dead in my ear, I sat there, thinking. Trying to make some sense of the jumble of facts. We had a kid no one knew about, a dead couple using aliases and the Feds had taken jurisdiction. Why couldn't I come up with something? Then it hit me. I wasn't using my talents. I was thinking like a victim, like a father protecting his child, like a love-sick puppy when it came to Patrenka. I needed to get back to my roots so to speak. I opened my laptop and got to work.

I started typing what I knew, which after only a few minutes, I realized wasn't much. We had the man with a bullet in his head and a woman named Ashley. We had a child called Joey. We had the Feds taking over the investigation. We had the mysterious stranger and rental car.

As I looked at the computer screen, a plan started to form. Whoever was behind this had some deep resources. That was the only explanation I could find for someone finding me at my apartment. I hadn't had so many visitors in the entire time I had lived there.

I couldn't believe that it had been less than twenty-four hours since Patrenka had walked into the newsroom and the world had tilted on its axis. Patrenka. It was so easy to bring her face into focus. I had memorized every detail, every plane, even her mannerisms.

Her quiet nature drove me nuts and her body, I couldn't wait to caress. As I remembered, it was as if I made her materialize.

Patrenka and Joey came in the room dripping wet with small white towels wrapped around their swimsuit-clad bodies. My puzzlement must have shown.

"The pool."

"Oh." I didn't really understand, but I knew the futility of asking.

"I purchased swimsuits for us at the mall. I figured it would be one way to work off her energy. You needed to sleep."

I was amazed. This was a flood of information from Patrenka. It was the most she had spoken since we'd met. As the towel dropped away, I drank in her body in a modest black one-piece. Her fuchsia shirt had hid some glorious curves. Her hair was piled on her head and fastened with some type of clip. I must have been drooling, because Patrenka scoffed and turned Joey's shoulders toward the bathroom. Joey smiled and waved until the door clicked shut.

I closed my eyes and leaned back into the pillow. My dreams began again as I called to mind her damp skin aching to be touched. I fantasized about taking off the form fitting suit as I heard the shower start. My imagination continued as I forgot about Joey and pictured Patrenka soaping her skin sans the suit.

My imagination streamed into overdrive when I heard a giggle and easily inserted myself into the shower with Patrenka. I'm not sure how long I kept up the fantasy when I was brought abruptly to the present with a click of the door. Joey came out with tousled hair wearing one of my t-shirts. It fell off one shoulder and easily made a full-length gown.

She shyly walked toward the double bed I wasn't occupying and attempted to climb up as the shirt wrapped around her legs and impeded her progress. I watched Joey struggle a couple more times before I rose and gave her a boost. I returned to the other bed. I watched Joey grab the remote off the night table between the beds and push the large green button. Sound immediately flooded the room and drowned out my fantasy as well as the sound of the shower. While Joey knew how to turn on the TV, she didn't know how to change the channel. She was watching the hotel's welcome screen and yawning.

"How about I find something to watch?" I said, reaching for the remote.

As I cruised through the channels, Joey get comfortable and her lids drooped. Before I had made it through the thirty options, Joey had nodded off.

I stopped at a local news program featuring the police chief and a dark-suited stranger talking to several microphones strapped to a podium. I recognized the police station's conference room and increased the volume.

"We are following up on some leads, but are asking anyone with information to call us or Silent Observer," the police chief said.

"Chief, is it true that the killings were a contracted hit?" someone yelled from off camera.

"I can't comment on that. I will let FBI Special Agent Gill Garrison answer."

"We haven't ruled out any possible motives in the double slaying," came the well-modulated voice from the dark suit with the serious face.

"What caliber were the shots?" came another voice off screen.

"We are not releasing details about the caliber or number of shots," the agent responded easily parrying the question and nodding to another.

"Is it true the bodies have not been identified yet?"

"We are not releasing the names of the victims until we have contacted the next of kin," the police chief replied.

"Do you know who the kin is?" persisted the reporter.

"We are not releasing any more details on the identity of the pair," the chief replied clearly irritated with the persistent reporter.

"Were they married or living together?"

"Both resided in the Third Street home but had only moved in days before the incident," the FBI agent responded with what I recognized as throwing them a bone. I saw the chief flash an irritated look at the agent before resuming his composed public persona.

Why had the FBI taken over the case? Murder wasn't a Federal crime. Was it because the pair was in the Witness Protection Program? Were they spies?

My concentration immediately fled from the press conference when Patrenka reappeared looking sexy, clean and ready for ravishing. She was wearing a towel wrapped around her head and I recognized one of my t-shirts and sweat pants looking better on her than they ever did on me.

Patrenka must have read my thoughts giving me a cold look that reminded me to keep my zipper up and my desires unsatisfied.

"What?" I said, licking my lips and trying to cure the dryness in my throat.

"Anything new?" she said pointing to the TV.

"Not yet. The dark suited guy is from the FBI. They've taken over the case. It's odd. I'm wondering why they're involved, whether they were asked or just showed up. I'd check with Dennis, but he's off the case." I stopped abruptly realizing I was rambling.

Patrenka dipped to plant a hip gently on the mattress without waking the sleeping form and drew the bedspread up from the bottom to cover Joey who snuggled deeper into the pillow.

I forced myself to return to the news show but the anchorman was detailing the latest glitch in the Grand River economy. I plotted ways to put my desires into action. I pictured myself walking suavely over, tilting her chin up with two fingers, and bending down lightly caressing her lips with mine. Slowly I would draw her up until we were hip to hip as we explored more than our mouths. I'd rip off her clothes and find satisfaction in those luscious curves. . .

"Noooooo. . ."

I jumped to my feet as the heart-wrenching cry broke into my fantasy. Where I was planning on laying my lust to rest was filled with Joey, tossing and turning in a nightmare or maybe reliving yesterday's shattering memories.

I wanted to follow my body into action on the other bed but my lust limped. The cries were eerie, haunting. I couldn't sit still. I looked to Patrenka for help and her eyes were sad pools. I panicked. Desire disappeared.

"I've got to get to the paper, write a follow up." I grabbed my jacket and was out the door.

It wasn't until I was going through the lobby that I realized I was still wearing yesterday's clothes and I didn't have a car.

Chapter 11

As I entered the police station, I garnered more attention than usual but chalked it up to my less than clean appearance and my arrival by taxi. Instead of cracking a joke about where I'd spent the night, the desk sergeant averted his eyes. Not a good sign. Something wasn't right. I picked up my pace and reached the hall to the detective's bureau, hoping to find Dennis.

I entered the detective's bureau and the rush of a big case was replaced by the doggedness of overwork and the chasing of details that may or may not pan out. Ties hung loosely, jackets draped on the backs of chairs and empty coffee cups and fast food wrappers littered the desks. Faces that looked up when I entered, quickly lowered their gaze.

I scanned the area for a friendly face or even a familiar one. No luck. The lack of eye contact was unnerving. I considered ducking out the officer's entrance on the side of the building by my SUV, when Dennis entered.

He looked right at me, gave an imperceptible tilt of his head, and then turned on his heel, leaving the room. I was seriously unsettled and the only word that fit was hinky.

I followed my intuition. I exited the police station out the opposite end of the hallway from the front. I felt the need to rush and didn't know why, but when in a building full of people carrying guns, you don't stop to analyze the situation. You follow your gut and my gut said get out, now.

I shoved the keys in my ignition when my cell phone rang.

"Malone here."

"Dunkin Doughnuts." was all the voice said before disconnecting.

I recognized the voice and the stress it contained pulled my nerves taut.

I dropped the phone back in its belt clip and started the Jeep. As I pulled from the lot, I headed in the opposite direction from the doughnut shop. Call me paranoid for feeling like a target, but I didn't want to be followed. I was only being cautious, I rationalized. This was not my comfort zone. I was used to gathering the news and not being pursued by it. I felt like I had a target on my back and I wanted to know why. Why had someone tried to break into my apartment? Why was everyone acting as if they didn't know me?

Officers often were annoyed by a story I'd written and they'd given me the silent treatment, but this was a different feeling. I was a persona non grata and I didn't know why. Could it be because I'd hidden the only witness to a grisly murder? That couldn't be. Dennis knew how to reach me. I thought about the stories I'd written, nothing potentially damaging there. The story about the double homicide that hit the streets this morning didn't mention any officer by name or few details. That couldn't be it.

I pulled into the newspaper's employee lot, driving parallel to the back of the building until I'd passed the loading dock on the far end. I parked past the last slot behind a cement abutment. It was mid afternoon but it looked like dusk with gathering storm clouds. The lot was usually packed during a normal business day but this was Saturday and it was only half full. I often parked in my current 'no parking' spot by the loading dock if I was dropping off something. I was sitting there feeling foolish, waiting for something but I didn't know what. I was telling myself I was obsessing, when a shiny black Suburban pulled into the lot and started down the rows closest to the entrance, farthest from me and perpendicular to the building.

I knew in an instant, that my paranoia was real and not an illusion. I was being followed. Few in my business can afford big, expensive cars and those that can, don't work the weekends.

A semi truck pulled into the lot to make a delivery of one of the many department stores preprinted advertising circulars for Sunday's paper and I saw my chance. The Suburban was heading down the first aisle of parked cars away from me and the building. The semi was making a wide turn to allow it to back into the dock between me and the Suburban. Before the truck started its turn to back into the dock, I shot out from the side and exited onto the street while the view of the Suburban's driver was blocked. When the SUV sped up and turned into the next aisle, I knew they were looking for me. My pursuers accelerated in my direction behind dark tinted windows, only to be blocked from the exit by the turning semi. To be sure I had lost them, when I hit the street, I turned left and then right and then made another left in quick succession trying to get out of sight and away.

Not bad, I thought, congratulating myself. I drove up an on-ramp to the highway and got off on another expressway and then took the first exit. I hadn't gone far in miles but was now approaching the doughnut eatery from the opposite side, away from the paper. I pulled through the lot and backed into a parking space near the rear exit. Dennis walked toward my idling car, and hopped in with a bag.

As soon as his door closed, we took off, not saying anything until I pulled into Lookout Park, a favorite place for teenage parkers to look at the stars at the end of a date. It was too early for any amorous couples but perfect for a little chat as we watched the building storm clouds roll in.

"I hope you have coffee," I said, turning the car off and feeling exhausted, now the adrenaline rush was gone.

"Yes and a Bavarian Crème."

Dennis handed me the Styrofoam cup and the long john which I quickly maimed.

Dennis sipped his beverage and chewed a bear claw.

The doughnut disappeared and I wadded up the cellophane wrapping and tossed it into the now empty bag sitting between our seats. As I sipped the hot brew, I raised my eyebrows in a questioning glance.

Dennis finished his doughnut and avoided my gaze, looking out over the city whose lights were blinking on in anticipation of the rainstorm.

"What's going on?" I finally asked to break the silence.

I could see Dennis looking around for another doughnut to stuff in his mouth to avoid the question. He had yet to make eye contact.

"You are." He stared out the passenger side window.

"What are you talking about?"

He turned to face me. "You are on the FBI's top list of suspects for the murders."

"You've got to be kidding." My heart pounded in my chest.

"No. They found one of your fingerprints at the murder scene and think you're the killer."

I didn't answer for a minute with a zillion thoughts coursing through my mind. How? What? Why? It hit me. My print was on the door of the bedroom when I pushed it to take the photo of the couple before running down the stairs ahead of the captain. I was getting sloppy.

Dennis continued. "They matched your print to one on file from an old Army record. I didn't know you were in the Army."

"That was a long time ago and didn't last long. Didn't you explain to them what happened?"

"No. By the time I found out about it, the FBI had been running with it for an hour. When I finally got a chance to talk to the captain, he said to let it go for now."

I couldn't believe I was wanted for murder and the captain would let them arrest me. He had to know I didn't do it. How could I go in a matter of hours from reporter to wanted man? I had covered the search for suspects but it didn't feel good being the hunted.

"The captain isn't happy about the FBI taking over the investigation and shutting out the department," Dennis continued. I was only half listening. "So far there's been nothing mentioned about the child by anyone."

"Joey," I said.

"Joey? Who's that?"

"The kid's name is Joey Smith." I could see the question but didn't wait for it to be voiced. "Maybe they wanted a boy."

"Anything else?" Dennis turned toward me.

"No. Was the couple who were killed the kid's parents?"

"We don't think so. According to the medical examiner, the woman hadn't given birth to any children but was pregnant. That isn't to say that Joey couldn't have been adopted."

"I don't think so." I said, but didn't know why except there wasn't enough evidence in the house of a child, even if they did only move in. "Any hits on missing children that fit Joey's description?"

"No. Wherever she belongs, no one is saying she's missing."

"What do I do about the FBI?"

"I don't know. I do know they have the paper staked out. All I could do was get that one phone call to you. I've been busy and haven't been able to sneak away. You almost got nailed at the police station but none of the guys were willing to arrest you. They all know the charge is bullshit."

"That explains the lack of eye contact and the bad vibes." I again lapsed into silence. "What is this all about?"

"Damned if I know. Once the FBI showed up, we were off the case. Period. No details. Nothing. So much for interagency cooperation," Dennis said, wadding up his napkin and slam dunking it in the paper bag.

"What can I print?"

"I don't care. It's not my case. But I wouldn't ask the FBI for a formal statement," he chuckled, a smile breaking out on his face for the first time today. "Hey, what happened to that hot number you were with?"

"Patrenka still remains a mystery but she's taking care of Joey and rather well, I might add."

"What's the story with her?"

"Wish I knew. She's supposed to be an intern at the paper but doesn't seem too interested in going to work. I don't know. Something odd about her, I can't figure it out," I said running my hand through my hair. I glanced into the mirror to make sure we weren't garnering any interest and realized my gesture had given my hair a punk look.

"No shit. You can't figure her out? That has to be a first. Actually, she's the first woman I've seen you with, ever."

"Yeah, yeah. Right. Like I'm celibate."

"You said it, man. Not me. Have you gotten any information from Joey? Did she say anything besides her name?"

"Nope, but I haven't really tried. When I've been there she's been asleep and I can't find the heart to wake her. She had a rough night," I said, thinking about her nightmares which had to be more than scary dreams.

"We need to question her."

"I thought Grand River PD was off the case?"

"We are, that's the damn problem. Captain doesn't want her anywhere near the FBI. That means no Social Services. You have to keep her for a while longer."

"Are you crazy? I took her just so she wouldn't get hurt. I can't shack up with a kid. I don't know the first thing about kids. I don't get along with kids."

My diatribe was cut short when my cell phone buzzed.

"Malone here."

My editor's voice boomed over the line.

"What the hell's going on? Where are you? FBI agents served the publisher with a warrant to search your desk. We're stalling on first amendment rights to free speech but you had better not have anything in there. Do you?"

I thought for a minute while Ken took a deep breath after his tirade.

"I don't think so..." Then the hammer fell. I had pictures of the murder scene on my computer. The FBI wouldn't believe they were taken with the cops. It would be proof I did it. Trophies of my handiwork. To confirm my suspicions I asked: "What crime do they think I committed?"

"Murder, but they refuse to release any details. What's going on?"

"My print showed up at the murder scene when I was ducking out of sight. The FBI have taken over the investigation and pissed off the locals. Other than that, I can't tell you anything, but I'm a wanted man."

"Well, don't show up here. By the way, what did you do with the intern? I haven't seen her since she left with you."

"She's with me, but let's keep that between us for now. I may send her out to do some legwork. What's her story anyway? I haven't had much time to find out."

"Don't know. A directive came down from the publisher to hire her temporarily. I had a feeling it was a favor for a friend. She seemed knowledgeable enough during the interview and had a couple of clips from the *Los Angeles Times*. I didn't get many answers during our interview."

I smiled. It was good to know that no one was able to pierce Patrenka's shell.

Patrenka had good reporting skills, I'd seen that at the murder scene and that fit with experience at the *Los Angeles Times* but as an intern? What was it about her? I stared at my silent phone realizing Ken had hung up. First on my agenda was to find out more about my intern.

"Earth to Mitch, earth to Mitch. I have to get back," came a voice to my right. I had forgotten Dennis was with me.

"What?"

"I've got to get back to the station. I do have a job to do."

"Yeah, right. Got any ideas where I could find answers and get the kid turned over to some relatives?"

"Nope. Keep your head down and keep me posted if you find anything!"

"And what will you do? Protect me from a killer?"

"Don't laugh, it could happen," Dennis replied as I started the car and headed into the rain that was beginning to fall.

Chapter 12

I dropped Dennis at Dunkin Doughnuts and headed back to the hotel, scanning the rearview mirror every few seconds. I did a couple of three-sixties around the block before getting onto the highway to make sure I wasn't followed. I parked in the mall's underground parking and jogged through the rain to the hotel on an out lot of the mall, my nerves on edge for strange noises.

As I opened the door, I didn't know what to expect. Patrenka was doing her nails and Joey was sleeping on the other bed looking sweet and innocent. I didn't want to waste any of Patrenka's few words on pleasantries. I also was unnerved with Dennis' revelations.

"Did Joey say anything about the murders?" I had decided on my drive back that I was going to get whatever I could out of Joey to help get me out of my mess.

Patrenka brought her index finger to her lips to signal silence. The TV was on, but muted. I went to the desk in the room's far corner to my computer. In frustration, I ripped off about twelve inches of copy, and emailed it to Ken via the hotel's wireless Internet. It wasn't the greatest story but what I could and couldn't print was becoming a blur. What was real and wasn't also was becoming fuzzy. Time to pull back and investigate.

I continued to work on my computer, trying to nail down what I could. I needed a plan. I still didn't have any idea who the couple was. That mystified me. If they could get my prints from the crime scene, they had to know who was killed. Why not release their names? What would be the harm in saying they were dead? Was it for Joey's protection or was it something else?

Patrenka appeared to be engrossed in a rerun of *Magnum PI*, then *Simon and Simon*. She had turned up the sound bit by bit. I stretched, trying to relax my muscles from the less than ergonomic hotel chair.

The opening bars of the ten o'clock news on Fox played. I watched the top story, which had nothing to do with the murder. The murder had been dropped to the third story. Nothing new and that meant it got buried in the newscast. By tomorrow it could be totally gone unless something new broke.

I was angry. How dare they drop it because there was nothing new? A young couple was brutally murdered and a child was now without a home. This was important. Pressure needed to be applied to the FBI to solve this crime. Instead the media was backing off as if the FBI were a great crime-solving god. The fifth estate was waiting for whatever tidbits the Feds threw.

I stopped myself cold. That had been me yesterday. Only following the stories that would get top play in the paper and forgetting murders and robberies the next day. What made this case different? Was it me? Was it Patrenka's involvement? Was it Joey? I didn't have any answers except to realize this was personal. They were looking for me and I didn't want to be found. I could outsmart the FBI.

I had to find a new theory of the case or a new angle. I was going to make sure it was news again if only to bring justice to whoever had made Joey parentless, I silently vowed.

I returned to my computer hoping that some new theory would magically appear during my musings and only glanced occasionally at the TV waiting for the weather. I didn't really care how hot and humid it was gong to be, but habits were hard to break. The last story before a commercial and the weather was a new development announced as The Cascade — touted as an environmentally friendly, multi-functional development.

I was turning back to my computer when I heard an eerie squeak that turned into a high-pitched scream. Patrenka went to the child, and I figured it was another nightmare. She had every right to them after the gruesome scene I had witnessed the night she crawled into my bachelor existence.

The screams continued. Patrenka was having no luck quieting the distraught child. At first all I wanted was for the noise to stop. The shrill sound grated on my ears and I tried to shut it out. It seemed like she'd been screaming for hours but had only been about thirty seconds. I focused on the TV because I didn't know what else to do. The developer discussed the new concepts of a festival grounds using natural features to create campsites, staging areas, and commercial complex that would be a self-contained community on the banks of the Cascade River for a music festival featuring headline acts. He touted it as a giant Woodstock of the environmental age.

Still screaming, Joey's eyes were glued to the TV screen as she pointed at Buck Rockwell, the green king of development in the Grand River area. This was the most personality I'd seen out of the kid. Joey was screaming, "It's him, it's him."

I felt like a light bulb had gone off. Had she seen something? Was this a major clue? I wasn't a professional investigator like a cop but a reporter had to be an investigator of human nature. I was good at that. Joey was scared and Buck Rockwell had caused it. This wasn't to be taken lightly. The news flipped to a commercial and the room became blessedly quiet again.

Patrenka was murmuring sweet words of nonsense and after a hiccup, Joey wrapped her arms around Patrenka and buried her head in her chest like I had dreamed of doing. I was suddenly jealous of our young friend, as my imagination caused parts of my anatomy to stiffen.

I picked up my cell and dialed Dennis. "Do you have anything on Buck Rockwell?"

"No, why?" Dennis' confusion was evident in his tone.

"Joey had a major reaction when he came on the TV and I thought it was worth following up."

"Okay, but I gotta run. Captain's on a terror." The line clicked dead.

I stood, stretched again and turned back to Joey who was already drifting off to dreamy land. "What do you make of that?" I asked, gesturing at the TV.

Patrenka shrugged her shoulders, the large t-shirt slipping off a shoulder. I walked to my suitcase and looted the last pair of clean sweats, t-shirt and boxers. I needed a cold shower.

While scrubbing two days of dirt and sweat, I had a heart to heart with myself. I don't know why I kept asking Patrenka for input. I never got anything, only gestures. A reporter had to ask questions even if they weren't answered. I again wondered about her career ambitions because she didn't seem to have the reporter instinct.

I exited the bathroom at least feeling refreshed, plumped the pillows on my bed and started watching the late season baseball scores.

The TV droned on. I drifted off to sleep and dreamed about charming a beautiful dark haired lady who was pulling my clothes off. She smelled like a garden after a rain, all warm and damp and welcoming. I moved to accommodate my seductress' instructions. I felt the earth cave in under me …

I came awake in a shudder of panic. I tried to focus but couldn't. Something landed on my chest. The darkened hotel room resurfaced as I drew in the stale air with a hint of flowers. I realized the feeling of falling was from the bedspread and other covers being tugged from underneath me and draped over me. I looked up into the warm eyes of the face in my dream. I smiled sheepishly to cover my embarrassment, glad the spread covered my erection.

I felt sixteen instead of thirty caught by my mother in my first wet dream.

"Get some sleep," came the throaty voice I ached to hear so often. I yearned to pull her in and join me under the covers but she was already moving away. My t-shirt barely covered her shapely buns and a hint of lacy black. I was jealous of my shirt caressing her curves. Its hem slapping gently against what I yearned to hug. She slipped between the sheets of the next bed with Joey sleeping peacefully again between us.

I wanted to pee but couldn't trust myself to walk past Patrenka's prone form without showing my dream's consequences through the slit in my navy boxers. I tossed and turned, trying to find a comfortable spot but my bed had grown lumps before I eventually drifted into a troubled sleep.

Chapter 13

I awoke to a narrow band of sun coming through a slit in the room darkening drapes. Groggily I rolled over and glanced at the clock on the table between the beds. Nine-thirty it read. The next bed was empty. Where were they? I glanced around. My adrenaline was climbing. I scanned the room again and I noticed the less than traditional sleeping apparel was tossed haphazardly across the bed but their clothing was still neatly folded on the dresser besides the TV. I took a deep breath to calm my momentary panic. They must have gone to the pool again. I grabbed the remote left on the bedside and turned it on. An all-day news show caught my attention for a few minutes.

Deciding to take advantage of the empty room, I climbed out of bed and headed to the bathroom. I looked at my face in the mirror and realized I could do with a shave. I was never heavily endowed with the need to shave but after two days, I was looking scruffy. In the harsh light of the bathroom I looked closer at a face that didn't look as familiar to me. I couldn't help but feel I was on the downward slant of life. Long nights, too many doughnut dinners, and lack of sleep were catching up in a way they never did in years past.

The shower was hot and had my senses awakening, allowing me to focus on the day ahead, Sunday, wasn't it? I wasn't sure anymore about the days. My ordered life and schedule had disappeared. I had gone from a mysterious bachelor in a rut to living in a hotel, toting a woman and child. The part that I was having a hard time coming to grips with was that it didn't trouble me. I didn't want to think about why this domesticity didn't worry me.

I've always been a loner, even when my parents were alive. It might have something to do with the fact that I was an only child and had no opportunity to make friends easily. I was my parents' token child. Their professional careers were important to them and their kid secondary. I often wondered if they had me to stop others from asking about children. Now I was finding myself cohabitating with a child, wondering how I would answer those same questions.

With the towel firmly in place around my waist, I stepped out and crossed to the suitcase I'd hurriedly packed in my apartment. It had been rifled several times for t-shirts and attire to outfit my compatriots who I assumed were swimming. I hoped my guess was right and they were at the pool. I didn't want to think about what could have happened to them if they weren't. I pulled out clean boxers and a polo shirt and grabbed my jeans from the day before. I pulled on clean white athletic socks when I heard my phone vibrating against the desktop.

"Malone here," I answered. I hoped it was a lead. I was tired of chasing my tail and not knowing what was going on.

"How are your traveling companions? Getting lots of sleep?" Dennis snickered.

"Yeah, yeah," I said trying to blow by his smart comments without reacting. "What gives?"

"Where'd Buck Rockwell's name come from?"

"Joey freaked out when he came on the news." I sat at the desk.

"Well, get this. He doesn't have much of a history either. About fifteen years ago he cropped up in the city doing his first development. Each year he takes on a bigger and better project. After nosing around, Buck's projects all go off without a hitch, if you know what I mean."

"No, what?"

"Well, one person was pretty vocal at a local city meeting and by the time the issue came up at its rezoning, that person had disappeared and has never been seen since. I also talked to the county building authority. Seems Buck always builds to code but never an ounce more than he has too. When I started to question further, the clerk got real antsy and wanted to know why I was calling him on a Sunday."

"You mean he could have underworld connections? Maybe Mafia?"

"I don't know if we can make that leap yet, but obstacles do have a way of disappearing, giving his projects smooth sailing every time. The odds of that are a long shot."

"Any police activity?"

"No, there is never anything to investigate. The department has looked into the people disappearing but couldn't find any evidence of foul play or a good connection to him."

"What about his newest venture?" I asked, pulling my notebook over and taking notes.

"Not many particulars. What you saw was the initial announcement. We're looking into it, but quietly. I think it's time for an exposé on the developer king. What do you think?"

"Great idea but I can't walk in there, especially if he sent Herman Munster to my apartment."

"Let me go." I jumped to my feet turning toward a voice at the door, knocking my notebook off the desk. Why did Patrenka have no difficulty catching me unawares? What was it about her that made my hormones go into overdrive but left me as skittish as an abused kitten?

"Dennis, I'll have to get back to you."

As I disconnected, I noticed Joey's head peeking out from behind her. They were still in their swimsuits but it looked like they had done their showering while at the pool.

"I'll run out and pick up some breakfast while you two dress," I said, making my escape. I had to think clearly and I couldn't think staring into those eyes.

"Doughnuts?" said a small voice.

I turned and stared at Joey. I tried not to let my surprise show by the request. I had grown accustomed to my silent companions.

"Any special kind?" I asked, dropping to my knees to get a better look at her.

"Sprinkles," came the soft reply and the face disappeared behind the long legs of my dreams.

"Sprinkles, it is," I said, rising. "Any requests for you?"

As per usual, Patrenka shook her head in the negative. I'm not sure what I expected but I kept hoping for more and was feeling doomed to eternal disappointment and frustration. The disappointment, I could live with but the frustration was putting my genial disposition on edge.

I quickly exited the room and headed for the underground garage to get my car. I flipped open my phone and called the paper, asking for the morgue. The morgue was a library of sorts for the paper. I had them email me all they had on Buck Rockwell, the developer king.

~~~

I started the SUV and pulled out of the garage, making a right turn and heading for the Interstate to take me downtown. It was chancy hitting the coffee shop by the newspaper and cop shop but I was willing to risk it to get some information on Buck Rockwell. Donna, owner of Donna's Doughnuts, was one of the most knowledgeable women in city politics. Not only did she have the best doughnuts, ones I was sure would have sprinkles, but hopefully a little information that was not in the morgue copies on Buck Rockwell.

I pulled into the nearly full parking lot. Donna's Doughnut Den was always busy no matter what time of day. I walked into the warm homey interior. There were large round tables through the center and a counter with stools along the left edge. Booths edged the outside wall. The smell of coffee and the sweet confections made my stomach rumble.

I couldn't believe that less than forty-eight hours ago, I had brought Patrenka here when I still thought I could grill her. I scanned the crowd looking for any familiar faces of the boys in blue and didn't see anyone who would be looking for me. I patted myself on the back for my daring plan of coming into their backyard. That was something they would never have expected. That it was a Sunday was beside the point.

Donna's was a local icon. Politicians came to air ideas and get the common man's view. Union workers and leaders gathered around the tables and hashed out issues reaching settlements that couldn't be done in the office. I used it to interview sources and hot
~~~

interns.

I wandered back to the old-fashioned bakery case. Donna's strictly forbade anyone but employees to serve from the display cases unlike the convenience stores that offered self-serve doughnuts. That employee was usually Donna, who prided herself on always remembering a face. Many a criminal was tripped up by Donna's sharp eyes. After serving a wanted man, she would pick up the coffee pot circling the room pouring out a hot refill, then whispering in a cop's ear about the felon at her counter. The law enforcement officer would rise and nab the criminal outside of the Den so as not to interrupt the patrons' meals. I was hoping Donna didn't know the Feds were looking for me.

"Watcha got in some sprinkled doughnuts?" I asked Donna.

She pointed to the bottom row of the case, a perfect height for little eyes. There were vanilla frosted doughnuts with pink and white sprinkles, chocolate frosting with green and blue sprinkles. Other doughnuts featured pink frosting with little candy shapes.

"What meets your fancy, Mitch?"

"How about one of each? I have a particular little lady who I want to please," I responded.

"Since when?" Donna asked smiling curiously at me.

"I've got a few secrets left, don't I?" I teased. I was a little stunned that the man of mystery wasn't a mystery to the doughnut queen, but I came for information. I was right. Donna did know everything about everyone. Might as well get started.

"How about letting me buy you a cup of coffee?" I said, trying to flirt with the gray-blue eyes that matched the salt and pepper hair that went light on the pepper.

"Okay, I'll bite," Donna said calling another younger girl over to handle the counter traffic. I grabbed the bag of doughnuts and signaled for a long john to be added to the mix and two coffees, black.

Donna followed me over to a booth against the opposite wall. She slid her ample frame in and pierced me with a look of complete attention.

"I need help, Donna, and I need it to stay confidential."

"Oooh. Sounds mysterious. Will I be an unnamed source in one of your big crime and corruption exposés?" she teased.

"No. I need some background. I'm working on something that's outside my normal crime beat. I need to do some investigating without anyone knowing I'm looking in their direction. Can you help?"

"Maybe. I don't know everyone but I'll do what I can. Shoot," she said.

I had to get the measure of the man and Donna was the best.

"Okay, I need to know everything you know about Buck Rockwell."

She stared at me for a minute then looked around the restaurant as if gauging how her business was for the day but her sharp eyes never missed a patron. I realized she was looking to see if anyone was paying us any attention or were near enough to hear our conversation.

I could feel the rosy color flow into my cheeks. I had let my guard down in the cheery establishment. I was not meant for this cloak and dagger work. I only wrote the news.

"Buck Rockwell, huh? You do pick 'em good. About time somebody started investigating that creep," she said settling back on the bench seat. I had somehow redeemed myself. I glanced around to see if anyone had heard. No one had. Donna talked to hundreds of people every day. She wasn't one to tell anyone's secrets. That's why the Den was the perfect place for high stakes negotiations and strategy sessions. And the doughnuts were top notch, too.

I took a bite of my custard-filled mass of cholesterol and sat back to enjoy the sweet taste melting on my tongue.

"Buck is a sly one. Don't ever turn your back on him. He has never graced my doors but I've heard plenty, but never for long and that is the key. He talks like he's the big philanthropist, making promises to help make the world a better place. All the time he's stealing you blind to line his own pockets."

She stopped her musings and took a sip of her coffee. I could see her weighing the pros and cons of what she was about to say. Giving me a hard look, she took another sip and then wet her lips with her tongue.

"Buck is not one to be trifled with lightly. About five years ago, Buck planned a thirty-house subdivision in the Cassville neighborhood, down the street. His plan was to put in some low-income houses. He touted it as quality, affordable housing for the working man. Neighbors were vocal at the first planning commission meeting but by the time the development hit the city commission, no one voiced their concerns.

"The houses went in and were thrown up and not worth what the owners paid but by the time anyone realized the financing Buck provided was mostly interest, few had the resources to move. Some grumble here and there but quickly stop. By who, I can't tell you for sure, but it's always wise to look at who would benefit the most." Donna lapsed into silence and took another sip of brew.

"No one has ever lodged a formal complaint?"

"No. They are either paid off or some literally disappear. Nothing ever sticks to Buck for long. Take care with your methods. You're wise to be cautious. Keep your target a secret for as long as you can," Donna said, grabbing her cup and starting to rise.

"One more question," I asked giving her my best smile.

She returned to her seat and nodded. "Do you know anyone who works for him that could provide any further information?"

"No. Most of his workers stay around his complex, a large place on the east side. It has a guest "cottage" on the grounds. Employees stay right there and a gate at the front rarely allows anyone in. One of his workers made it in here a few months ago and was nice enough in a tough guy way, but he's not been back. He was looking for a hamburger, not doughnuts. Wasn't talkative about what he did or about Buck either."

"Curious for an upstanding member of the community," I said.

"Isn't it? Now I need to get back or we really will be drawing attention to ourselves. You best be getting on your way before others get wind of your location. Don't forget the sprinkles for the little lady," she added with a wink as she moved the bag in my direction and headed back behind the counter.

I finished my now lukewarm coffee, grabbed the bag of doughnuts and headed back to the hotel. As I neared it, I decided to fill up at a gas station. While there I grabbed a pint of chocolate milk to go with the doughnuts.

I pulled into the underground garage and, as a precaution; I did a tour around its three floors. I thought it was odd that it was empty until I realized it was Sunday morning and the mall didn't open for another half hour or so.

As I walked across the parking lot toward the hotel I remembered the last time I brought doughnuts back. I quickened my pace. I didn't want to get back and find my ladies gone. I rushed through the hotel's side door using my card key and down the hall. I saw no one in the hall and inserted the key.

When I entered I took a deep breath and relaxed. I didn't want to examine why I was so relieved. Instead I brandished my goodies. Joey was watching some kids' program and Patrenka was looking out the window. Both turned and followed me over to the desk. Within seconds we all were enjoying the holed breakfast treats and the sprinkles were falling around us in a colorful rainbow.

Joey looked up at me with the brightest eyes of a happy child I had ever seen and she smiled, a big toothy smile with chocolate icing outlining her ruby red lips. She was cute and innocent. She didn't deserve what happened to her parents. She impressed me with her spunk and the pleasure she took in the doughnuts. This was some kid. Smart too. I never took a personal interest in anyone I wrote a story about. Sure, I felt sorry for wives of drug dealers or victims of horrible crimes, but never personally cared. They were subjects and the idea was to get the most information possible about what happened and print it. Period.

The kid was worming her way under my skin. I didn't know what to do about it. I did know I never wanted her to be unhappy again and I would do anything to prevent it. Some could say I was becoming paternal; maybe I was. I knew I liked this happy, smiling face better than her guarded expression, the wary look, the fear.

Chapter 14

As Joey settled into a cartoon, I booted up my computer and downloaded the articles about Buck from the newspaper's morgue. I started reading but my concentration kept slipping as I caught whiffs of Patrenka's haunting scent. I glanced behind me and realized I was looking at Patrenka's stomach as she read over my shoulder. I followed her body higher, proud of myself for only pausing slightly at chest level before reaching her eyes. I wanted to hit the power key to turn it off, to protect what I was doing. It was an inherent reaction from the newsroom days of not wanting to be scooped. Then I relaxed, remembering we were in this together. I moved over and she pulled up the only other chair. We read in silence. There wasn't much in the clips and certainly no smoking guns or possible hints of impropriety, but that seemed fishy. All we had were screams of a small child. Was that enough to move forward on? We had to. It was all we had.

In my gut, I trusted Joey. She didn't have any motives or agenda. My other companion, I wasn't so sure about. As if sensing where my thoughts were headed, Patrenka looked at me. I pulled my gaze from her chest and continued reading.

The stories consisted of new housing developments in various suburbs. An initial announcement made at a planning commission meeting, then another story when the project received the green light. Everything was so neat and tidy — too tidy. Everything I had read in the last few minutes had my instinct on full alert. This was our man. I was sure of it. I needed more information on how he worked. Where he got his ideas, who brokered the real estate deals and where were the neighbors that objected? Neighbors always objected. However, Donna's comments about the fortress and men who went in but didn't come out had me hesitating. I needed another way. I would love to interview Buck and deftly probe about the development and land and see what kind of reaction I got. The only problem was anyone who read the paper knew my byline was crime, not zoning or development.

"I can interview him," Patrenka said surprising me by offering herself without my having asked a question or even knowing what my thoughts were. Maybe the connection I felt wasn't only one way.

"It could be dangerous," I said, trying to dissuade her.

"I can handle it," she said her chin arching up.

"Okay. Let's see." I reached out my hand. "Buck Rockwell. Pleased to meet you ma'am."

"Thanks for meeting me so quickly. I wrapped up a story on green building when I saw your development on the Associated Press wire service and knew it would be a perfect complement. Can you tell me about it?"

I started at her. She had seemingly slipped into a chatty newswoman filled with her own importance. The transformation was amazing. I couldn't speak.

She continued unfazed in the least. "How did you come to build a green development? Have you always been interested in the environment?"

I finally found my voice and did my best imitation of J.R. Ewing from the *Dallas* reruns. "Well, little lady, I believe we all should do our part to save the earth and if we can, then that is our responsibility."

We parried questions back and forth and I was surprised by her depth and seemingly innocent leading questions.

The battle of wills with each stepping deeply into our roles and sidestepping questions and answers had my admiration for Patrenka increasing as well as my libido. This was one smart babe. I wanted her and wanted to prove to her that I was worthy of her.

"Whatcha doing?" Joey asked, popping up from the pillow where we had wrongly assumed she was watching TV. We had forgotten our small guest as we had tried to trip each other up.

"Practicing."

"Practicing what?"

"Just something I might have to do, sweetheart. Nothing to worry about." Patrenka smoothed the hair on Joey's head.

"I'm hungry."

I looked at Patrenka who shrugged her shoulders. The chatty reporter was gone behind the piercing eyes. Might as well get something to eat as I realized I was famished too.

"Let's get out of here," I suggested, suddenly feeling lighthearted and carefree as I ruffled Joey's hair and she gave me a dirty look.

We grabbed our coats because the humidity was a memory after a thunderstorm had ushered in a cool front. We were nearly out the door when Joey turned back to grab her Tigers cap from the nightstand and race back to the door. "I don't think its going to be that cold," but Joey only pulled the bill down close to her eyes and raced down the hall.

"What sounds good?" I asked after quickening my pace to catch her.

"Doughnuts," Joey said.

"No, we need something besides doughnuts," Patrenka said sounding like a motherly authority.

"Pizza," Joey responded without a beat.

"Pizza, it is." I remembered seeing a Chuck E. Cheese's on an earlier trip to the mall.

We ordered at the bright colored counter and got a small cup of tokens. Joey was jumping up and down ready to take a spin with all the bells and whistles pulling her forward into the dining room arcade. I had never been inside the famed children's pizzeria and wasn't comfortable. It was however, a child's playhouse so I tried to blend in.

I watched as Patrenka led Joey to a machine that had five holes in the top. She fed it a token and grabbed a mallet handing it to Joey.

Joey shook her head and Patrenka started hitting what looked like squirrels as they popped up out of the five holes one at a time. Joey watched and took her turn next. Her reflexes were fast as she knocked several back. The game was over and Patrenka grabbed the tickets. Joey took them and came to show me.

It was fun to watch Joey run on her short legs from machine to machine and try to figure what each was about. I thought she would get bored but she would study a game, play it and then move on to the next. We tried a couple other simple games and she mastered those as well. I wondered not for the first time how old Joey was. When we first found her she seemed so small and I thought she was barely two. Now, I wasn't so sure. I didn't know much about child development but hers seemed incredibly advanced for only two. Maybe she was small for her age and could have been four. I had no idea what capability children had at what age.

I watched a couple other children who seemed about Joey's size. They flitted from game to game never really getting it. Joey studied each game before starting and then quickly figured it out. She was able to give each a run for the money instead of letting the time waste away. We, of course, followed like dutiful parents and collected the paper tickets that spewed from the games upon completion. Patrenka was running out of hands to hold them. I reached for the next batch counting out twenty-three. I looked at the wads in Patrenka's hand pondering how many we had and if that was normal for a small cup of tokens or if maybe Joey was smarter than the average bear.

A tug on my pant leg brought me out of my reverie.

"You do one." Joey held out a token to me.

"No, you use it." I shook my head and held up the tickets in my hand.

"No. You." She shook the token in my direction.

I took it and started looking around. Patrenka had disappeared and I had no idea how to play any of these games. Pinball was my game. We settled on Skee-Ball where you roll the ball up a ramp and try to get it to land in the circle with the most points. I rolled three of the five balls with varying degrees of success. Joey was watching me intently. I picked up the fourth ball and offered it to her. She shook her head and backed away.

"Go ahead. You try," I encouraged.

She hesitantly took the ball and moved to the front of the ramp. She stood there for a minute and then let it go. I was afraid it wouldn't make it all the way up the ramp, but it did and popped neatly in the fifty-point circle, the smallest one with the highest points. I lifted her up under her arms from behind and twirled her, congratulating her on her great shot. I set her down and handed her the last ball. She quickly grabbed it and again studied the ramp before her roll. This time her shot was only forty points. I gave her a high-five.

"Great job." We collected the tickets discharging from the machine. I turned and straightened, trying to collect the long snake into a reasonable mass.

Patrenka reappeared, bringing the pizza to our table. We joined her and I grabbed Joey's cap and set it on the table. "No caps on at the table," I said, realizing I sounded like my father in one of his long lists of rules that I never understood.

Joey grabbed it and placed it back on her head, then hurriedly dug into her slice. I didn't push the point. We ate in silence, apparently too hungry to make conversation or deep in thought about why we weren't the perfect family that we appeared to be.

After eating, we gathered the mass of paper tickets and headed to the counter. I was afraid it would take hours for her to decide from all the choices of cheap toys. Instead it took less than a minute to count the tickets and for Joey to make her choice. She walked away clutching a small green bear to her chest. It was a painful reminder of the brown bear in the evidence bag at the grisly crime scene. I silently vowed to get the bastards that made her an orphan.

We still weren't conversing but by silent agreement, no one wanted to return to the small hotel room yet. We wandered around the mall. After a half hour of window shopping, Joey finally broke the silence.

"I want to swim. Can I swim again?"

"Sure," Patrenka and I chorused and returned to the hotel. While Joey and Patrenka swam, I called an old friend for some advice.

"Stephen, Mitch here. How's academia treating you?"

"Great Mitch. You can't believe what they pay me to do research and to impart a little bit of knowledge to some grad students. It's great work if you can get it."

"Yeah, rub it in. You know I'm still on the night shift. Hey, I have this preschool witness I want to interview. She was found at the scene of a double homicide. I want to tread lightly but need to see what she knows. Any suggestions."

"Take her to the police, Mitch. Don't try. Let the professionals handle it."

"I can't. It's a long story but if anyone knows she's alive, she will be in danger. The fewer people that know, the better."

"I don't like it. You could influence her responses that might mess up the case if she ever needed to testify. How old is she?"

"Don't know, preschool for sure. I don't know much about kids. She hasn't answered many questions at all. I didn't want to push it. I wanted to do it right." I could hear Stephen laughing at my understatement of my knowledge with kids. When we were in college together we had to take a child development class that required community service at a day care. I withdrew on the first day because I couldn't even imagine being in a building with small children. Stephen, however, loved it and changed his major to child development with a minor in child psychology.

"The best thing you can do is ask broad, open ended questions. Don't react to any of the answers. She will be looking at you for cues if the information is correct. She may embellish if she thinks that is what you want to hear."

We talked for several minutes and he gave me several more suggestions and again reiterated that a professional should be involved. We finished when "my gals" returned.

Chapter 15

"Mr. Rockwell, Patrenka Peterson from the *Los Angeles Times*. I'm finishing a story on green building practices. I am in town on a personal matter and was reading about your development. Would it be possible to get an interview with you?" There was a pause. "Your development that I saw on the news would be a perfect example of what can work when concerned environmentalists are willing to try." Another pause. "This afternoon would be great. I'll reschedule my flight. About two?"

"No need to pick me up. I'll get a rental. Yes, I've got the directions. See you then."

I called Dennis and he was arranging for a vehicle and would be over soon.

Dennis showed with doughnuts and Joey was content. Patrenka closeted herself in the bathroom to get ready.

"Any new leads on the murder?" I whispered so Joey wouldn't hear.

"No. The damn Feds have it locked. Nothing. It's like the murders never happened. Something's going on. Anything out of our young witness?"

"No. I'm going to try and talk to her while you're gone. It's like the kid won't say anything with Patrenka around." I stopped. Where had that little bit of trivia come from? Thinking about it, I realized it was true. Joey never talked much around Patrenka.

I'd get something out of Joey this afternoon. I hadn't thought much about being alone with her. I'd handle it.

Patrenka emerged from the bathroom. My mouth dropped open. I wasn't sure it was her. Within twenty minutes she had transformed into a completely different person. Her dark tresses were pulled back into a tight chignon, all smooth and lacquered. Her eyes were still green but not the luminous quality I dreamed about. They were narrower and more oriental looking.

I realized I was staring.

"Is there something wrong?" she asked.

"No. Sorry. You look different," I said in wonder. My heart hammered. I wanted to pant and beg for her attention like a lap dog.

She returned my stare lapsing into the silence I knew so well. I shook my head still confused by the transformation. She was another person I didn't know. She wasn't the intern that had captivated my senses. She wasn't the caring mother figure I had seen with Joey. Now she was more hardened, a professional, but still beautiful. It was like she was a multiple personality but it was more than personality and much more subtle. It was attitude too. I couldn't help but be impressed. I thought she would make a superb undercover cop. That niggling suspicion started to take hold and needed more thought.

Who said she wasn't? I actually knew little about her. I didn't even know her name for sure but I doubted that would be an alias. It fit too perfectly. I wanted to unravel her to find the inner core the same way I wanted to strip off her clothing. My lips longed to discover every inch of her skin. I wanted to unwrap her layers until I found out what was at her core — investigator, reporter, nurturer, or seductress.

"Ahem," Dennis coughed. I'd forgotten he was there and blocked his view of the vision. Patrenka balanced on little strappy heels and grabbed some papers from the desk that I assumed were her notes for the interview. She moved effortlessly on three-inch heels that completed the almost traditional, two-piece, herringbone suit with the low cut V in front showing ample curves and valleys. I caught a whiff of musky jasmine and contemplated having Dennis take Joey for a walk. I wanted answers and also to satisfy my lust. I could get her to talk, I just needed to satisfy her sexually first and then she would be mine.

"We need to go," Dennis said. I dropped my gaze to the floor and tried to clamp on a firm control until I saw fuchsia toenails. Oh, how I wanted to suck on those toes.

As if she knew, Patrenka hurried to the door. Dennis followed, handing her a set of keys.

"You ready?" he asked as I watched him look her up and down. I wanted to remind him he was married.

I had to say something, establish dominancy in some sort of knee-jerk caveman type of way. I peeled Dennis with a look and asked: "What do you have for protection?" I groaned inwardly realizing it sounded like I was asking if he had condoms. My face must have flamed by the look of pure mockery that crossed my Irish friend's face making his green eyes turn to slits when he smiled, giving him the look of a snake.

Dennis covered my embarrassment by picking up the conversation in the way I had meant it. "I'll be outside parked near the entrance to his estate. I can't get too close because it will look suspicious." He attached a pewter pin in the shape of a butterfly to Patrenka's jacket lapel. "I should be able to hear and tape the conversation. I don't think he'll try anything but I want to know what he says. I want to beat those Federal boys to their own case. It pisses me off that they cut us out." His fingers lingered at his task much longer than needed.

I walked to Patrenka wanting to take her in my arms and breathe in her erotic scent. I wanted to beg her not to go because it could be dangerous, but knew I had no right. Instead, I put my hands on each of her shoulders and looked into her eyes. "Please be careful. We don't know what, if anything, this had to do with Joey. Make sure you stay safe," I said looking deep into her eyes. Her look changed to the luminous quality that struck me from the first. She nodded and the look was gone, making me wonder if I had imagined it.

I felt a tug on my pants and looked down to see a scared Joey looking bewildered and on the verge of tears. Her mouth had a ring of chocolate frosting from the doughnut. I wasn't sure what to do but something inside me guided my actions. I picked her up and hugged her close. Her head melted into my shoulder and her arms encircled my neck in a fierce lock.

"Patrenka is going for a ride with Dennis. She'll be back soon."

Dennis opened the door and extended his arm to usher Patrenka through it when she stepped around me and back into the room. She went through a couple of her shopping bags and picked one up. Crossing back to Joey and I she said: "I bought this. Thought it might make the afternoon easier."

With that she walked out the door and closed it with a click. I looked in the bag, surprised to see a bright orange flowered swimsuit in what appeared to be my size. I certainly wouldn't get lost in the pool with my neon attire.

"Hey Sport, how about a dip in the pool?"

Joey struggled to get down and ran into the bathroom, coming out in her suit. It was the perfect distraction and I made a mental note to thank Patrenka for thinking of Joey and wondered if she knew how uncomfortable I would be entertaining her.

I changed and was surprised the suit fit to a tee. Maybe she had been giving me more than a passing glance I thought, straightening my shoulders. I sucked in my gut trying to find a six-pack of abs that had clearly never existed. Swimming was not in my workout routine. I looked way too white in the garish bathroom mirror, which had never bothered me before. I vowed to cut back on the doughnuts and vigorously swim at the pool. With that, I emerged and off we went.

We had a fun time frolicking in the warm water. After an hour and a half I could see Joey tiring, so we headed back to the room. I was a little awkward as I helped Joey out of her suit and adjusted the water temperature to rinse off the pool chemicals as I had watched Patrenka do on their earlier visits. Joey dressed and crawled up on the bed and I turned the TV onto her favorite cartoons. Her eyes fluttered and she was soon asleep. I felt a little guilty for not trying to press her for information at the pool but we were having fun.

I jumped in the shower and dressed. I hadn't really missed my solitary life, which was a serious revelation for a confirmed bachelor. I adjusted too easily to the cozy living arrangements. Fluffing a couple of pillows, I grabbed the remote, changing the channel to the news and hoped to get an update on the investigation. As the local headlines were about to be repeated, soft moans came from the other bed that turned into a scream.

"Mommy! Mommy!" came the terrified voice of my sweet charge. "I don't want to go." Joey started thrashing around. "I'll be quiet. Please! No!"

The heartbreak and terror I heard in the voice had me scrambling off my bed and gently shaking her trying to make her come out of the dream into wakefulness. She grabbed hold of me in a terror grip. I didn't know what to do. I crouched on the edge of the bed and patted her back feeling awkward and inept. She was starting to wake up more fully now and clutched at my shirt, pulling me down. I perched my hip awkwardly on the edge of the bed. I tried to lean her back on her pillows but she crawled into my lap. I again started the patting motion and her cries eased to sniffles. I attempted to move her back against the pillows, but if anything, her grip increased in strength. A lot of strength for a small mite of a girl, I thought.

"You okay?" I asked hesitantly. She shook her head.

"Can you tell me about the dream?" I asked, ever the reporter and hating myself immediately after as I saw the terror return to her eyes. "Sometimes it helps to tell someone." She snuggled deeper into my arms and hid her face. "Was the dream about your mommy and daddy? Can you talk about it?"

I could feel her head shake side to side against my chest. I brought my hand up and patted her head in what I hoped was a comforting gesture. I felt like a schmuck but knew she had to get it out in order to deal with it. "Was the dream what happened to your parents?"

Her arms reached out from her small frame and snaked around my stomach like a python going in for the kill. I felt her nose making a permanent indention between my two lowest ribs.

"Joey, you have to get it out, talk about it."

Joey didn't move and as tight as she held me I wondered if she could even breathe.

"You don't have to tell me. But you have tell someone," I negotiated.

She cautiously lifted her head. She looked up at me with her big brown eyes. Tears rolled along the bottom edge waiting to spill out and run down her cheeks.

"My daddy's in Afghanistan," she said so solemnly it broke my heart.

I decided knowing wasn't worth the pain. This was a real breakthrough for a hardened reporter like me. Mitch Malone didn't consider others when he was on a story. He did or said anything to make people talk. I tried to rationalize that the key person in most stories hadn't been ensconced in my hotel room for days and I didn't take them swimming, but it didn't help.

Her father was in Afghanistan in the military maybe. Okay, at least he was alive. At least I hoped so. I could get Dennis started on finding him, maybe through the Red Cross. "What's your daddy's name?"

"Sgt. Joseph Smith." I heard her sharp sucking in of air and knew she was close to tears. Her bottom lip was quivering.

Great. A crying kid with only one of the most common names. I had all the luck. Bad, that is. Finding her father might be a bit more difficult. Then it hit me. Joey. Joey was named after her father. If she was named after her father, then it couldn't have been him who had taken the bullet to the forehead.

I wanted to ask about her mother. I needed to know I rationalized silently. I patted her back thinking of various ways to go about it and discarding each one. I held her and tried not to look in her big trusting eyes. I felt so sorry for her. To have had so much happen in her short number of years. I was not equipped to deal with this.

I felt her chest expand and then exhale. She felt more under control and I lifted my arms to extricate myself when her voice started out high and shaky.

"My mommy disappeared because they wanted to hurt me. She was protecting me," came the small voice I was beginning to care for and that scared me. I didn't know what to say.

"Really?" seemed so inadequate but it was the only thing that came from my mouth.

"They wanted something from her. I don't know what." Again the nose was between my ribs. I could hear a large sucking in of mucus from her nose.

After a few more minutes she continued. "Mommy said no. The bad men tried to grab me. I didn't want to leave." Again the story broke off and I felt the little button nose rub across my ribs. This shirt was shot but it didn't bother me. I didn't have time to analyze why because the voice started again after a quick hiccup.

"Mommy got really mad and hit the man holding me. She told me to run. . ."

It seemed once she started talking, she couldn't stop.

"I ran. I heard loud noises. I wanted to go back. I was so scared." She turned her head back into my chest and I could hear her sobs again. I awkwardly tried to comfort her and ran my hand down the back of head, surprised by how soft her hair was.

I thought about what she had said. The murder scene I saw didn't look like any kind of struggle. Had they posed the body? They couldn't have. If the man in the bed had been shot moving, there would have been blood spatter, but there wasn't. Had someone had time to clean it up? Who was the man? It couldn't have been her father if he was overseas. How had Joey gotten in that stair cabinet? She couldn't have climbed in by herself.

"Where did you hide?" I heard myself ask.

"I ran to the rood seller."

"Where?"

"Rood seller. It was cold and dirty but I stayed there."

Root cellar. She hid in a small area usually hidden under the floorboards where families stored their vegetables for the winter. "Who found you?"

"I don't know, a man."

"What did he look like?"

Joey hunched her shoulders and thought. After a few minutes, she replied: "He was big. He gave me a sucker and told me I was brave."

"Where did you go?"

"He took me to a nice man and lady and said they would be my new mommy and daddy. I don't want a new mommy and daddy."

What moron would take a child to a new place and introduce them to new people as new parents like the old ones were yesterday's trash. I was pissed at the insensitivity.

"They were nice but I like you and Auntie Patrenka better." Joey must have seen my anger and tried to fill the void.

I couldn't be anyone's foster parent. No way. I had to get her off this subject. I had to get back to my quest for information and get this kid off my hands.

"What happened to the people the big guy gave you to?"

She shook her head. "I woke up and I was with you in the car. Patrenka always smells nice. She smells like my mom. The next thing I knew, we were eating French fries in a big bed."

That must have been the night we took her from the murder house. So the dead couple wasn't her parents but her mother was dead. How did the dead couple fit into this? "What did your new mommy and daddy look like?"

She looked at me quizzically and shrugged her shoulders. I could see she was trying to think about it. "She had a slippery dress that was really pretty but I would slide off her lap," she finally said.

Could the dress she described be the red dress of the woman on the porch? If I was a betting man, I would say yes.

"I'm hungry," Joey said.

I looked at my watch and realized that it was nearly five and Parenka hadn't returned from her two o'clock interview. I didn't want Joey to worry. I wasn't sure what to do. I didn't really want to move. I was comfortable with Joey snuggled next to me. Her grip had loosened but there wasn't a lot of wriggle room. I reached for the remote on the bedside table and flipped back to cartoons hoping to distract Joey while I rehashed what she'd said. It seemed to work and she rolled away and became engrossed in *Dora the Explorer*.

Chapter 16

As I considered calling Dennis's captain to see if he was in communication, the door opened and in walked Patrenka and Dennis in one piece. I sighed in relief. Why was I so worried about someone I had only met a couple of days ago? How had someone pierced my defenses in such a sort time? It wasn't just Patrenka, it was Joey too. What had happened to my loner existence, my master reporter aloofness that never let anyone close?

"Well?" I said, jumping to my feet, waiting for something.

"It went well," Dennis said. "She did fine." He patted her on the shoulder and I ground my teeth.

"Great, but did you get anything that would help us?" My blood pressure was already high from worry and I was about to blow a fuse.

"Yes and no. Mr. Rockwell is definitely a person of interest. He didn't give anything away but he got upset a couple of times when Patrenka deftly led him into traps. Mighty fine questioning, I might add." Dennis grinned at her. "It came across loud and clear over the radio and is now on tape." He patted his pocket.

I could feel my eyes rolling at the compliment but I wanted details, something to go on. "Do you think he is behind all this?"

"I don't know. He's suspicious. He's definitely running some type of shady business, a touch outside the law. I would bet on that, but if it includes murder, I don't know," Dennis added.

"How so?"

"When Patrenka probed about other developments being green, and how people don't normally like things that are different, I thought he was going to launch into how he intimidated them, but he caught himself. What was it he said?" Dennis scratched what was left of his reddish thinning locks.

"'Other people's opinion don't bother me and I don't let it get to the planning commissions. It's all about,' and then he stopped, realizing what he was saying. That sure was a mighty fine way to get at the truth of his nature. We could use your talents in our interrogation rooms." I wanted to wipe the lecherous grin off Dennis's face.

"What did he say about Joey's parents and the disappearances of people opposed to his developments?" I could feel the red infusing my face and took a breath to cool down.

"Yeah, right, Mitch. Patrenka walked in and demanded to know if he had killed Joey's parents. We would have gotten a lot of information that way. What's wrong with you, man? Have you lost your mind?"

I gave him a warning look and we glanced at Joey who hopefully hadn't heard his crass statement. I knew I was acting crazy and not the cool professional reporter but I needed information. I started pacing back and forth.

I turned to Patrenka. "What did you think?" I expected the tell-all stare I normally got when I asked her questions. Again she surprised me.

"He's slime," she whistled out between set jaws and hard eyes. This was more emotion than I had ever heard out of her before. I wanted to take a step back, but was unable to. The hatred in her eyes riveted me to the floor. I couldn't believe this was the same person, but she was wearing the same herringbone suit.

"He made my skin crawl," she added with a curling lip. Her accented voice reminded me of the old gypsy fortune tellers in the movies. I thought she was going to spit right there on the carpet but of course she didn't.

"What was it that tipped you off?" I moved toward her ready to shake her if she didn't give me more information.

"His whole manner. He was above the law alright. He was so

cocky. So full of himself," she said with the disdain dripping in her voice. "He thought he owned me," she continued. "Mr. Buck Rockwell wasn't laughing when I asked him why all his objectors mysteriously disappeared. I wanted to crow with laughter." As she talked, she slipped off the heels.

I was amazed. She was volunteering information. We were conversing and I was enjoying it. I was also enjoying the outline her breasts made against the jacket and hoped that would be the next to go.

Dennis cut in then to break the mood and I wanted to strangle him.

"You could hear him gulp right through the mike. It was like she had him trapped. It was incredible. I was in awe." Coming from Dennis that was high praise. I sucked in a breath and looked at Patrenka. She was obviously in her element, the center of attention and basking in Dennis' praise, something I didn't like one bit. I wanted to break the mood, the camaraderie. "So what did you learn?" I asked rather sharply then glanced at Joey, noticing her attention on us and not the TV show.

"Not much," she said back to the two syllable answers after her diatribe only seconds before. I wanted to call the words back. I wanted her happy and proud and talking. I wanted her to explain everything — not clam up into monosyllables. What could I say to bring it back? The moment was lost.

"What made you think to ask him what he was like in high school?" Dennis asked. "That was pure genius."

I said a silent prayer of thanks to the Virgin Mary for Dennis and the saint he was, not withstanding that I had damned him only moments before.

"I wanted him to feel safe and what safer place is there than reminding him of being the big man on campus during his youth . . ."

"He never even realized he told you he played football at St. Mary's High School. We can find out a lot more about him now," Dennis preened.

"Wait a minute," I said, aggressively slamming the mood back, jealous at their camaraderie. "I thought the FBI ordered you to hand over the case and all the documents. You can't investigate."

"I'm not investigating the murder on Third Street." Dennis's smile was that of a petulant child and his green eyes sparkled in mischief. "I'm investigating complaints of violence and disappearances. This has nothing to do with the murders."

"Tell that to them FBI boys," I snapped.

"I tried to get more out of the Feds, but I was lectured about case loads when I tried to find out more about the identifications," Dennis snapped. I watched Patrenka stiffen slightly.

Then I remembered. I couldn't believe I had forgotten, but my jealousy and worry over Patrenka had driven Joey's revelations from my mind and may be a way to redeem myself to Patrenka.

"The dead couple wasn't Joey's parents," I dropped into the conversation. It landed there like a ton of bricks. Dennis stared wide-eyed, but Patrenka looked at the floor.

"Why do you say that?" Dennis prodded.

"Joey said so. She told me her father is in Afghanistan. She also said someone came to their house looking for something her mother had. I think it was Buck coming to their house judging by her reaction to him on the TV. Joey said she hid in a cellar with fruits and vegetables. Then a big man came and took her to live with this couple. The man told her it was her new mother and father." I paused to see what effect my words had. Dennis was amazed. Patrenka looked angry.

"Joey said the couple was nice but she didn't know what happened to them. All she remembers is waking up in my apartment. I guess it's a good thing the Feds don't know she was there because she slept through the whole thing."

I was waiting for a 'good job' or some kind of acknowledgement. Dennis stunned expression was enough, but Patrenka wouldn't meet my gaze. She was beautiful when she was angry but why was she angry?

Then it dawned on me. She already knew this latest bit of information! How could I be so stupid? She had spent a lot of time with Joey and probably gotten the same information. Why hadn't she shared it? She was going to use the information on her own exclusive. My hands clenched. What else did she know that she hadn't shared? I was mad. This wasn't about my lusting after her and finding a traitor. This was about Joey and our quest for the truth. I thought we were working as a team, but apparently not. My fury increased with my blood pressure. We deserved to know.

"Really?" Dennis asked, breaking into my silent tirade.

"Yes, but I don't think that comes as a surprise to all of us." My voice dripped with betrayal. Patrenka didn't look up. She glanced at her wristwatch. She didn't acknowledge the conversation. Dennis looked from Patrenka to me and back again and shook his head.

"I'm hungry," said a small voice who gripped my hand. It was moments like this that were quickly breaking my cold heart when it came to Joey. I looked down at the little squirt.

"We can get something here real quick. I think we're done," I said hoping Patrenka would get the double meaning I intended.

"Yeah, I need to get home," Dennis said quickly escaping my dark mood.

I stood and went over by the door and picked up Joey's shoes. "Here, Sport, put these on. What sounds good?"

"Pizza." Joey jumped off the bed before I had the last one tied and ran to the door.

"Pizza, it is," I said following her to the door and ruffling her hair in an almost paternal gesture. Joey ran and grabbed her Tigers cap.

"Coming?" I turned and looked at Patrenka. I didn't care if she came or not. She nodded her head in the affirmative and I turned my back on her letting her hustle to catch up.

Chapter 17

Dinner was a disaster. Joey spilled her soda reaching for a second piece of pizza. Patrenka and I jumped at the same time grabbing napkins to stem the tide before it reached the edge of the table. Our hands connected and we catapulted back into our seats. We dabbed futilely at the spill as it spread across to our respective laps. We all picked at our pizza slices like they were pieces of cardboard. I didn't want to leave, knowing Joey would soon be asleep and there would be no buffer. Patrenka was having difficulties meeting my gaze. I enjoyed her discomfort because I was still mad that she withheld vital information. We finally called it quits and headed back to the hotel. No one spoke much, even Joey was solemn, catching our somber moods.

When we returned to the room, Patrenka gave Joey a bath and I did research on my computer looking for all the St. Mary's High Schools in the United States hoping to nail down Buck Rockwell. My first search showed hundreds of St. Mary's schools. Then I narrowed it and added Buck's name to the search. There was only one – St. Mary's High School in Chicago. It was close but not so close where someone would recognize him. Still he could have some less than savory connections even though, according to the Chicago public relations machine, the days of Al Capone were long gone. He was involved in something, but whether it was organized crime or not remained to be seen.

I was engrossed in my research, hot on the trail of Buck Rockwell. I didn't realize that Patrenka was tucking Joey into bed until I smelled her perfume. My back straightened, then my shoulders sagged, and my forehead rested on the top of my screen. What did I want? I lifted my head and rolled my shoulders to release the tightened muscles. Did I want Patrenka to spill all her secrets? Yes. Was I afraid I wouldn't be attracted to her if the mystique was gone? I wasn't sure, but I knew I wanted to know her better. I felt my blood rush between my legs creating a rise I wasn't ready for emotionally. I wanted her to trust me. I wanted her to talk to me, but I had never had any luck in that regard. I gripped the arms of the chair in frustration. It seemed she let her hair down so to speak with Dennis but not with me. Did she not like me? Why did I make her uncomfortable? Did I stare too much at her incredible body? Was she a spy? Anything was possible. I wanted answers. My closed fist hit the arm of the chair. I deserved answers. The other fist connected with the other chair arm. We'd been cooped up in this room for three days. I deserved honesty. In some cultures we would be considered married and we were parents at least in the fostering sense.

Joey snuggled down and went right to sleep, worn out from the pool, our emotional discussion and the silent treatment at dinner. Patrenka disappeared in the bathroom. I started channel surfing to keep me occupied, my research forgotten. Patrenka re-emerged from the bathroom in my t-shirt and sweatpants she used for pajamas. How I wished I was in those same clothes. I did a mental slap and reminded myself I was still annoyed with her. We needed to talk and she needed to give some answers. Now.

I knew she was stalling but I wasn't willing to call her on it yet. I was still hoping she would trust me without having me pry it out of her. She hung up her suit from the interview, straightened the items on the dresser and I saw her looking around to find something else to keep her from the issue at hand.

I rose and grabbed her hand and pulled her to the chair that I vacated. I turned the chair around facing the bed. I sat on the bed our knees a mere centimeter apart. She was looking at her hands.

"Spill it. What do you know?"

She looked up into my eyes and I thought I saw pain there. I wanted to make it better but wasn't willing to make it easy. I waited in silence knowing the trick wouldn't work but hoping she would volunteer. I didn't want to interrogate her. I wasn't sure I could control my anger if I had to start pushing. I could easily start shouting and that would surely wake Joey, possibly scaring her. I didn't want to torment our young charge with any more loud arguments.

"I'm sorry. You deserved better," came the low reply. I thought I had imagined it until she lifted her head and looked into my eyes. They were glossy and ready to overflow but I could see she was trying hard to control them.

"I didn't know who to trust. When I figured out you were one of the good guys, I didn't know how to tell you, so I kept silent."

"Who are you?"

"My name is Patrenka. My last name has changed several times. Peterson is a former cover that worked well for what I had to do here. I am an FBI behavioral specialist. I've worked undercover quite successfully bringing down murderers that prey on women. Unfortunately, I was too late to save my step-sister. She called me for help but I didn't get the message until my current case was completed. I was in deep cover and the case was ready to break wide open. My supervisor made the call. Maybe I could have stopped her death. Joey's mother has to be dead. She'd never leave Joey. I haven't been able to find her body. All I have left is my niece. I will get whoever killed her if it is the last thing I do." Patrenka looked over at Joey's sleeping form, taking a deep breath.

Now that she was talking, it was as if the dam was overflowing and I didn't want to stop to ask the many questions that ran through my brain.

"When the call came in, a friend of mine in the bureau went to check it out. When he arrived at my step-sister's home, they were gone. Luckily, he did a thorough search and discovered Joey in the root cellar. My step-sister was different from me. I wanted excitement, challenges, big cities. She wanted an Amish existence - a simple life, growing their own food, raising chickens and cows and being self sufficient. She supplemented their income by taking nature photos for postcards, greeting cards, anyone who would pay. Joey's father was deployed about year ago and is scheduled home soon. I don't know how to reach him."

She stopped speaking and disappeared behind the veneer I

knew so well. I was happy with her confession but knew there was more. I watched her carefully, unwilling to let her stop now.

"I don't know what happened. My friend placed Joey with the couple who were killed. I wasn't done with my case yet, but he knew I would take her on my return in a day or two. The couple was former FBI agents who left the bureau for a normal life. They had gone out to celebrate her pregnancy. They'd been trying for years for a child. Everything my friend did was off the books. The FBI took over because of the couple and their former identity. They never knew about Joey and still don't. I don't think they should. It would only complicate matters. I'm not sure their death is related to Joey.

"I'm currently on leave as I always am when I'm done with a long mission. My plan is to leave the bureau and raise Joey as my own. First I need to find out what happened to my sister. She would never have left Joey voluntarily. She can only be dead." Patrenka's composure seemed to crumble talking about her worst fear. Her head dipped and her dark tresses covered her face. I heard her suck in some air and her head lifted. Her iron control was back.

"Joey woke up shortly after you left your apartment. I told her to pretend she didn't know me and not talk to anyone who asked her questions. I reinforced it every time we went to the pool."

I had to remind myself to close my mouth. She had told Joey not to talk. Good thing I was a better reporter and Joey opened up. Before I could say anything she continued.

"I think my sister was an impediment to Buck Rockwell in some way that he couldn't resolve so she disappeared like all the other complications he has come across."

I sat there and stared. I couldn't help it. I knew I was making her uncomfortable by the stupid look on my face, but I was trying to process the flood of information and categorize it. The problem was it didn't work. I felt like I had been dropped into the plot of a B movie. I could recite her speech, word for word, but I didn't know what any of it meant.

"How did you get hooked up with me?" I asked. "Why did you want to be a reporter?"

"That was luck on my part. Two assignments before, I worked as a reporter for the *Los Angeles Times* where my cover was Patrenka Peterson. I slipped into that persona. I had my friend call in a couple of markers and get me the internship. I asked to work with the person on the cop beat. Your editor — Ken, isn't it? — warned me against working with you. He said you were a real loner. I would be better off with someone else, but I resisted. I convinced him that I needed experience on the crime beat. I implied I could pull some more strings upstairs so he relented. He didn't like it but he gave in."

I knew what it felt like when she turned up the heat. I could even feel sorry for Ken; he was way outmatched. That made me feel better about getting stuck with her, although I knew I wanted to be stuck with her from the minute she walked through the door.

"Let's step back a minute. When were you here last?"

"It was about a year ago. I read your piece on a simple murder suicide that turned out to be a conspiracy and a double murder. Your story had more information than the cops would have provided and I knew you could get me into places. I was right." She smiled knowingly at me.

"I had no idea how quickly I would get on the case," she said, her smile widening then dropping. "On the drive to Third Street I couldn't believe how well my plan worked. I didn't know we were going to the house where Joey was. I saw a panicked Sam talking to one of the officers at the scene after you went in the house. I approached and he told me Joey was inside. You reappeared outside and when I turned, Sam was gone. I was so scared for Joey. I thought she was dead, but you never mentioned a child. I couldn't face seeing Joey in the same condition as Ashley on the porch. I couldn't believe it when you said there was no child, and I had to do something. I had talked to the neighbor but she didn't know about the child. I made it up."

I never thought her intuition was a lie. I thought she was an incredible reporter. Boy was I stupid. I couldn't help but shake my head.

"It's true. I'm telling you the truth." Patrenka said, thinking my head shaking was a statement of unbelief instead of the sad state of my intuitive skills and how gullible I had been.

"Who is Sam?" I asked.

"He's my handler. You saw him at the door to your apartment. You've been calling him Herman."

I had my answers but it didn't make anything clearer. We weren't any closer to finding Joey's mother and presumably never would if she was wearing cement shoes. The couple we, — or correction —

I thought were Joey's parents, were dead former FBI agents. Patrenka was Joey's closest relative which explains the "auntie" I heard and why Joey was so comfortable with Patrenka.

"When was the last time you talked to your step-sister?" I asked.

"It was before the start of my last assignment. I had stopped by to visit for a week." Patrenka paused and I could see she was remembering her last visit. She was talking almost to herself.

"My niece had grown so much and I wanted to keep in touch. I taught her how to upload photos of them to a secure website I created so when I was on assignment, I could still keep in touch and not break my cover."

I watched her eyes sparkle as she remembered a happier time. I didn't want to bring her back to the present, but I needed more information. I touched her hand and her head snapped up, the pain returning to her eyes. I wanted to take it back but couldn't.

"Evelyn never said anything about problems. Her husband, Joe, had been sent overseas. I was undercover for about six months when she called looking for me and I didn't know it. Two weeks later I had the proof I needed for a conviction and wrapped up my investigation. Only then did I know Evelyn was trying to reach me and what Sam had done to protect Joey.

"When was the last time you checked the website?"

"It's been several weeks."

She turned around to my computer. "May I?" I nodded and she plugged in a website and clicked the keys entering the username and password. I stood, looking over her shoulders.

"HELP!" came up in red on the screen and underneath it a blurry photo of the woods with shadows. I put my hands on Patrenka's shoulders and leaned in closer to get a better look. Patrenka muttered and the scene disappeared. A list of dates and times came up.

"What is it?"

"This is a listing of when the website was last updated. It was at 2:13 p.m. on September 23 when the photo was uploaded. The connection timed out. She never finished uploading the rest of the photos. What does this mean?"

She clicked more keys and the photo was enlarged to the full screen. "It's in the woods," I added.

"Yes, and this is the outline of someone, but I can't see who."

Frustration sharpened her words. I squeezed her shoulders liking the way she felt under my T-shirt. I started massaging her shoulders and her neck and felt her begin to melt. I felt my reaction stir and was glad she had her back to me.

Finally, I thought, I was getting somewhere. I felt a tinge of guilt using Patrenka's distress to my advantage but I figured I was entitled. We had been sharing a room for a couple of days. My fingers started wandering farther down her front. I leaned down and was ready to continue my massage with my lips and let my hands flow further to those mounds that I was sure ached for my touch. Patrenka stood, pushing the chair back into my midsection and smacking my chin as I was leaning in to nuzzle her neck. Patrenka neatly sidestepped my bent-over form and started pacing back and forth. I tried to get my dignity back but I doubt she even noticed or missed my touch.

"What did she find in the woods? Whose woods was she in?"

After the second question, I realized she was totally focused on the image we found on the web and hadn't even realized my seduction. I was crushed, then ashamed. We were supposed to be in this together to help Joey. I glanced at the small child in the bed relieved to see she was still in slumber land.

"Was she interrupted while uploading the photos? Maybe the rest of the photos are still on her computer. We need to find her computer."

"It's gone. Sam couldn't find it." Patrenka lapsed deep in thought, still pacing. I had my libido nearly under control.

"If Sam hadn't answered the call for me, Joey could have died in the cellar or came out and been taken by Buck, although I can't prove that, yet."

"Tell me about this Sam guy," I said getting jealous at the way her voice softened when she said his name.

"His name is Sam Sloan or at least that is the name he uses. I believe you met briefly. He was coming to check on Joey and me at your apartment. I was about to let him in when I heard your tussle in the hall and pretended to be asleep. I've only talked to him once since then although briefly and he has been trying to get in touch since."

"You're sure he is a good guy? He can be trusted?" I asked.

"I'm sure of it. He's had my back since I started undercover," she said and my stomach clenched in jealousy.

"Let's get him here then and compare notes. Maybe with the three of us, we can make some headway," I said wanting to see my competition and what spin the FBI had on who killed their agents. Maybe I could do an update to the double homicide story and get it back in the news.

Patrenka stood and walked to the desk. Opening her purse she pulled out a slim cell phone and powered it up. It jangled immediately but she ignored it. Instead she punched in a couple of numbers and waited.

"Sam, it's me. He knows. Meet me at the Best Western, Room 228." She disconnected and returned the phone to her purse.

"He will be here quickly. He knew I was by the mall but not exactly where. I didn't want him underfoot until I was sure you could be trusted."

I looked at her in amazement. "Trusted? I didn't even know the half of this until a minute ago and you were worried if I could be trusted? That's rich," I scoffed.

She didn't answer. I was used to that. She didn't offer explanations or even an apology. In a way I had to respect that. She stood her ground and followed her instincts. At least she had confidence in me now or at least I hoped so. "What made you tell me this now?" I asked curiously.

"Joey. She trusted you enough to talk about Ashley and Mark. If she had faith in you, you couldn't be wrapped up with Buck."

"Oh," I said, pleased that Joey was on my side. I never had wanted trust like that before. Now I had it, I wasn't sure what to do with it. But Joey's faith and then Patrenka's made me feel warm in a place that had not been in a long time. Maybe my heart of stone was not as hard as I thought. Maybe it took the hand of a toddler to break it.

"You trust a two-year old's impression?" I said nearly to myself.

"No," Patrenka said. "Joey, short for Joanna, is nearly five and smart for her age. She takes after her aunt," Patrenka said with pride I had never heard in her voice before. "People underestimate her because she is small for her age."

My comment was swallowed without verbalizing, when a soft rap sounded at the door. I watched Patrenka go to the door and peer out the peep hole surprised when a small caliber gun was at her side.

Where had that come from? Why didn't I know she had it? She was certainly full of surprises. I wouldn't mind hunting for the holster because believe me, there weren't too many places she could hide it.

Patrenka undid the chain and the bolt cracking the door open. The giant of a man, I had labeled Herman, gracefully slipped into the room despite his size. The room seemed to shrink and I did take a step back as his arm struck out.

"No hard feelings huh?" came the deep baritone voice as I stared numbly at the outstretched hand.

I belatedly grabbed it and shook it, surprised that the handshake was firm but not crushing. "No problem," I answered, unconsciously standing taller and thrusting my shoulders back.

"Now the male bonding is done, let's compare notes," Patrenka said taking charge in a manner I found intoxicating and annoying.

"Sam, did you find a computer when you found Joey?"

"No. The place looked like a scuffle had taken place but there was no computer."

We powwowed around the small table for an hour but I didn't hear anything new. Sam didn't have much to add about Ashley and Mark's death. That was at a dead end, too. The only lead we had was Buck and few ideas how to proceed. I was beat. It had been a long day. I was ready to drop. Patrenka must have sensed my exhaustion or was beat herself.

"Let's wrap this up and meet for breakfast at nine when we are all refreshed," she said in total control. Sam stood and she walked him to the door and he was gone. She relocked and chained the door and then turned to me. "I'm turning in" and disappeared into the bathroom.

I could see how Patrenka could be a good cop. She had a natural authority that even Sam respected even though I suspected he was the senior agent.

I wasn't sure how I liked her calling the shots. I was used to being my own boss.

Chapter 18

The next day dawned cold and dismal with a misty rain falling. Joey was up and bouncing on the bed. She threw a pillow at my head, which woke me as well as an alarm clock. I shuffled into the shower, hoping to revive myself. I felt like I had been on a week-long drinking binge with none of the carefree revelry to remember.

After the shower and dressing, I realized I was going to have to do something about my dwindling wardrobe. My clothes adorned a different frame than my own. If Sam was not a bad guy, maybe we could go back to my apartment. I wanted to broach that subject at breakfast but wasn't sure I was ready to let Joey and Patrenka out of my life. The hotel room kept us connected and together. Maybe it was best to keep quiet.

We met at a Denny's down the street. Joey was excited to be out and ordered strawberry pancakes. Patrenka had fruit and yogurt and Sam and I had eggs, over easy. After we had eaten, we again discussed strategy. I worried about Joey or others overhearing but no one else seemed to notice. Joey slid across the booth's seat to sit closer to me and her hand wound its way into mine. She gave me a dimpled grin, reassuring me.

As the waitress refilled our coffees, Patrenka said Buck's new development adjoined her step-sister's property and his denial of any opposition. "During my interview with Buck, I asked him about options for all the property for the development. He said he had them all wrapped up." Her hands tightened around her coffee cup as she brought it to her lips. She was even more beautiful when she was angry.

"He was so smug, I wanted to scratch his eyes out," she said slamming her cup back on the table. "We have to get this guy."

"How can we break him? We need ideas," I said.

Sam looked at Joey and I wanted to shield her from view. "We could leak that there was a witness and be there when he makes a move."

A kid as bait? Over my dead body! I wanted to plant my fist in his mouth. Lucky for him, I didn't have to.

"No," came Patrenka's steely voice. Her eyes were hard, cold and penetrating. I gave a small sigh, glad they were not trained on me.

The waitress stopped again and dropped the bill on the table. Patrenka picked it up without looking at it and slapped it down next to Sam. "You won the bill with that stupid idea."

Silence reigned at the table and Joey started moving back and forth in the booth shaking the table every time she came forward. I reached out and grabbed her half-empty glass of milk before it toppled.

"Joey, honey, do you remember anything from the night you hid with the vegetables?" Patrenka asked.

"Like what?" came a small voice. Her boisterous behavior of only seconds before had disappeared.

"Can you describe what you saw and heard?" Patrenka asked gently. Joey seemed to lean closer to me but that could have been me reaching out to her, afraid of what she heard and afraid she hadn't heard anything.

"Fighting," came the small response.

"Who was fighting?" Patrenka asked.

"My mom and the men."

"What men?"

"I don't know. The man with the raspberry on his finger."

"Raspberry?" I asked.

Joey's only reply was a nod. Time for a new tactic.

"Was one of them the man you saw on TV?" Patrenka probed

reading my mind. Joey didn't make a verbal response but shook her head up and down then buried it in my chest smearing snot across my last clean shirt. I rubbed her back trying to comfort her but not sure I accomplished the task. I wanted the questions to end but knew they couldn't. We needed information to break this case.

"Did you hear sounds or words?" Patrenka asked gently.

Again Joey nodded and we waited while she tried to tell us.

"Momma said she wouldn't give in and, and, and," Joey started to sob.

I didn't know what to do. I felt powerless, unable to give this small person what she needed most. I struggled with my inadequacy and was moving closer to hug her tightly when she took a deep breath trying to get herself under control. "He hit my mom. I heard a crack and then she cried."

"What kind of crack? Like two hands clapping or like a metal sound?" asked Sam, leaning across the table.

"Both" and the sobs started again.

"Joey, do you know what a gunshot sounds like?" Sam probed.

She shook her head no. Patrenka scowled at him. "That's enough," she hissed.

"You were brave, Joey," Patrenka said reaching across the table running her hand down the child's cheek and cupping her chin. "We will find out what happened to her, bet on it." There was such confidence in her voice I even found myself believing her.

As if we had a prearranged signal, we all rose from the table and headed for the door. I hung back as Sam stopped to pay the bill at the hostess stand. Patrenka and Joey crossed to the car. "She's the best undercover agent there is," Sam said as we watched Patrenka hold the door for Joey to scramble into the back seat. Patrenka shut the door and opened the passenger door looking back toward us.

I nodded. "Sam, I need those bogus murder charges to disappear so I can move around freely. These close quarters are a killer," I said trying to make light of the situation.

Sam studied me for a minute and glanced back at Patrenka. "Torture, I imagine," he said with a sly grin.

I wanted to do the macho thing and make some comment about it being tough sharing a hotel room with a babe, but I couldn't do it. Patrenka wasn't some babe to massage an inflated ego. She was so much more than that and I didn't want to go there. "When do you think you could clear it?" I probed, steering the conversation back on track.

"Soon, but I think it best if you lay low a while longer. Two people missing and another two dead. We don't know what we are dealing with yet," Sam advised as we walked back of my car.

"Two people are missing? Who else?"

Sam blanched, looking guilty. "Sorry, I meant the two agents who were killed." I knew he was lying but tried another tack. Sam was not the smartest at undercover work.

"Do you really think there's a chance that Joey's mother is alive?"

"I want to stay positive," he said, staring at Joey who was putting on her baseball cap and talking animatedly with Patrenka.

"What about a will?" I asked. "If they had a will, killing her would only have the land pass to the heirs and then only after a lengthy probate."

"We're checking into it but don't want to tip our hand with Buck Rockwell yet. We don't want him to know we're suspicious. When Patrenka interviewed him without letting us know, it almost blew the whole operation. We're looking into his financials and studying deeds to the property surrounding his. He'll have to document his ownership when he goes before the Thornapple Township Planning Commission. That's in a couple of days."

"I want to be there," I said quickly.

"I don't think that is a good idea, Mitch."

"I need to do something. Hiding out in a hotel room is not the way I conduct business."

"I know," Sam said and I knew he was placating me. "It's important to keep Joey hidden and Patrenka's cover intact."

I understood the necessity, but I didn't like it. I let him think he had me convinced. I fished the keys out of my pocket and moved around to the driver's side, leaving Sam.

"I'll keep in touch," Sam said not quite meeting my gaze and nodding a farewell to Patrenka.

We drove back to the hotel and I didn't add much to the conversation. I was thinking about what I could do. The waiting was killing me. I was used to finding out my own answers, not hiding while others did my legwork and only coming out when the coast was clear. On the other hand I had never been responsible for two others and never a child. The weighty responsibly felt odd on my shoulders.

As we walked into the hotel, I felt a small hand reach into mine. I looked down at Joey and smiled. She frowned.

"What's the matter, Sport?"

"I'm sorry," she said pulling off her baseball cap.

"Sorry?" I asked. "For what?"

"I can't remember it all. I want to find my mommy but I can't remember it all," came the small sad voice and my heart turned again. I stopped and bent down on one knee.

"It'll come back. Wait and see," I said.

"I miss her," she said breaking into a fresh round of tears that tore at my gut. I wanted to do something, but I didn't know what. I had to do something. As tough as it was for me, I now knew it was time for Joey to find out what happened to her mother – good or bad. We needed answers.

I grabbed Joey and swung her up in my arms. I had never lifted a child before but I wanted to provide warmth and strength. I carried her into the hotel room on my shoulders and sat down with her on the edge of the bed. I had totally tuned out Patrenka, a first since I met her. She had been following unobtrusively. She joined us on the bed waiting for Joey to calm down. Before I knew it, Patrenka suggested a swim and Joey bounced up and ran to change. Oh, the ease of youth. I was still thunderstruck at the violence Joey had endured. I raged at a faceless opponent. I needed to vent my fury.

I needed to quit being part of the case and be the investigative reporter. The cops and Feds weren't doing enough. I needed to find some clues. I needed to do something productive. Instead, I was picking up Joey's cap from the bed and laying it on the dresser along with the clothes she left on the bathroom floor. I needed to be more than a glorified maid.

I dialed the only person I knew would give me answers if he had them.

"Hey Dennis, anything new on the case?" I said, lounging on the bed with a couple of pillows behind my back.

"No, how's beauty doing with the beast?"

"Knock it off." I was in no mood for banter. "Did you dig up any more on Buck Rockwell? What about the murders?"

"Nope. The Feds have it locked up nice and tight. What do you know?"

"Not much more than I knew a couple of days ago." I flipped through my notebook, scanning my notes from the previous day's activities. "Hey, can you check out Sam Sloan? He's a Fed working the case. I want to see if he is legit. Got any contacts that can check him out from within the agency?"

"Maybe, but it will cost you."

"How's this? The Feds are investigating Buck Rockwell too and were mighty upset when Patrenka went in herself."

"Glad they didn't know I was listening in. I'm sure they would have confiscated that as well. Who is this Sloan guy anyway?"

"The moron who found Joey and placed her with a couple of FBI friends for safekeeping only it wasn't so safe. Get this, he then apparently forgot to keep looking for Joey's mother and went back to his caseload."

"What an asshole."

"Yep. He wasn't even any good getting caught breaking into my apartment."

"That guy was a Fed? So much for upholding the law," Dennis said.

"Yeah, whatever you say. Get back to me as soon as you can." I disconnected without waiting for any smart replies.

Next I punched in Ken's number.

"Are you still alive? I figured with you being on vacation, I wouldn't hear from you for another week," Ken said.

"I'm on vacation?"

"Yup. It was either that or fire you for not showing up for work or calling in. Rules are rules. Suddenly, your vacation request was in my 'in' basket. Next time remember to sign it."

"I didn't know you had an 'in' basket," I said chuckling. It felt good bantering about something pseudo normal and inconsequential.

"What can I do for you?"

"I don't know. I guess I wanted to check in," I said hesitantly. Feeling needy was definitely a new thing for the lone ranger.

"Where are you?"

I wanted to tell him I was holed up in a hotel room with a beautiful woman I couldn't touch and a cute little girl. I stopped. I almost let it slip. I didn't know what to say next. I shouldn't be talking about Joey at all but yet I wanted to claim her as mine too. I was thinking of Joey as my child. I didn't even know she existed a week ago. And now she was mine? Some secretive reporter I was. I wanted the world to know about my roommates.

"Mitch, are you there? Did I lose you?"

"No, sorry, just distracted for minute."

"Hey, what happened to that woman intern? She hasn't shown up since you left and no one has inquired about her either. It's odd. You ain't shacking up with her, are you?" Ken said and I could hear the laughter in his voice at the absurdity of his own joke.

"Is the FBI still checking in on the arrest warrant?" I asked to deflect his interest.

"No, not in a couple of days. After the initial barrage, there hasn't been much. Your fill-in isn't much for digging out info and it seems no one is talking. Any suggestions?"

"No. I'm not having any luck on my end either." I heard some noise in the hall. "Ken, my vacation is calling. Thanks." I hit the disconnect button as the door opened and Joey walked in.

"Uncle Mitch, I did the big slide and went really fast," Joey said climbing up on my lap and in great detail outlined her journey down the slide. I hugged her and she hugged me back. "I love you, Uncle Mitch." I didn't even mind the damp spot she left in my lap as she headed for the shower.

I looked up. Patrenka's smile had softened her features but she looked away when she realized I was staring. She quickly busied herself, grabbing her clothes and disappearing into the bathroom. I would never understand that woman.

Chapter 19

It took a few seconds for my eyes to open. I didn't want to wake but the prodding in my ribs was insistent. In my dreams, I'd wanted something with green eyes and curves, but it was floating farther and farther away.

As the sensual touches turned into sharp jabs, I moved to open my eyes and quickly shut them against the harsh light sending spikes of pain into my fuzzy brain. Another poke, this one sharper than the last, and I again opened my eyes. I tried to focus but the pain intensified again. I wanted to drift back.

I recognized Joey through small slits. Joey's face was only inches from mine and looked worried and alarmed. My senses jerked awake as the pain intensified. I tried to lift my head. Something was wrong. What was wrong with me?

"What's up, Sport?" I croaked in a sleep-soaked voice trying to sound casual while my adrenaline started to race.

"Gone," came the garbled reply around the thumb in her mouth. Something horrible must have happened to have this self-possessed child sucking her thumb.

"What's gone?" I was trying to make sense of what had made her upset. The pizza from last night?

We ordered a pizza delivered and I went to a party store for beer at Patrenka's insistence. I was recharged with testosterone after Joey dropped off to sleep. I groaned as I remembered drinking several of the beers and going to bed in a sulk. Patrenka never drank any and my lack of inhibitions crept into my unconscious thoughts. I was determined to move our relationship to first base; it was the least I deserved with our close quarters. I remembered patting my side of the bed once as she came out of the bathroom. I'm sure I had an invitation on my face. I watched her gracefully stride to the bed with Joey and lower herself down to lean on the pillows against the headboard and stretch her feet out, wiggling her toes. I remembered suggesting I suck on her cute little fuchsia toenails to see if they tasted any different from other ones. She had ignored my double entendres and subtle gestures. I finally turned in but didn't sleep for the longest time listening to the breathing of the ladies in my life and wondering if anything would ever make sense again.

"Auntie Pat's gone." Joey's voice brought me back to the present.

"I'm sure she's in the bathroom or ran out to pick up some doughnuts. You like doughnuts, don't you?" As I said the words I realized that Patrenka had never gotten breakfast for us and rarely left the room except to go to the pool. I sat up, rubbing the sleep from my eyes as more pain shot through my head. I surveyed the room and realized the pounding in my head was directly related to the beer cans haphazardly arranged around the wastebasket. Everything else seemed to be in place but something nagged me. I looked around more carefully and realized the suit Patrenka had worn to interview Buck was not hanging on the rod behind the door. Further searching showed her purse, shoes and other items were gone.

"I'm sure she stepped out for something, honey," I said soothingly, but not really believing it. I swung my legs out of bed and trudged to the bathroom, surprised to discover Joey right on my heels.

"Honey, wait a minute for me and we'll find her," I said, stopping at the door before she had a front row seat to my morning routine.

I quickly finished and opened the door to find Joey hadn't moved an inch and looked even closer to tears. I had to do something. But what? I must have taken too long to decide. Another tug and my attempt to remain clothed in my plaid flannel lounge pants would be history. I had begun wearing them for the sensitivity of the ladies and to mask the aroused state of my affairs when Patrenka was near.

Crap, the kid was going to cry again, I thought as I looked into the big round eyes that seemed to be all pupils. I reached down and brought her up and hugged her. I was surprised to find myself comforting her despite the foreignness of the gesture. It was not as awkward. I was getting better with practice. While I wanted to focus on reassuring Joey, I had to figure out a plausible explanation for Patrenka's disappearance and my gut told me we'd be on our own for a while.

That thought didn't terrorize me as much as the first time I found myself alone with Joey. What did scare me was where had the woman who had done fantastic things in my dreams gone?

"Why don't we get dressed and then we can see what we can find?" Joey obediently went and got her clothes and I helped her make sure they were on right side out.

If anyone had told me I would be this domesticated a month ago, I would have laughed so hard, I would have pissed myself. Surprisingly, that thought didn't bother me now but my gut clenched when I pondered Patrenka's whereabouts. What was she doing? Why did she have to sneak off without a word? That in itself – while making me crazy with fear – also pissed me off. How dare she do this to us – especially Joey who had already been abandoned too many times in her young life?

I looked over by the desk and I noticed my organized chaos was ruffled. "Hey Sport. I bet she left us a note." I said, realizing as I carried Joey toward the desk that I'd be making up a note, if I couldn't find one.

"Here it is." I snatched a scrap of paper. "'I had to run out and do a couple of errands. I will be back as soon as I can. Signed, Patrenka' See. She'll be back soon," I fabricated, my anger hitching up a notch. "There. How about you watching a couple cartoons while I take a quick shower and we will go out to my favorite doughnut place and see what I can find? I'll leave the bathroom door cracked in case you need anything."

I moved around the room retrieving my clothes and still looking for a note or some other sign of what had happened to Patrenka. I didn't know why I wanted to protect Joey so much but I couldn't face having the child worry or lose anyone else in her young life. I surreptitiously grabbed my cell and headed to the bathroom.

I waited for Joey to become engrossed in the cartoon before turning on the shower. I flipped open my phone and hit Dennis's number code in memory.

A groggy voice said: "Flaherty. This better be good. It's my day off."

"Dennis, did you set up something for Patrenka today?" I said in a hushed rush.

"What? Where are you? I can hardly hear you."

"I'm in the bathroom and don't want Joey to overhear. We woke this morning and Patrenka's gone. So is the suit she wore to see Buck. I thought maybe she returned there to try and get more information."

"I don't know. I haven't heard from her, but I did get some information on Sam Sloan."

"Shoot."

"Funny you should say, shoot," Dennis said warming to his subject. "Seems our FBI guy is known for tying things up nice and tight. He always gets the guy and the guy always ends up dead."

"What else was in his file?" excitement tingeing my voice.

"I didn't exactly see it, but I have friends. None of his fellow agents really like the guy. They don't trust him."

"Anything specific? Anything I could check with my sources?"

"There was an incident in a Chicago bank robbery where none of the suspects came out alive when he went undercover to join their group. They had a string of successful robberies and lost one of their members. Sam went undercover as an ex-con with knowledge of the banking industry. The next robbery, Sam walked out without a scratch and his three compatriots were killed. My friend didn't know what happened inside the bank."

"I should be able to find that. What name did he use?"

"Don't know, but it was First National Bank."

"Great." I had a lead to pursue again. "Hey Dennis, how's that beautiful wife of yours?"

"Fine, whatcha want?"

"Why would I want anything?"

"You always want something when you compliment my wife."

"Okay, you got me there. How about Joey coming over to play with your kids today and allowing me some time to investigate?"

"Yea, right. You're going to find Patrenka so you can ring her bell."

"I'm a reporter. Cut me some slack. I can't take Joey and I don't want her know anything's amiss."

"Okay, give me some time to sweet talk Colleen, so say in about an hour the coast should be clear."

A soft knock sounded at the door. Was I busted? I covered the receiver with my hand. "I'll be right out, Joey."

I turned back toward the shower and muttered into the phone. "I gotta go. See if you can't poke around and find Patrenka. Something tells me she went after Buck on her own."

"I might have a line on her. I'll check it out and let you know." Dennis disconnected.

I washed my face and ran some water through my hair to give the appearance of showering. I quickly dressed and opened the door. Joey was ready to go with her shoes tied and her baseball cap on, waiting patiently on the edge of the bed. There was no sign of a carefree child. She looked bereft.

"How would you like to play with kids today?"

She nodded up and down quickly, then looked wary.

"You remember Dennis?" Another nod. "Well, he has two kids. One about your age and then a younger one. How would you like to play at their house?"

"Okay, I guess. Do they have a dog?"

"I don't know but I bet they've got toys."

"What kind?" she said stubbornly, but I could see she was intrigued.

"Don't know. You'll have to investigate like Uncle Mitch does as a reporter." Joey's eyes sparkled in excitement. She had been trapped with adults, and she was looking forward to a little free time. I was looking forward to some time to track Patrenka down and wring her neck.

⁓⁓⁓

As I pulled into Dennis' driveway, Joey was craning her neck to see. I could see she was excited. "Uncle Mitch, they have a swing set.

Can I swing?"

"I'm sure you can. Let's see what's up, shall we?"

Joey bounded out of the car and started pulling me toward the front door. Before I could ring the doorbell, she was pulling on my hands and I bent down toward her face.

"Uncle Mitch," she whispered, which got my attention.

"What?" I whispered.

"You're going to come back aren't you? You're not going to disappear? These aren't going to be my new mommy and daddy?"

I didn't know what to say. What could you say? I wrapped her in my arms and hugged her. "No."

The rest of what I said was drowned out by two loud voices coming from inside.

"She's here. She's here."

Chapter 20

I cruised past the Rockwell estate, amazed not only by the height of the walled fortress but by the sheer size as well. I glimpsed the main house along with several outbuildings through the wrought iron gate as I coasted by. After two trips past in short order, I decided anymore would be pretty obvious to anyone watching the gate via closed circuit TV.

I never saw any sign of Patrenka, not that I expected her to be out front waving a white flag. But I had hoped. I knew she left of her own accord. No one else could have gotten out so quietly. What bothered me was why? What sent her off without a word and without Joey? Although I never asked Joey if she knew where her aunt had gone, I don't think she would have confided in her. I could be wrong. Seems Patrenka confided in everyone but me.

But then the logical part of my brain asked why she would confide in me? She knew I only wanted her confidence to worm my way into her secret passages. Last night I had acted like a jerk, a drunken jerk with a headache to prove it. We didn't even know each other and most of that time I treated her like a lowlife intern or my personal Playboy bunny. I needed to solve this and soon. I couldn't have a four-year-old dogging my heels. That wasn't my style. Patrenka was my style but it didn't look like anything would be happening anytime soon. Before my train of thought could continue to lusty dreams and fantasies, I needed to think like Patrenka to find her.

My stomach growled and I realized it was noon. I didn't necessarily need to eat but the thought gave me an idea to find Patrenka. If I were a Rockwell employee, where would I go for lunch? It was a long shot because Patrenka said the complex was self-sufficient, kind of like that new development that was supposed to be environmentally friendly. Yeah, right. I bet the closest thing to green was the lining of Buck Rockwell's pockets.

If nothing else I had direction. I had seen a restaurant/bar called the Roadhouse a mile beyond Buck's estate. I headed there.

The gravel lot was half-filled with an eclectic mix of vehicles from Beamers to pick-up trucks in the front and commercial vans and Chevys parked out back. The front looked neat and tidy to fit the upscale neighborhood but I was betting on the clientele being as eclectic as the vehicles they were driving.

I pulled open the solid metal door and paused for a minute to let my eyes adjust to the darker interior. I walked past the "please wait to be seated" sign and up to the wooden bar. I perched on a high stool. I glanced around and was disappointed I couldn't see more of the tables. The Roadhouse was divided up into intimate rooms of four booths, two on each side and a table or two in the center. From my perch, I could only see a couple of booths in the bar area. Their cushions had seen better days. The noise level was muted and a fan slowly circulated the stale air. I wouldn't be able to see or hear any conversations. It had been a good idea, I fumed.

"What'll ya have?" came a gravelly voice. The woman looked like she'd been kicked hard by a horse leaving a dark-red, horseshoe-shaped scar that traveled from one ear and around her chin and up the other side to her flattened nose.

"What's good?" I countered.

"A wise guy, huh?" She muttered before reciting the house specials in a voice that wasn't conducive to eating.

"Steak's good if you want it burnt, burgers have baskets with fries for a heart attack waiting to happen. No fresh greens to speak of. Special today is meatloaf — if you're living dangerously."

"How about a Coke to start and I'll ponder my choices?"

"Suit yourself." She left.

I again surveyed the room and noticed the steer horns mounted on the wall along with coils of rope and other rodeo paraphernalia barely visible in the dim interior. The place was nothing special but a great place for an illicit rendezvous. How I wanted to meet Patrenka here for a drink and then retreat to a hotel to peel off her layers. How I wanted to feel those curves caressing my loins. I ached for her and shifted uncomfortably on the stool.

What was it about her that had me acting like a bitch in heat? I never was one who fell in lust. Long term commitments were not in my plan. It wasn't that I didn't like women. I did. I dated occasionally. No one woman captured my imagination for more than a passing glance. That is until Patrenka strutted into the newsroom. I was a loner. Always had been and always will be. I could feel a smile come to my face as I thought about my week sharing a hotel room with a small child and the woman who was making me think of an illicit rendezvous.

"Have you decided your poison?" The bartender set my cola on the bar in front of me. She licked a pencil and was poised to jot my stomach's desire.

"How about the steak, medium rare. Fries."

"Anything else?"

"No thanks." She scratched the order on her pad and slapped it on the cook's queue and spun it. She grabbed a dishcloth from the bar sink and wiped the end of the bar clearing away an empty glass as she went.

"Not very busy here is it? I thought you'd have a busy lunch crowd."

"Some days, yes, other days, no. It's hit and miss. Usually we have a big group of construction workers and such. They must be working out of town today," she said as she washed the glass she had cleared and set it on a drainer to dry.

I wondered if her construction workers were Buck Rockwell's. I tried to put on my friendliest smile and flirt a little bit. That was rarely if ever needed on the police beat. Cops would punch me in the face if I tried that with them. Cops weren't swayed by a friendly male reporter. Patrenka would only have had to smile and every cop with a Y chromosome would start gushing details.

"There's some kind of big environmental development going up around here, isn't there? I thought I saw something about it on the news."

"That's Buck Rockwell's, he's got some big plans, but if you ask me it's all a scam."

I acted dumb. "What makes you think that?" My poker face must have given way to surprise because she continued.

"Everyone thinks he's such an upstanding citizen, but I know better." She turned and started to retreat as if she thought better about what she was saying.

"Wait." She turned and looked at me suspiciously. "It ain't healthy to talk about Buck," she said again turning her back on me.

"Please, my girlfriend has gone missing and I'm afraid she went to shack up with Buck," I said in a rush. She continued down the bar. I dropped my head to sip my Coke disgusted with myself for coming on too strong.

The next thing I knew, a short heavy tumbler with an amber liquid appeared next to my taller glass. "Here, this will help take the edge off. It's the only thing that works for me."

I looked into the sympathetic eyes and shook my head. I wasn't planning on playing a part. I drained the glass and did a quick, sharp shake of my head as the liquid fire made my eyes water.

Her head nodded imperceptibly. I licked my lips and tried to find my voice. "What do you know about Buck Rockwell?" I rasped and wondered if her voice wasn't derived from her beverage of choice.

"He's a hoodlum. My Frank can't even show his face around here anymore because of Buck."

"What'd Frank do?" I asked, trying not to let my eagerness tip her off. Luckily the lunch crowd was slow and no new patrons claimed her attention. She leaned her large bust over the bar and lowered her voice.

"My Frank used to work for Buck. He'd come in here for lunch and dinner every day. My Frank was really something. He had plans and dreams. He was saving his salary from Buck. Going to buy a piece of land. We were going to start our own business, a restaurant and use vegetables we grew ourselves. I think that's where Buck got the idea for his environmentally friendly project," she sneered. "Buck doesn't like it when one of his men wants to leave."

"It's a free country. What can he do?" If I could keep her talking about Buck and a little less on her cowboy, I might learn something useful.

"Buck is a dictator. You do it his way or you disappear." Her chin dropped to her chest and her shoulders sagged in defeat.

"How did Frank disappear?"

She looked up at me, surprised. "No. Frank got away, but I didn't. I'm stuck in this rat trap. I can't go. Buck's men will follow me and then take care of Frank. I can't let that happen." Her tone was flat, accepting.

This was my lead. I had to get her to hook me up with Frank. He could be my source.

"Do you know where Frank is?"

"Hey, who are you?" she snapped her shoulders squaring. "Do you work for Buck? You think I know where he is? He left me, now you get out of here!" Her scar was a vivid red. She looked like a woman who had gotten the better of the horse that marred her face. She looked like she was going to kick me and I was a little scared.

I looked around making sure we had not captured anyone's attention. Her threat, while lethal, did not carry in her raspy voice. I pulled out my wallet and continued to scan the premises for interest. I drew out a dirty-edged business card and slid it to her. She picked it up and eyed it skeptically. "*Grand River Journal*, huh? I've heard of that."

"My girlfriend and I were working on a big exposé to blow Buck out of the water and force him to leave town. Now she's gone and I don't know where," I whispered. She set the card down on the bar and I slid it back and deposited in my wallet. "It's hard to find witnesses to speak against Buck. They seem to disappear. I have to find her."

My status as a reporter seemed to impress her and she looked less severe. The red of her scar was less noticeable. "I'm sorry I got in your face," I apologized. "I'm frustrated I can't find anyone to give me the straight scoop on Buck Rockwell, upstanding citizen." I tried for the sincerest look before continuing.

"I got excited when you talked about Frank and now I realize he's like all the rest. It sucks that every time I get close, people disappear. Most recently my girlfriend." I was playing a part but realizing my acting was coming close to the truth and that hurt. Patrenka had betrayed me and Joey when she left. This was personal. I had to find out something.

I caught a glint in her eye. "My Frankie was a smart one. He knew what Buck was like. Yes, he did." With that she turned and walked to the kitchen. A few minutes later she returned with my lunch. Dropped it on the counter so hard the steak bounced. Before I could ask for ketchup, she was gone again.

I didn't think I was hungry. I took a bite of the steak, which surprisingly was both tender and juicy. My fries would have been better with ketchup, but they were crispy and hot. I ate in silence and watched a late season ball game on the TV mounted above the bar without really seeing who was playing. As soon as the last bite had been chewed, I set my fork down. The bartender reappeared, slapped my bill down and took away my plate — all without a word.

I watched her go and wished I knew her name. I thought all service workers should be forced to wear name tags, but then I figured hospitality wasn't her strong suit. I picked up the bill and reached for my wallet, resigned to another dead-end. Under my bill was a smaller piece of paper with a phone number on it. I glanced around to see if anyone saw it. I dropped the bill back on top of it and made a show of pulling out a twenty for a twelve dollar meal. I deftly dropped it on the bill and slid the smaller piece off the table and into the fold in my wallet.

"Keep the change," I told her as she took the bill. She gave me an imperceptible nod.

"Come back again."

I guess that was the best I could hope for as an endorsement.

I walked out of the Roadhouse to my car. I pulled out looking carefully both ways. I was trying to act normal but was itching to open the paper and look at the phone number more closely. I cruised up a busy street with gas stations, fast food, and retail strip malls lining the way. I saw a Meijer store and pulled into the busy lot. I cruised down a couple of aisles looking for a parking spot checking my mirrors to make sure I wasn't followed. I was good at this cloak and dagger thing. I finally selected a parking spot and pulled in next to a large van.

I left the car idling as I pulled out my wallet and looked at the number. The area code was for the area north of Grand River. I grabbed my cell phone. I was sure this was Frank. I started punching in the numbers and stopped before the last digit. If Frank was a true lead, anyone could track him. There was too much to be lost. I needed to use every precaution. With that I thought about Joey and figured I should check on her and I could use Dennis' phone to try Frank. A cop would have a secure line.

I pulled into the yard and Joey was in the back swinging with Dennis's kids. She looked happy and normal. Not like a child who had seen too much violence. She saw me and her face lit up. I sucked in a breath and she jumped from the highest point of the swing's forward arch and landed gracefully on the ground and ran into my arms. "Uncle Mitch, come and see what I did," she said, grabbing my hand and pulling me toward the sand box. Four tall towers with a wall connecting them and a moat encircling it all with a small princess figurine in the center. "Do you like my castle?"

I couldn't speak. The castle was brilliant for a small child. My little princess had safely ensconced herself behind towers, a wall and water to protect herself. She needed to be rescued and I was going to do it. I didn't want her to feel scared anymore.

My thoughts may have been a bit melodramatic, but the castle didn't have any frills like a flag or fancy turrets. It was solid walls. I again wondered if she was exceptionally gifted or what. I wasn't sure what preschoolers were capable of.

"The castle is beautiful. You go on and play some more. I need to make a couple of calls." I turned and walked toward the house as Dennis's wife, Colleen, stepped out.

I had to admire Dennis's taste in women. Colleen had shoulder length strawberry blond hair and a thin frame that childbirth hadn't changed. The photo on his desk didn't do her justice.

"Just wanted to make sure it was you showing up in my back yard," she said, smiling at me.

"Sorry I didn't ring the bell. I was drawn back here." I glanced at Joey who was chasing one of the other kids around the swing set.

"It's okay. Joey's a great kid. She hasn't been a bit of trouble. Actually, she has kept my hellions busy so I could get some things done. Want to come in for a Coke?"

"That would be great. Could I use your phone? It's long distance but I'll pay you for it."

She waved away my offer of payment as we entered.

"Use the phone in Dennis's den. I'm sure he won't mind. I'll get your soda."

While Dennis and I had been friends for several years, I had never socialized with him. Until today I had never visited his home or met his better half. I liked his wife's open, friendly spirit. I felt guilty for the times I kept him from coming home to her and the kids. She, however, either didn't know or it didn't bother her. I liked her and vowed to be less troublesome for Dennis.

I dialed the number and waited holding my breath as the phone rang. I glanced around Dennis's den and studied the family photograph framed on the desk. They looked happy, smiling into the camera. In the time I had known Dennis, I never put together the family man and the cop, until today. He was successful at work and had a beautiful family to come home to. I felt like I had been missing something but couldn't put my finger on what it was. I realized the phone was still ringing. I had expected an answering machine after the fourth ring. Realizing I had no idea how long it had been ringing, I was reaching to return it to its base when the line crackled and clunked.

"Darn," I heard.

"Hello," I said.

"Sorry," came a female voice. This couldn't be Frank. Maybe the Roadhouse waitress had some competition. "I dropped the phone."

"Is Frank there?"

"No. Can I tell him who called?" The voice was warm and friendly which didn't match my image of Frank.

"Do you know when you expect him?" I said trying to decide whether to leave a name and number or not.

"Around seven is my guess."

"I'll call back then. Thanks." I hung up.

I stared at the phone and wondered if I dialed wrong. Maybe he was staying with a daughter or sister?

Colleen came in and set my drink on the desk. "Everything all right?"

"Yes, just surprised. Do you mind if I use your Internet connection?"

"No go ahead. Let me know if you need anything."

"Thanks." I went to my car and retraced my steps to the den. I powered up my computer and connected to the Internet. I pulled up Google and entered the telephone number. I got a half dozen good hits as well as the usual garbage that came up whenever you search for anything. The top listing was George Bednarek at 4053 Five Mile Road, in Bromley. I'd never heard of Bromley before. I looked at a couple of the other listings but it was basically the same in several different reverse directories.

I next opened Mapquest and put in the address. The address looked like a rural area about 90 minutes north. I tried another option and pulled up satellite photos of the area. It looked like there were open fields, a river or stream running where I thought the address was. I could make out a roofline surrounded by trees.

I then returned to Google and put George Bednarek in. The last entry on the first page was an obituary. I pulled it up. George Bednarek Sr. died June 30, 1999, after a short illness. I skipped through the funeral arrangements and went to survivors. Survivors include his son George Bednarek of Bromley and step-son Frank Stolnek of Chicago. Bingo! This had to be the Frank I was looking for. Maybe he had been working for Buck since they both were from Chicago and knew some secrets. I couldn't wait until seven when I could call back.

I shut off the computer after making notes of all I had found and headed to the back yard. Joey ran into my arms. I picked her up and hugged her, silently promising that I would make the men who took away her parents pay.

Chapter 21

Seven o'clock was drawing closer. I was reluctant to leave the hotel room hoping Patrenka would return. I wished she would have left a message, but there was nothing when we returned from Dennis'. I was angry and worried but pretended like nothing was wrong, which I don't think fooled Joey. Luckily she asked no questions or commented on Patrenka's absence.

We decided on pizza at Chuck E. Cheese again. After dinner and game tokens, we went through the mall. I went to a pay phone to call Frank. I deposited the coins and waited for the connection. Again the phone rang several times and was answered on the seventh ring.

"Yeah," came a deep voice.

"Frank, please."

"Who wants him?" Somehow I knew I had the right person. This rough around the edges voice was the perfect match for my raspy waitress.

"Mitch, Mitch Malone, reporter for the *Grand River Journal.*"

"What do you want? I don't need no newspaper delivered."

"Frank, a waitress friend of yours gave me your number and said we might be able to help each other. Could we meet and discuss it?"

"How is she?" His voice softened.

"She's fine but misses you." I didn't think she would mind.

"My Daisy," was all he said in a voice choked with emotion.

After a few moments of silence, he said: "Denny's. Exit 131, Cooperstown. Noon. Sit at the end of the counter. I'll find you." The line clicked dead. I hadn't even used my whole three minutes.

I grabbed Joey's hand and we wandered the mall for a half hour and returned to our room. After Joey was fast asleep, I returned to my computer and started putting my notes in order. I called Dennis again and updated him, asking if Joey could spend another day. With that taken care of, my hope for the next day lessened my concern about not hearing from Patrenka. I turned in early.

As I pulled out I dropped my shades on and cranked my car's air conditioning to max for my trip north to meet with Frank. As farm fields dropped away and more trees lined the road, I tried to come up with scenarios on how best to approach Frank. How to convince him that I was trustworthy? I tried to gauge how intelligent he would be, knowing he worked for Buck. Daisy hadn't said much except he wanted to grow his own food. Was he a hillbilly? Denny's wasn't the classiest place so maybe he would be easy to convince. I'd go for the friendly, honest approach with my wholesomeness.

I figured Denny's was about a half hour from where he was staying or maybe that was his contact number and he went there to get calls. I wondered if the public meeting place was to throw me off or if he had a new job in the area. The more I thought the more questions and scenarios I came up with as I expanded my conspiracy theory during the hour and a half drive north from Grand River. The parking lot was comfortably filled with pickup trucks sporting NRA bumper stickers, and an occasional late model sedan, but little else.

The smell of bacon and grease greeted my senses as I made my way to the end of the bar. "Hello. Coffee?" The waitress in a nondescript polyester dress with large double pockets on the front plunked down a cup on the chipped Formica counter and filled it with the black liquid. She moved the coffee creamer and sugar containers within reach and moved on.

I put a little powdered cream and a healthy teaspoon of sugar in the opaque fluid. I glanced around the dining room, looking for my mental image of Frank. No one. I'm not sure what I expected. I was thinking six feet tall, covered in tattoos, muscles the diameter of light poles. I continued to sip my coffee, scanning the menu. When I walked in, the seat next to me was empty waiting for Frank. After a few moments a short, thin man sat down beside me His receding hair line sported several thin stalks in a ridiculous comb over.

Probably still lives with his mother, I thought, glancing his way. I gave him a mean look hoping he would move down a seat or two to make room for Frank. He glared back at me and I went back to studying the menu.

The waitress returned and I ordered a hamburger and fries. The man next to me duplicated my order.

"Mitch?" It was the gruff voice from the phone

I glanced up and around looking for the tall body the voice came from. I couldn't figure it out.

Mitch!" the voice was impatient. I looked at my nerdy neighbor, surprised to see him glaring at me.

"Frank?"

"Yes. What are you looking for on Buck?"

I looked at him and he kept eye contact, each of us assessing the other. My idea of acting like the boy next door vanished. His voice still held a touch of annoyance. I thought about shaking his hand but decided against it.

"Thanks for meeting me. I'm working on a story on Buck Rockwell and the disappearances that follow him wherever he goes."

I paused to see his reaction, but there wasn't one. I continued.

"Your friend said you were forced to disappear because of Buck. I thought finally, a witness that hadn't vanished permanently. Did he try to get rid of you? Can you corroborate any of my suspicions?" I wanted to get everything out on the table. I didn't think this wimp of a man would be much help in ratting out Buck. It had been a waste of time driving up here. I wanted to eat and get out.

"Maybe."

A long pause ensued as the waitress returned with our hamburger platters.

I didn't want to say anything about Joey. No one knew about her and I didn't want to tip anyone off. I took a bite of my burger, surprised by how tasty it was.

"Burgers are good here, ain't they?" Frank said.

I nodded in agreement and he continued. "Of course, they ain't like the Roadhouse but I don't dare go there now."

It was the perfect opportunity. "So tell me why you are hiding?"

"I couldn't cotton to what Buck was up to. I'd worked for him for ten years doing his accounting, books, ordering his supplies for his development and construction company. Then I started noticing things. We would be getting checks that I couldn't trace to accounts receivable. I asked Buck about them. He told me not to worry. The checks disappeared and never showed up in any accounts. One day I got the mail and there was an envelope of cash. Again I was told to never mind. I did, sort of. I kept looking but under the radar if you know what I mean. I was able to trace a couple of things to events related to the new development on the river, the one that is environmentally friendly." Frank paused and took a deep breath and looked me right in the eye to see if I was getting the message. He held my stare for a minute and seemed to sum me up. He let the air out. "Let me tell you this. Buck doesn't give a tinker's damn about the environment."

Frank stopped to take another bite of his burger and I processed what he told me.

"What do you think is going on?"

"I'm not sure. I started asking questions and such and Buck told me it was none of my business. He suggested I let it drop or I would be gone. I knew by the way he said it that he meant six feet under and not fired. That's when I started making my plans. I kept my nose clean and never said anything to anyone, but I made extra copies of things. He wanted me to take care of a few loose ends. He wanted me to get my hands dirty. The night of his big environmentally-friendly development announcement, I disappeared. No one but Daisy knew that I was going and she only had the phone number. She must have seen something in you to know you weren't one of Buck's men. She is a great judge of character."

"She's a peach," I said smiling thinking that she was as far from a Daisy as you could get.

"You better not be interested in my Daisy," he said gruffly. I wiped the smile off my face. He was welcome to Daisy. I had Patrenka to fantasize about. "I would have been gone a lot sooner if it hadn't been for Daisy. I raved about the burgers at the Roadhouse for an excuse to get out from under Buck's scrutiny for a few hours. I do love the burgers, but mostly I went to see Daisy. At first, she didn't give me the time of day, but little by little she started opening up. I told her about my life and she didn't judge me. Daisy is one heck of a strong woman but I'm worried about her." His voice trailed off and then I saw his fists clench.

"Just as soon as I can, I'm going to get her out of that Roadhouse. She's a bit stubborn and old-fashioned. Won't live in sin with me even if it means risking her life. I respect her, but hope it doesn't come to that. You need to keep her out of this." His stare didn't brook any argument. He meant business and for a small man, he looked tough. My first impression was way off. It wasn't like Mitch Malone to misjudge someone so badly even if it was only the first time they met.

"I have a sweetie all my own," I said thinking of my missing roommate and wondering if I would ever make my fantasies come true.

"Daisy was sure that Buck was just talk. I think she's changed her mind now. One of Buck's boys was asking questions and none too nicely. I'm worried about her."

We ate in silence for a few minutes, each absorbed in our own thoughts.

"If I help you write your newspaper story, will you help me get my sweetie out of there with none the wiser?"

I readily agreed. I wasn't sure what that was going to cost me or how I would do it, but a promise was a promise and who was I to stand in the way of true love?

"What do you think is going on with that development?"

"I don't have any proof but I think he wants to use it for some type of smuggling. I'm not sure what. I couldn't ever find any papers that had anything interesting. I do know what he plans to build will be for show on the top, but is supposed to have an underground layer that will be much larger. No one is supposed to know about the underground part. He kept talking about that UFO place out west, Area 51 in the Nevada desert, and laughing. I don't know what that means."

I was surprised to realize that while Frank had talked, I had finished my burger. Frank was quiet for a few minutes while he finished his last bite. Then he licked dripping ketchup from his fingers.

"You can't find many places with good burgers. That's what first drew me to Daisy," Frank said getting all dreamy-eyed. I needed to bring him back to the point.

"Anything else you can think of that I should look into? Can you tell me what the routine was around Buck? The more I know, the more I can help."

"Buck is strange. He's an early riser and goes to bed late. He thrives on only a couple hours of sleep a night. He likes his ladies and there are a lot of them."

"Anyone he is particularly fond of?"

"No but he likes them tall and lanky with long hair," Frank said.

My heart plummeted. That was Patrenka to a tee. Add her intriguing eyes and Buck wouldn't be able to help himself. A sudden swell of anger shuddered through my body in a sense as foreign to me as compassion and concern. I was worried for Patrenka. The thought of Buck Rockwell so much as caressing her cheek made my fists ball in anger. So much for my vow of passivism and unconcern, the traits of a good reporter.

I brought my attention back as Frank started to speak again.

"Buck likes the finer things in life. Always talking about how much things are worth but if you ask me he don't know nothing about nothing."

"What about his accounts? Does he have a lot of cash on hand?"

"Yes and no. There are times when his accounts are full, then poof. The accounts are empty again. I got a lot of invoices that at the beginning I would question him about. Later I quit asking, figuring they were frauds but if he didn't care, I didn't either."

"What do you mean frauds?"

"He'd get these bills for cement work from companies that weren't listed in the phone book and only had post office boxes for addresses. We'd get them when he didn't have any developments going. None of the other boys said they ordered any cement and when they did buy cement, it would be from a different company. I may not be a CPA, but I know accounting. You don't pay for cement you didn't use and stay in business long."

"How did you end up working for Buck? Answer a want ad?"

"Very funny. I knew someone who worked for Buck. I needed money to pay off some medical bills. I had an accident when I was going to college and was working third shift to pay for it. I mixed two chemicals I shouldn't and burned my lungs and throat with the fumes. Gave me the bass voice the ladies find sexy." He laughed at his own joke, then sobered.

"I figured I'd stay as long as my paycheck cleared the bank. Buck quickly discouraged me from asking him or the other employees any questions. That's when I was promoted. That's a laugh. Buck called it a promotion but to me it was house arrest. I had to move into the mansion from the guest house and was only allowed out for dinner a couple of times a week. Buck's taste in food is horrible. I couldn't stand it. There were never any burgers on the menu."

I nodded to continue his story. It was good to know as much as you could about the man you were going after.

"After that I never let on any of my business. Never asked another question. I paid the bills when they arrived. Buck allowed my trips to the Roadhouse. He thought I went for burgers and not my little flower."

I smiled, encouraging him. I didn't know what any of it meant yet but a good reporter listens to everything and then puts the pieces together. People never talk in an organized fashion.

"Buck also had some visitors that he didn't like others to see. I saw them on account of I had to run up some reports for him in the middle of the month for his investors," Frank said using his fingers to make quotes around investors. "I was leaving for the Roadhouse and I saw them. Now there were some fancy dressers. Their pinstripe suits were cut perfectly and their hair always looked too good, you knew it was fake with a hint of sheen holding it in place. They arrived with brown leather briefcases. Later, I was told to make a deposit. It was in cash and the bills were wrapped and laid neatly in a brown leather briefcase. Most investors use wire transfers or cashier checks. They don't walk around with briefcases of cash."

Now that I had Frank talking, he wasn't stopping. Our food was gone and the waitress refilled our coffee cups and dropped the bill on the counter. I threw a twenty on it and it disappeared.

Frank wiped his mouth on his napkin and wadded it on his plate. "Thank you for dinner. Before you print one word, I want my Daisy safe. I know what Buck can do and I won't put her in danger."

"I'll let you know before my story goes to press, so you can get her out."

"Wait a minute. If I show my face back there, it will be the last time I'm seen. You have to get her out before your story goes to print. When they find out I'm alive, it will be too late."

Frank looked scared, then straightened, squaring his shoulders and drawing himself up to his full five feet, two inch frame. "I got the goods on Buck. You want them? You get Daisy out. That's my deal. No Daisy. No proof. Deal?"

"Deal, but I need something, some proof, sort of a good faith gesture."

I watched Frank scratch his head and think. "Be right back." He left the restaurant and a few minutes later returned with an envelope. "Here's your good faith gesture. Now get my Daisy out of danger."

"I'll get to work on it right way, but if she doesn't want to go, I can't force her." I said sliding the envelope into my lap.

"I understand. I believe she's ready. You see that she's kept out of this and safe."

We shook on the deal and he headed out. I followed and watched him climb into a faded green Ford pickup that was covered in dust. I hastily memorized the tag number and headed to my car. I wanted to open the envelope but didn't want anyone to see its contents. I worried that it contained blank paper. After getting in my car, I jotted the license number down on the outside of the envelope. I unlocked the clasp and hauled out a half dozen sheets of paper. It was a purchase agreement to buy forty acres of land belonging to one Joseph and Evelyn Lippistan Smith. Smith was Joey's last name. This property had to be connected to Joey. It was too big of a coincidence with the last name being the same although Smith was the most popular surname. I read the agreement again.

It was a standard agreement with the purchase price a measly $10,000, way below market value for forty acres. The last page was signed by Buckwald R. Rockwell.

As I pulled out of the lot, I called Dennis to check on Joey and gave him the license number to run. As I continued my drive back to civilization, I thought about what Frank said and his theories. I had nothing to go on except a parentless child, a dead couple, a missing mother and a purchase agreement. I had no idea what tied them all together except for a pintsized witness. I needed to get more information out of Joey. Suddenly my burger and fries weren't sitting so well in my stomach.

Chapter 22

What was the altercation between Joey's parents and Buck? Were there other conversations with Buck saying how he was going to get the deed to the property? His development was moving forward and he couldn't wait for it to be probated if he killed her to get his hands on it. The property would only be sold if the husband signed or had signed a power of attorney for his wife.

I wanted to ask Joey but I couldn't do it dispassionately. Joey would want to please me and tell me whatever she thought I'd want to hear. I had seen this a dozen times especially in cases alleging abuse of a child. One parent accused the other of abuse and the child would say whatever he thought the parent wanted to hear. I didn't want to put Joey in that situation.

I needed to do more research on Buck's days in Chicago. The only thing I knew was the school. I chuckled when I read the name in the yearbook under the austere face, Buckwald Randolph Rockwell. What a name. No wonder he'd shortened it to Buck Rockwell. I wondered about the Randolph and if that was his father's first name or a mother's maiden name. Originally I thought he was Texan, because of his pompous nature and the cowboy hat he wore. But my Internet research revealed he was from the south of Chicago like Bad, Bad Leroy Brown — rather fitting and a chip off old Leroy's block.

I headed back to the Cascade Hills area. I wanted to touch base with Daisy and I also wanted to check out the property on the purchase agreement from Frank. I decided to do the land first. I stopped by the nearest library and hopped on a computer. After a quick search, I had the address and maps thanks to Google Earth and Mapquest. Even from the slightly blurry satellite image, it did look like a prime piece of property with the river snaking through, barely visible between towering oaks and pines. I searched the county records online for tax information and learned it was a forty-acre parcel, surrounded by property listing the taxpayer as one BRR Development. I could only guess that BRR Development was Buck Randolph Rockwell.

I found the drive to the property. A shiny steel cable stretched across it. I wondered if it was to keep people in or out. Did Buck order the property locked? Could it be that Evelyn locked it when she left voluntarily? No, I couldn't believe she would willingly leave Joey behind. Could Buck be behind keeping people out? Could Buck be holding Joey's mother hostage on their own property waiting for them to crack and sign whatever papers he wanted? Was it closed off so he could bury the bodies in peace? Too many possibilities and none of them were the happy ending I'd unconsciously been hoping for, for Joey's sake.

I parked in the drive and noted it didn't have a "no trespassing" sign. However, gravel had been kicked into the weeds along each side by the road. Had someone left in a hurry? I looked for tire tread marks but found only small indentions from the spin out. I parked as bold as could be next to the chain and ducked under the cable.

I walked about a half mile up the road and was enjoying the wildness and the nature. Birds chirped and I could hear the rustle of small animals in the ferns along the drive. I could see a clearing in front of me and suspected I was getting near the house. I didn't feel a need for caution although I probably should have. Maybe it was the brash reporter who crossed police lines or maybe it was too nice of an Indian summer day to worry about bad guys. It was a serene walk through the woods.

"What are you doing here?" came a stern voice to my left. I jumped, startled and couldn't speak as I hastily swallowed. The man was large, beefy and dressed in black with three pockets on the outside of each leg making him look wider. I was thinking fast, trying to come up with a plausible story. My initial thought about saying I heard the property was for sale didn't seem to cut it. I needed something else and I needed it fast.

"Sorry. I was looking for Joseph and Evelyn Smith." I moved to the right to go around.

"They ain't here," the mastodon said, moving to block my path.

"Come on. She's always home," I said. Again I dodged right, trying to move around his bulk. I saw the house around the next bend and I wanted a better look.

"They're on vacation. I'm house-sitting."

"Vacation? They've never taken a vacation before," I said flying by the seat of my pants trying to make it like I was good friends and edged forward further. "I talked to them two weeks ago and they didn't mention any vacation. They knew I was coming for a visit. I admit I'm a day earlier than I told them, but they've never minded before."

"They're on vacation and won't be back for some time. Now move it." He stepped closer, casting a dark shadow and cutting off my path forward.

"Then let me stay here tonight. I don't have anywhere else to go. At least let me use their phone to call a hotel." As I talked I glanced around nonchalantly. The house was a mess even from this far away. Curtains were hung half across the windows. Plants were knocked over on the porch, Adirondack chairs were laying on their sides.

"They don't want any trespassers." The tone was all steel. I took an involuntary step backwards as he stepped toward me. He was a solid six feet tall and immoveable.

"Well, fine. Tell them Lenny stopped by when they return. Have them give me a call." I turned and trudged back up the drive. I felt like I had a target on my back and knew hitting the bull's-eye would be child's play for that soldier.

By the time I trekked back to the car, I was starving and headed for the Roadhouse.

I walked in and headed right for the bar, not waiting for my eyes to adjust to the darkness. A burger sounded really good and I had Frank's recommendation after all. Daisy came out from behind a swinging door to the kitchen and paused momentarily. Her eyes quickly darted around. My friendly greeting was squelched at the imperceptible shake of her head and the fear in her eyes. Being an unwelcome guest was starting to make me feel edgy and nervous.

"What can I get you?" Her raspy voice lacked any hint of friendliness. Her eyes continued to dart this way and that.

"How about a Corona, burger and fries? A friend of mine told me the burgers here were the best in the state." I watched her eyes widen in surprise. She nodded in understanding, but still the reserve was in her eyes and a little bit of fear. Something had happened. She hadn't seemed fearful on my last visit.

"Your friend is right, I'll get your order in. You look a mite hungry," she said, walking away.

A few minutes later my Corona was set in front of me and she hurried by with a couple more beers in her hand. She took them to the end booth furthest from the door. The two occupants seemed in deep conversation, one on each side of the table. I could see their hands, emphasizing their conversation points, lit by a candle on the table. I couldn't see the one person's face but something made me take a second look. The hands were big and beefy and attached to large muscular forearms. I realized what caught my eye. Something red flashed when the candle caught something on his finger.

Why the gut reaction to that? Think Mitch. Where had I seen it before? I hadn't seen it, but then I thought of something Joey had said about a raspberry. I took another swig of my beer and casually looked at the men again. The light was from his right hand and looked like a large gold ring. The flash was from a blood red stone the size of a pistachio set in the center.

Joey had talked about a man with a raspberry on his finger when she talked about the man who was hurting her mother. That must be what she meant. I again marveled at my small companion's description.

I needed to find out who this was. I kept trying to keep an eye on the table without being obvious. Luckily, a large-screen TV carried a Tiger's postseason game in the corner close to their table. I pretended to watch the game while taking quick glances at the pair.

The second man was tall, thin and dressed in a dark suit and paisley tie. His looks were dark and intense and freshly pressed. In contrast, the other man's arms were bare and brown as if he'd spent a lot of time outside. He seemed unperturbed, raising his hands a few times to emphasize a point but remaining relaxed.

I swiveled back to the counter as Daisy slapped my dinner on the table.

"What do you think of them Tigers?" I asked, trying to break into Daisy's hard shell.

"No matter how good they are, they're always the Tigers," came the enigmatic reply and then she was gone.

I turned my attention to the burger. I was ready to put Frank's taste buds to the test. I lifted the burger and tried to keep the trailing condiments from hitting my shirt and lap. The bite was even juicier than I expected as another rush of fluid slid out. I leaned in slightly and caught myself as the flavor enveloped my mouth. It was delicious. I could see why Frank recommended it. I could only describe it as nirvana. I could understand his taste in burgers, but his taste in women was unfathomable.

I took another bite and didn't even touch my fries. I didn't want to put the burger down. I wanted to compare it to a sexual experience but lately that had been limited and then only to my dreams. This was no dream and I didn't want to cheapen it in comparison.

I took a few more bites, chewing slowly. I looked up and realized I'd let my pseudo baseball game surveillance lapse. I was no private dick that was for sure. Reporters were allowed to eat. I turned in time to see my quarry get up and shake hands. Sure enough, the bronze man was Buck Rockwell. They shook hands and walked toward the door. The skinny man must have said something funny because Buck let out a belly laugh and slapped the skinny man on the back so hard I thought he was going to choke. It was obvious the suit didn't care for Buck, but tried to mask it. Interesting, but I didn't know what it meant. I watched them leave. When I returned to my burger, Daisy was right in front of me.

"How's the burger?"

"Great," I took another bite, chastising myself for having left it unfinished for even a few moments. She seemed content to watch me enjoy the burger and I saw a little of what Frank must see in her. Her presence was comforting.

I finished the burger off in a few more bites. "That was wonderful. Frank was right."

"You saw my Frankie? How was he?"

"He's doing okay but he sure misses the Roadhouse burgers," I said.

Daisy smiled like a cat that had eaten a mouse and found it satisfying.

"He misses you and wants you to join him," I said. She glanced around as if the walls had ears. "Any chance you might make an honest man out of him?" I hoped this would help her see that Frank was looking long term.

Daisy blinked at the ceiling, but never said a word. I couldn't figure it out.

"What's wrong?"

"I can't go," she blurted out, turned and left me to nibble on my fries. What was going on? She was obviously mad about him, but she couldn't leave. What was it? My reporting skills had deserted me. I wasn't finding out anything to help Joey and I couldn't figure out what was standing in the way of true love.

Daisy returned after a few minutes to take my now empty plate. I touched her arm lightly to hold her.

"Can't you tell me what's going on?" I asked, trying to put a brotherly tone in my voice to inspire confidence.

Daisy stopped and her frame slumped and the harshness of her face softened. "Did Frankie look okay? Is he taking care of himself?" she whispered.

"He looked good to me but I only just met him. We had lunch and his appetite was good." There was no way I was bringing up his cheating on her by eating another place's burgers.

"That's good. I'm worried about him," she said, sniffling at the end. I didn't know what to do if she started crying.

"He was worried about you too. He made me promise I would watch out for you."

"He did?" A smile broke out on her scarred face that didn't make it look any friendlier until you saw the sparkles in her eyes.

"Yes. He wants to get you out of here. He's worried Buck's boys will be tough on you because of him. He wants you to join him."

"Do you really think so? You're not just saying that, are you?"

"No. He . . . " I stopped as two guys came in and sat at the other end of the bar.

Daisy wandered over, her expression shutting down into the gruff exterior. "What'll you have?"

"Burgers and a couple of beers, drafts."

Daisy turned to go when the larger of the two grabbed her arm.

"Heard anything from Frank?"

"No. Why would I?" she responded, shortly, yanking her arm from his grasp and disappearing behind the swinging door.

I saw why she couldn't accept Frank's proposition and why Frank was worried about her. He knew about Buck's beasts of burden and their visits to the Roadhouse.

I nursed my beer, unwilling to leave Daisy, although I was sure she could take care of herself. Buck's boys gave me the once over and without saying a word, I got the impression they wanted me to hit the road. Well, too bad. I had caved for the mastodon on the driveway and I wasn't moving to make these guys happy. I was a tough reporter and this was a public place.

Daisy came back and drew two beers from the tap, failing to stem the flow of foam by tilting the frosted mugs, walked to the pair, dropping them in front of them. She headed for the kitchen. I needed a reason to stay.

"Hey, waitress. I need another beer, like yesterday," I slurred. "How about some service here." I pounded on the counter.

Daisy grabbed another mug and filled it. She slapped it down in front of me and winked. She disappeared through the swinging doors. I buried my nose in the beer, ignoring the pair and their daggers but trying to listen to their conversation.

"Jim is really getting on my nerves. I'm going kick his ass if he doesn't quit snoring. I can't sleep." said the brawny one who grabbed Daisy's arm.

"I know. You don't have to smell Doug, though. Whew, can that guy let loose. Sounds like a bazooka and stinks like rotten eggs," said the second who must be six feet tall and the same width through the shoulders.

"Two weeks and we can blow town with that five thousand dollar bonus. That's the only thing that's holding me to this job. Whatcha going to do with yours?"

"Get out of this Bible, do-goody city. That's for sure. They don't even have decent hookers. I strolled Division Avenue and all I found were men in drag and cops on bikes wearing spandex. What I wouldn't give for a little pussy."

"Know whatcha mean. Our barmaid is even looking good."

"Hell, even a donkey is looking good," the tall one said, laughing at his own joke.

Yikes, these guys were lower than leeches with half the brain.

Daisy returned with their baskets of food and pulled three more beers. Two for them and another for me without me asking, and was gone again. I continued to act like I had already had a few.

I didn't want to hang around, but I didn't want to face Frank's wrath if I left Daisy and something happened to her. I continued to nurse my beer and watched the ballgame on the TV.

"Whatcha think got Buck all nervous?" the tall one asked.

"Beats the shit out of me, but he's as grumpy as a bear waking up in the middle of winter."

"Just a little hitch with some damn land he wants. Word has it the owner up and dropped out of sight before she could sign over the property nice and legal. The paperwork disappeared when she was supposedly taken care of."

"Jake, shut your fuckin' trap. We ain't supposed to be talking about nothing or we'll end up as the camp's target practice. We're only here to watch the bar bitch and get her to tell us where Frank is."

"I don't think ugly there knows nothin'. I mean Frank wasn't no piece of work but the bitch is ugly," Jake said.

"Don't matter. We follow orders or we don't get paid. Keep your head down and we'll get our bonus and be gone within the month."

Daisy came back and slapped their bill on the table but didn't move fast enough. Jake grabbed her arm and twisted. Daisy didn't flinch. "Where's Frank?"

"I told you, I don't know." Daisy yanked her arm back and returned to the kitchen.

"We won't be learning anything here tonight."

The uglier one crumpled the bill and threw the wad toward the table but it missed. They laughed and strutted out. The door had barely time to close when Daisy was drawing another beer. She gulped it down without taking a breath.

"You okay?" I asked.

"Yes." She clunked the empty glass on the counter. "Bastards. Even a donkey's too good for them." I thought she was going to spit on the floor but she didn't.

"Did you hear them talking about looking for Frank?"

"No, they don't know where he is, do they?" her lip quivering slightly.

"No. They were sent to get any information from you, but they gave up. Said Frank disappeared with an option for some property. You wouldn't know anything about that, would you?"

"I know the last thing Buck asked him to do didn't set well with him. He'd been talking about leaving but..." She turned red and seemed sheepish. "He talked about not wanting to leave somebody special. I wasn't sure if he was talking about me. I wasn't ready to leave without some kind of promise or future. He came in one night right at closing and was real upset. I've never seem him like that. He said he was leaving and wanted to know flat out if I would come, right then. I said no. I thought he was nuts for leaving. I was wrong. I'm nuts for staying."

"Would you leave now?" I needed to know if there was any hope of getting her away as Frank had demanded.

"How could I get away? Buck's hoodlums keep getting nastier and nastier. I don't know. They'd track me down. If I went to Frank, they'd follow me. I'm not sure I can start over."

"Do you think you could work for Frank? He talked about opening a place and serving the best burgers?"

Her eyes brightened. "If I knew I had a job to go to, I think I would get out of here."

"I think Frank would be happy to give you a job," I said not mentioning that she may not get paid and the job would be wife but they could work out the details.

"What's the plan?" Her eyes took on a crafty look, all sentimentality gone. She was ready to plan her escape. I didn't know what that plan was going to be.

I started to say something when I noticed Daisy stiffen, and then began wiping the bar with her rag. I had heard the door open. A shaft of sunlight penetrated the smoky atmosphere and then quickly disappeared. I turned to look and my heart stopped — Patrenka.

Chapter 23

I watched Patrenka scan the area and our eyes locked. Hers widened and mine thinned in satisfaction at her shock. My first reaction was where had that dress been hiding at the hotel? Its plunging neckline making me wonder what was holding her glorious breasts in. The hem was an inverted V in the front teasing me with hints of her inner thighs. It was teal and shiny and begged for hands to glide along her hips and to all points above and below. My second reaction was to launch myself off the stool, straight at Patrenka. I wasn't sure if I would kiss her or strangle her.

I resisted both options and sank lower onto my stool. Her laugh challenged my resolve to stay uninvolved. I took a long drink of my cold brew, hoping it would cool my hot-headed impulses. Instead, my desire escalated with her giggle, until I heard a hearty, deep voice join the laughter. My eyes traveled to her escort. Buck. I knew she was on an investigation of her own.

She turned to Buck, said something and they disappeared into another area of the restaurant, out of sight.

I started to rise when I felt myself being pulled back by a vise grip on my arm. I turned ready to fight. Daisy glared at me.

"Leave it." I saw understanding in her eyes. "You can't do anything now. Just wait."

I wasn't sure if she was talking about Patrenka or Buck, but the advice was good either way. I knew Patrenka wouldn't acknowledge me. It was part of her cover and I didn't want to chance getting her hurt. I could wait and kill her later.

I hoped we were on the same side — Joey's side.

Thinking of Joey, I knew I needed to pick her up. I didn't want her to think I abandoned her at Dennis's house.

The grip on my arm lessened. "I think I'll head out."

"When will you be back?"

"In a day or two. Be ready to go. I'm not sure of all the details." I scanned the area to make sure no one could overhear. "Will have to check with my contact. I'll let you know. If I come in and don't order a burger, be ready to hit the road in a hurry. That will be our code."

"I'll be ready," she said, a sense of strength infusing her words. I threw a few bills on the table and headed out. I couldn't stop myself from glancing in the direction where Patrenka disappeared, but I couldn't penetrate the room's dark recesses.

The sun and heat hit me full force when I exited. It seemed like the Roadhouse had been a separate planet or I had walked out of a spaceship of aliens and back onto Earth. I scanned the lot trying to find a hint of what car Patrenka came in but found nothing. A couple big, expensive ones that could be Buck's were in the lot, but I had no idea which. What was Buck doing back there so quickly after he left? Was it for dinner with Patrenka or did he have more sinister plans?

I sighed in frustration, started the engine and headed toward Dennis' house, anxious to see Joey and not willing to examine why.

As I rolled up along the curb I barely had time to get out before Joey saw me from the backyard and ran to meet me, throwing her arms around my neck

"Uncle Mitch, Uncle Mitch. I made a picture for you. Wait till you see it."

"That's great, Sport." Dennis's wife appeared from the back yard with two other small fry racing out the gate behind her.

"Hi. How about staying for dinner? We're about to sit down."

I started to shake my head. She had Joey all day and I didn't want to impose on her good nature. It was as if she read my mind.

"It's no problem. It's only macaroni and cheese with hot dogs in it and a little Jell-O."

I looked at Joey. "Please, Mitch. I'm hungry."

"Okay, if you're sure it's not a problem." I glanced at Colleen.

"Then it's settled." She smiled. "Kids, why don't you go wash your hands?" All three took off at a run with Joey in the lead.

"Joey's a sweetheart. She keeps my two from fighting. It's actually easier having her here. I don't have to mediate. Joey does it for me."

I wasn't sure if she was serious or not, so I let it drop.

"Will Dennis be joining us?" I no sooner got the words out when he pulled in the drive.

"He called about fifteen minutes ago and said he was on his way." Her smile said she knew some intimate secret about the timing of his arrival. I wished I shared that closeness with a raven-haired witch.

I'd never had dinner with three preschoolers. The kids talked a mile a minute about nothing that needed to be said. With their chatter, there wasn't a chance to get any adult discussion going as Dennis and Colleen kept responding to the kids' need for refills on their milk, more macaroni or dessert.

I could hardly keep up and wasn't paying much attention until I heard my name.

"Uncle Mitch, how come bananas can float in Jell-O?" Luckily, Colleen saved me by asking if anyone wanted a brownie for dessert.

After dinner, Joey looked ready to drop so we made a hasty exit. I was preoccupied, puzzling out what Patrenka was hoping to gain and a little exhausted from the boisterous dinner.

"Can Sean and Kelly come visit at the pool?" Joey asked breaking the silence.

"I don't know. I'm not sure how long we'll be there. I was thinking of going back to my apartment."

"But how will Auntie Patrenka find us?"

I met Joey's gaze in the rearview mirror.

"She knows where I live. When we are not at the hotel, she'll know where to look."

"Are you sure? I don't want her to be lost."

I didn't want Patrenka to be lost either, but at this point, she'd made her decision to investigate Buck personally. She didn't choose to be with us. I was still smarting from her defection.

"She has a job to do, Sport. We need to let her do it. She'll be back with news any day now."

Wise advice I knew, but I wasn't sure I could follow it. I was mad and hurt. Why did she leave us? Was it because I was such an idiot after a few beers? Did she leave because I made a play for her? It didn't sit well, when I looked into Joey's eyes. I needed to make contact with Patrenka if only to make sure she was coming back.

"Tell you what. I'll try to call Sam and see if he can get a message to Patrenka that we miss her and where we'll be. How's that?"

She nodded, but didn't seem to brighten any. If anything, her features became more severe. I wondered if she didn't like Sam any more than I did. I had nothing to base it on. I glanced at Joey. What was it like to be so little and have lost so much? I was older when I lost my parents and it wasn't easy then. Maybe when you were small, the loss didn't seem so bad. Then I realized what a ludicrous idea that was. I was getting soft. I was losing my edge, the objectivity that is vital for a reporter to have.

How in such a short time could I have been with Patrenka, have Joey thrust upon me and be living out of a suitcase in a hotel room? When had I become part of the story? I knew the answer and it burned me that it was Patrenka who lured me in and now she was off.

I needed to get back to my usual routine. I needed to get the murder charges dropped. I needed to quit hiding out. I needed to pull back and get rid of these entanglements. Mitch Malone was a loner and liked it. I pulled into the hotel lot and parked, turning to Joey. I saw both determination and adoration in her eyes. My resolve to be objective faded as a single tear slipped from her eye, slid down her smooth cheek and silently dropped into her lap.

Okay, I rationalized. I still had a few days to get this puzzle solved and figure out what would be best for Joey. I stopped suddenly. What was best for Joey? I had never before thought about someone else in my life. I was putting Joey first instead of my career, the next big scoop. When had that happened?

Why had that happened? When could I get rid of Joey? Then a small pain started in my chest building into a tight mass. What was wrong with me? My heart was breaking at the thought of dumping Joey somewhere. I couldn't do that and live with my conscience. I had a duty and an obligation. I wasn't a blood relative, but I'd grown to love that little girl in the short time we were together.

I needed a plan and time to figure out what all this was about. If I was a good reporter, I had to get this story. I wanted to give Joey closure. I needed to know what happened to her mother and the even bigger questions of why. Joey deserved to be able to make sense out of it. She needed to know her mother didn't leave her voluntarily. She deserved to know if her mother died trying to save her. That none of it was her fault.

Joey deserved the whole story and Mitch Malone was the guy to give it to her. That would be my mission. When we got back to the hotel, I was anxious to get going on my computer, but Joey found a second wind. She wanted to swim so swimming we went. I was amazing myself how I fit into the father role.

After swimming, Joey's busy day caught up to her and she drifted off to sleep as soon as her pajamas were on. I kissed her good night, then I turned on my computer and connected to the wireless Internet.

I was on the hunt.

Chapter 24

I clicked the mouse button in frustration, turning my computer off. I had been hunched over the keyboard since eight and it was now midnight. I had nothing to show for my efforts. Stretching, I glanced around the dim interior. How had I gotten here? A nondescript room. An uncomfortable desk chair that wasn't the right height for me to work comfortably without kicking in carpal tunnel. I was trying to work the kinks out of my back and relax. A soft rap sounded at the door. I tensed and looked at Joey sleeping peacefully on the bed. Was it my door? I was about to chalk it up to thin walls, when I heard it again. No one knew where we were except Dennis and Patrenka. I scurried to the door as if it was an oasis in the desert. I wanted to throw open the door and welcome her back with open arms. I reached for the safety bar and stopped. What if it wasn't Patrenka?

I peered out the peephole and saw nothing. Had I dreamt the knock in my research-induced comatose state? Had she changed her mind and left? I wanted to fling open the door but something kept me back. I didn't know who was out there. Was someone deliberately hiding out of sight of the peep hole?

What if one of Buck's goons had found us and wanted to take out Joey as a witness? I held a silent war and, surprising myself, I opted for safety over Patrenka – Joey's safety.

If it was Patrenka, she'd understand my caution. She'd knock again. I was antsy and needed to pee. I turned to the bathroom when the knocker rapped again. The peephole revealed the long arm and blond hair of Sam Sloan.

What a moron I thought and not for the first time. Why couldn't he stand in front of the door. Probably part of his FBI training or something stupid. I opened the door but left the safety bar on so the door would only open a few inches.

"What do you want?" I whispered to not disturb Joey. I glanced out but couldn't see much more of the hallway than from the peep hole. "If you don't show yourself, I'm calling the police," I said, knowing I wouldn't, but I was tired. This cat and mouse game with Sam pissed me off.

The hell with this. He would wait while I peed. I pushed the door to close it.

"We need to talk." Sam wedged his foot between the door and frame.

"Fine." I kicked his government-issued, steel-toed hiking boot and winced realizing I didn't have any shoes on. Sam moved his foot back.

I shut the door and hopped up and down in pain a couple times, then removed the slide and schooled my features. I opened the door wide enough to allow his massive frame to enter. I made sure the door latched behind him, then retreated back to the desk and shut my laptop. I pulled the chair around from the desk to face the easy chair in the near corner. I took the comfy chair and watched him try to load his girth onto the small desk chair and felt some retribution for his door high-jinks.

"What's up?" I asked to get the ball rolling. I had tried contacting Sam through the FBI earlier but had been unable to reach anyone who would admit he was even an agent. I had enlisted help, but even Dennis had been unable to find his location through his Federal contacts.

"I have a message for you. Back off."

"Back off? Back off from what?" I said, playing the innocent but surmising his visit coincided with my Patrenka sighting earlier.

"Don't play coy with me. What were you doing at the Roadhouse today?"

"I was having lunch. I was surprised to see my former roommate playing it cozy with the man responsible for Joey's mother's disappearance, especially since I had no note, and my calls to a certain FBI handler weren't returned. How was I supposed to know I might be intruding on an FBI-sanctioned investigation?"

"You knew damn well there was an investigation. You're a smart guy and all, being a reporter. This is none of your business. Stay out of it before you get hurt."

"None of my business, huh? Am I just the baby-sitter? Well, Mitch Malone doesn't baby-sit for anyone. You tell that to Patrenka. Because of me, she found her niece. If she thinks I'm walking away or going to be stuck on the sidelines, she's wrong. I'm writing this story with or without the FBI's help. I will go where I want, when I want." I stopped my tirade and we locked eyes, each refusing to give. There was so much testosterone flashing I was surprised we didn't come to blows or wake Joey.

Sam started to rise out of the chair but I put up my hands to forestall his leaving. I took a deep breath. I needed to outsmart him, which I didn't think would be difficult. A softer approach might get me somewhere.

"Okay. This isn't getting us anywhere," I said and glanced toward Joey to make sure that our voices hadn't awakened her. She appeared to be sleeping but I saw a flutter of eyelashes and wondered if she was faking. I lowered my voice and asked: "Are you and Patrenka getting any closer to solving this?"

"No."

I thought that was all he was going to say and I needed more. I watched him try to get a grip on his breathing. The silence stretched. I was staring down the steely eyes of a hardened agent. He looked away. The silent treatment worked.

"Patrenka's fine and making progress. This is what she does best. She's infiltrated the operation without anyone being the wiser and we want to keep it that way. Your presence could jeopardize that," he said, returning eye contact. No warmth. No compassion.

"I had no idea I would find her there. I cruised the area trying to get a handle on why Buck would have wanted the land. I was hungry and there was the Roadhouse, down from Buck's estate." I stopped abruptly realizing I was rambling but I don't think slick realized it.

"Don't do it again." The reply seemed childish and at odds with the big frame. I gave this guy way too much credit in the brains department.

"What has she found out?" I looked at him, trying to give him my most sincere, hero-worship look. "If I know the investigation is moving forward, I won't feel like I need to do anything. I didn't know until today where Patrenka had gone. For all I knew, she could have hit the road. Joey needs some kind of answers."

Sam looked speculative and I tried my best to look earnest, humble and trustworthy. I must have been successful.

"Okay. Patrenka has infiltrated the network. Seems she made quite an impression on Buck during her interview and the story published in the *Los Angeles Times* was positive and featured Buck substantially."

"There was a story in the *Times*? When? Today?" Something wasn't right here. I spent four hours researching Buck and didn't see a *Times* article. "I didn't see it."

"It was a special copy for Buck. She took it to him personally this morning."

"Wow, the Bureau pulled out all the stops, huh? I suppose she's working on a follow-up article?" Sarcasm tinged my comments but Sam didn't seem to notice.

"She's staying with Buck while on vacation from the *Times* or so he believes. She hasn't found out much yet, except that his accountant disappeared about the same time as Joey's mother. She's not sure it's related but the timing is too close to be a coincidence."

I wanted to add that I'd found the accountant but something told me not to share. I still didn't trust Sam — he was a Fed and they never gave, only took, unless they wanted something. At least in my experience.

A couple of years ago I was covering a string of bank robberies. The robber wore a mask and no one ever saw him before he entered the bank. A pair of FBI agents was helping the local police crack the case. I had printed as much as I could to keep people aware of how the robber was pulling it off, hoping people would come forward with information if they saw someone putting on a Halloween mask, a gorilla head or Richard Nixon. The robber literally disappeared once he left the bank and officials were no closer after a half dozen robberies.

Dennis was a new detective and was assigned to the task force that was formed after the sixth robbery. He allowed me to accompany him as he examined each location with a fresh eye. We had visited five of the six locations when the call came in for another branch. We were only blocks away. We arrived and I was forced to sit in the car until the scene was secured. While waiting I noticed two things. One, it was one-thirty in the afternoon and the bank didn't have many customers and two, there was a bus stop across the street. I noticed that each of the branches were on a main bus route.

After getting the details of the current robbery, I returned to the paper and started looking at the times of the robberies. I then visited the transit authority and bus routes and times. Sure enough, each robbery was within a few minutes of a bus stop. I mentioned my observations to one of the agents and he laughed and told me to go back to what I know best, making up stories. I was ticked off and returned to the paper. I tracked down the bus driver of the number ten bus that ran in front of the Fifth Third branch that day.

Through my work, the robber was caught, because the transit authority was testing video surveillance on that bus. He was wearing reversible clothing and walked out of the bank and quickly took off his mask and turned his coat inside out and walked leisurely to the bus stop. Turns out the city buses run on a pretty tight schedule and the robber never had to wait long for his getaway car. The Feds were not too happy that I figured it out and printed it with Dennis' help before they were briefed.

My memory of the incident was jarred back to the present with Sam's caustic voice. "Mitch, you still there or did you drop the phone?" I ignored the jab.

"Anything on why he wanted the land?"

"No. She hasn't made any headway on the project. He keeps promising to give her a tour but something always changes his plans and it's making her suspicious." Sam stopped suddenly and then asked: "How's it going with Joey? Any more information?" He glanced in the direction of her sleeping form and my instincts went into overdrive. Something about the way he looked at her made my skin crawl.

"No. I hate to bring up bad memories. I don't want to force it."

Sam shook his head in agreement. I still wanted Joey to be questioned by a professional. Sam wasn't even an option. I needed to talk to Dennis about it but I was in no hurry to bring up bad memories for Joey.

Sam stood to leave when a small white object hit him at the knees.

"Where's Auntie Patrenka? I want to see her. Now," came the high-pitched cry. Joey wrapped her arms around his legs and held on tight.

I had never heard Joey whine in agitation. I almost smiled at Sam's panicked look. Joey pulled on the creases on his black slacks, making Sam clutch at his waist to stay decent.

I started to move toward him when I caught Joey's look transform with a smile before it turned back into the irrational child. I had to blink several times to make sure I hadn't imagined it. She had more of Patrenka's talent that anyone knew. A fatherly pride consumed me and I let her go.

"Tell me where my auntie is. Is she dead?"

Sam was immobilized and speechless. I was enjoying the show.

"Your aunt is fine. I just left her."

"Tell her to come back," she fired back, with a strong tug on his pants to accentuate the point. I thought she was going to unmask his grey briefs beyond the couple inches already showing.

"She will, as soon as she can," was the lame reply. Sam looked at me and started to raise his hands in a gesture seeking help, but Joey pulled again and his hands returned to his waistband to keep his dignity intact.

"I want her now. Why can't she come back? I want her now." Joey's tirade continued.

"She can't. She's making the bad man tell her his secrets."

"What secrets?" and a sob broke free.

"Joey, Patrenka will find out if Buck has anything to do with the terrorists working in the area. She'll be back soon."

A heavy silence filled the room as we each understood the statement. Joey let go of Sam's pants.

"Shit," Sam muttered, fumbling with the safety bar then slipping out the door. I was in shock and I think Joey was too. She turned and threw herself into my arms.

Damn. I forgot to get his cell phone number and his opinion on whether we could go back to my apartment. I needed some serious laundry done.

Joey peeked out from my shoulder and asked quietly. "Is he gone?"

"Yes." I walked to the door and relocked the safety slide and dead bolt. I didn't want any other surprises tonight.

Joey popped up and looked me square in the face. Not a single tear marred her soft skin. She wiggled her way out of my arms, ran back to the bed and jumped in, pulling up the covers.

"Did I do good questioning the bad guy?" she said a guileless expression on her face.

"Yes. You did. What made you think to do that?"

"Auntie Patrenka. When we went to the pool, she would tell me stories of her work. She told me different ways she got the bad guys to talk."

"She did huh? Tell me more."

"Patrenka said you needed to find out what the person hated the most. Sam's easy. He hates kids."

"How do you know that?"

"When he rescued me, I pretended to be asleep because I wasn't sure if he was a good guy or a big fibber." Joey stopped to take a yawn.

I should stop this and let Joey go to sleep, but I wanted to hear it. I wasn't sure she would remember in the morning.

"He talked to himself. He kept saying 'Why did I have to be the one? What am I supposed to do with a kid? I don't even like kids." Another yawn punctuated this statement. I walked over to get her settled.

"You did well. I think I'll call you my little secret weapon for your surprise attack. You did good." Joey held up her hands and arms to me. I bent down and she wrapped them around my neck.

"I'm glad I'm with you, Uncle Mitch." She let go and slid back onto the pillow. She was soon asleep.

I stood but didn't move from the edge of the bed. Not for the first time I wondered how smart Joey was compared to other kids because she had moments of sheer brilliance. Without her help, I wouldn't know I was facing terrorists and that there was a reason for the FBI to be hanging around. I finally moved from Joey's side and went back to my computer to research my latest lead, but exhaustion hit like a runaway train. Morning was soon enough to figure out the next step.

Chapter 25

Joey and I didn't wake until the bright rays of the sun cascaded through the nondescript, room-darkening blinds. We both were moving slowly but Joey perked up when I mentioned doughnuts for breakfast. I needed to see Dennis and also wanted to check in on how things were going at the paper. Through all this, I hadn't read the paper in over a week. It surprised me that I hadn't missed it.

Time to start revisiting my old haunts and find out what was new. Doughnuts were the best start. On the ten-minute drive to the doughnut shop, I told Joey we needed to go undercover. She was all for it. I told her our cover was going to be I was on vacation and caring for my nephew. Everyone was to think she was a boy. I didn't want anyone putting it together with our real objective. I warned her it was better to say nothing than to let something slip.

I could see the excitement in her eyes and it would be an interesting exercise. I didn't think there'd be much danger. Joey was full of surprises and maybe she could even help this ace reporter scare up a few details.

Donna's was pretty slow when we arrived. It wasn't breakfast and lunch was still too far off. I sat in my normal spot and Joey perched next to me, the baseball cap pulled low over her eyes. She bounced up and down, but I couldn't fault her eagerness. Or maybe, she was hungry.

Shirley strode over with a cup and stopped dead when she saw Joey.

"Can I see some ID? This is Mitch Malone's booth and he hasn't been seen in days."

I laughed and it felt good. "Sorry, Shirley. Meet my nephew, Joey. I wasn't expecting to be called in to baby-sit, but figured I needed a vacation anyway. If you can't help your family, what good are you?" I hoped no one would remember that I didn't have any siblings.

"Never figured you for the baby-sitting type," Shirley responded, then lowered her girth to Joey's height.

"What'll you have, partner?"

"A doughnut with lots of sprinkles."

"Anything to drink?"

"Milk," I replied.

"Chocolate" added Joey daring me to overrule her. I didn't. I relaxed against the booth. Shirley didn't seem suspicious at all and Joey was milking her part for all it was worth.

Shirley invited Joey to pick out her doughnut from the case in the back. She happily agreed and skipped off. She returned a few minutes later with Shirley in tow. After Joey climbed up, she deposited a doughnut frosted in a neon rainbow of color in front of Joey. "Fine choice. I hope you don't mind, but Joey picked one out for you, too."

I smiled and nodded and a Bavarian Crème long john was placed in front of me. My smile grew and I nodded at Joey in thanks. Joey beamed. Shirley clucked in amazement and moved off only to return within a minute with an empty glass and small carton of chocolate milk.

"Shall I pour?" she asked.

Joey shook her head, her mouth full with sprinkles dangling from her lips. Shirley set it down and left us.

"She's nice, Uncle Mitch. Do you like her?"

"She's a good friend. I eat here often and she takes good care of me."

We both perused the place while we ate in silence. I was looking for anyone from the paper and after a few minutes a metro editor on days sauntered in and gave me a nod. I knew him, but I worked mostly at night with Ken. The metro editor was not one of the day editors I enjoyed working with. He edited heavily whether it needed it or not, just to say, I do have a reason to be in this job.

He approached the table.

"How's the vacation?"

"Good." I recognized the instant he spotted Joey in the opposite seat. "Let me introduce you to my nephew, Joey. The reason for my hasty vacation."

"Oh, I thought . . ." and his voice trailed off as he realized how rude it would sound to say it was because I was running from the FBI. He collected himself enough. "Well, it was kind of quick," he added lamely.

Another black mark against Sam. The creep hadn't cleared me yet of the murder charges. I should have let Joey rip off Sam's pants. That would have been a sight. His large girth trying to slip out of our room with his pants tripping him up at the ankles.

"Care to join us?"

"Sure, but I only have a few minutes. Just needed a little Java to get me kick started after deadline. We sure miss your expertise on the beat. Your replacement is a little cavalier on the details. We end up making calls to verify things right up 'til the last minute to make sure we get it right. When are you coming back?"

"In another week or so. I think Joey's parents will be back then."

Shirley appeared and handed a Styrofoam cup to him and a small white bag. "I gotta get back. Good to see you."

I figured we'd done all we could and I didn't want to hang out too long. I got up and motioned for Joey to follow. She didn't. I looked back and she had a stubborn look on her face.

"What's the matter, Sport?"

"We have to wait for the bill." Joey crossed her arms on her chest and glared at me. What had I done?

Then it hit me. I never got a bill here. Shirley always put it on my account and I paid at the end of the month with a generous tip for her. "I eat here a lot when I'm working at the paper next store and she keeps track and I pay her once a month."

That seemed to satisfy her. She jumped down and grabbed my hand.

As we headed to my car, Joey asked: "Can I go see where you work?" I mulled that over for a few steps wondering if our story would stick. It seemed to go over with one editor. Maybe I could see where the investigation was and poke around. Then I realized I owed the librarian a favor for the research material. That seemed like a lifetime ago when our twosome was a threesome and the woman of my dreams was sleeping in the bed next to mine. I pushed that from my mind.

"Sure. Let's go. I'll give you the five dollar tour."

It seemed odd walking in the public entrance in the front. I nodded to the receptionist and grabbed the escalator to the second floor which was where the news, features, sports, business writers, and editors were housed. I'd never noticed before but the public entrance was classy. After the initial wood-paneled office and receptionist, the lighting changed to garish and the plush office became a tile floor and nondescript cubicles.

"This is the newsroom, Joey." At her blank expression, I elaborated. "This is where all the people write the stories that go in the paper." She nodded.

"Where's yours?"

"Right this way." I led her halfway down and then over two aisles, gesturing for her to enter. I followed and sat in my desk chair. It seemed like a lifetime ago that I was here pounding out story after story about the big crime news of the day. I glanced over my shoulder and stopped. The last time I did that, Patrenka had captured my attention. I shook off those thoughts and turned on my computer. I pulled up a couple of old stories up on the screen and then pulled the newspaper clippings from a stack buried under my desk and showed her the same story in print.

That seemed to impress her.

"Mitch, I thought you were on vacation," I turned to see Ken at the entrance to my cubicle.

"I am. I'm giving my nephew the dime tour. He was interested. Also thought I would pick up my paycheck and restore my finances."

"Nephew, huh? This must be some vacation," he added with a twinkle in his eye. A couple of years ago on a snowy holiday eve, he and I had talked about our families or lack thereof. He knew I didn't have any siblings.

"Yes, this is Joey. Joey, this is my boss, Mr. Clark."

Joey nearly got me all choked up. She was the perfect gentleman in a small package. She held her hand out, waited patiently for Ken to extend his, shook it and said: "Pleased to meet you, Mr. Clark."

Ken's chuckle was a belly laugh that shook the whole building. "Great kid, err nephew, you have there, Mitch."

To get him off the subject, I asked: "Ken, what are you doing here so late? Aren't you usually gone at sunrise? It's pushing noon."

"Yes, but your replacement requires a lot of direction and editing. I can't wait for your vacation to be done. We haven't had a good crime story in over a week. He can't even follow up the double murder you started. Any chance you want to pound anything out while you're here?"

"What have you had in the last few days?"

Ken looked at me sharply, surprised I wasn't reading the paper cover to cover as was my normal custom. "Hmm, let me think. We have no progress on the investigation and he can't get the FBI to return his calls. There are no further details, no motive and no arrests. That's the mantra he's getting. Want to take a whack at it?"

"I'm on vacation. Remember?" I grabbed Joey's hand and led her toward the back of the newsroom and to the rear entrance. We passed the newspaper's morgue and I remembered my promise. We took a detour inside.

"Lucy," I said. "I'm here to pay up."

"About time. I thought maybe you had done a rabbit and hopped down a hole never to return."

"Sorry, I kind of had a family emergency. Meet my nephew, Joey."

"Please to meet you, ma'am," Joey said, holding out her hand, which Lucy took.

"Nice to meet you, chillin," Lucy said, bending down and looking Joey in the eye.

She straightened and looked me right in the eye. I knew I was in trouble. "I don't know why you're passing this girl off as a boy or even why you are calling her a nephew when I know you don't have any siblings, but don't mind me. I run the morgue and mind my own business."

"Thank you, Lucy. I will explain when I can." I opened my wallet and pulled out the rest of my cash which was only about twenty dollars and gave it to her."

"Lucy don't take no bribes. I trust your reasoning," she said pushing the money back in my direction.

"But I owe you for your help last week."

"Don't you worry none about that. When everything is cleared up, then we'll settle up and you can really introduce me to your friend," she said, nodding in Joey's direction. "Now go on, I got work to do. Just cuz you're not here writing stories doesn't mean the paper isn't coming out with all the news." I watched her bulk shuffle to the back of the morgue. She was an amazing lady. She was almost like a mother to me and I never felt guiltier for my deception. I couldn't wait to fill her in. I needed to get back to work and get out from under this.

I glanced at Joey and she was looking at me. I felt guilty anew like she could read my mind about getting rid of her quickly. Her little hand welded itself to mine and I smiled at her to reassure her. "You'll figure it out, Uncle Mitch," and she squeezed.

I couldn't let this little girl down. She deserved answers and I needed to find them.

"Let me show you the presses. Now those are cool." We exited the library and disappeared down the back stairs to the basement.

Joey was suitably awed by watching the big presses move and the cylinders of newsprint taller than she was, unroll at lightning speed. I took her up a catwalk over a press and she was able to see the black blur as the ink was put on the pages.

"Cool, Uncle Mitch. Do your words get on the pages?"

"Yes they do when I'm working on a story," I answered unsure how much detail to go into for her young mind.

"When are you going to write another story?"

"I don't know. I hope soon," I prayed we would find answers and I could write about Joey and not worry about something happening to her.

Chapter 26

After the foray into the newspaper, I decided we needed to make a stop at my apartment and at least get the mail. I didn't have any pets or plants to worry about but I did enjoy my digs.

As we approached my apartment door, I had a moment of trepidation about bringing Joey into danger. I stopped and pulled back into the recess by the elevator and stair landing.

"Joey, if anyone is waiting for us or if I tell you to run, I want you to run. Do you hear me?" I put my hands on her shoulders to make sure she was getting the message. "Maybe I shouldn't have brought you, but we're here. I'll go in first and if anything happens, I want you to take the stairs." I pulled my phone from my belt clip and flipped it open. "You know how to use this?" She nodded. "I want you to call 9-1-1. You tell them Mitch Malone needs help at home. You got that?" I searched her eyes and saw the alarm. I hated to put it there, but I needed to keep her safe.

"Understand?"

Joey shook her head solemnly.

"Repeat it back to me."

"If anything goes wrong, I call 9-1-1 and tell them you need help."

"Good. Now stay here while I enter." I pointed to an area behind a fake palm tree beside where the elevator jutted out. I walked to my door and looked back making sure Joey had stayed put.

I inserted my key in the lock and turned, slowly opening the door to keep noise to a minimum. As I glanced around I was disgusted to see dishes overflowing in the sink. Fast food containers littered the coffee table. Half a dozen water rings marred my table. I was drawn into the mess like a trance. My caution fled. My apartment was trashed, not like it had been ransacked but like the three little bears, Goldilocks and all the fairy tale characters had moved in and no one had cleaned up after himself.

The bedroom door was closed. I moved stealthily to it and pushed it open, knowing the lock didn't catch right. There was somebody sleeping in my bed and it wasn't anyone from my dreams but it did remind me of Papa Bear — big and large.

I could feel the blood pounding through my veins. Someone not only came uninvited into my home, but was sleeping in my bed. I advanced into the room, not sure what I had planned to do. I was almost to the bed when an arm pulled from under the pillow and a gun was pointed at my chest. I followed the arm down to the face and saw Sam Sloan.

"Mitch, is everything all right?" came Joey's small voice laced with worry.

I swung toward the voice and mentally kicked myself for forgetting Joey in my rush to uncover who had violated my sanctuary. "Yes, Sport. I'm fine. Come on in and shut the door."

I turned back to Sam in my bed and noted the gun had disappeared.

"Care to explain yourself?" I tried to keep the anger from my voice but I didn't succeed.

Sam smiled and I wanted to launch myself at him and wipe it off his face. He didn't look tough lying there on my percale. I wanted to beat him bloody. Sam rolled over fully on his back and brought his hands behind his head infuriating me further.

"You weren't using it."

"I wasn't using it because some moron tried to break in. I didn't know that the same moron just wanted the California king mattress."

"I must say I did notice it when I was here with Patrenka, and after you were settled at the hotel, I decided it shouldn't go to waste."

"You have been here the whole week?" I sputtered, so angry I was rooted to the spot.

I felt a tug at my leg and looked down at Joey. "I gotta go."

I took a deep breath and let it out slowly trying to remember some relaxation techniques but came up empty. The best I could come up with was leaving the bedroom. Taking Joey's hand we retreated. When we entered the living room, I pointed to the right.

"The bathroom is through there. Remember?"

I took another step into the living room and turned a slow three-sixty, disgust welling up with each degree. Sam was a pig. He was a tall, gangly man who never learned how to pick up after himself. What had the FBI seen in him?

As my turn reached the bedroom doorway, Sam entered, having thrown a t-shirt over his upper frame and running shorts on the bottom showing more leg than anyone should have a right to. The bathroom door opened and Joey stepped out looking from me to Sam and back, uncertainty written in her eyes.

I walked forward, picked her up and swung her around.

"Whatcha think of my place?"

"It's okay." She wrapped her arms around my neck.

"Think we should move in here?"

"Where would I sleep?"

"I could fix up a little room for you in my office. It would be yours. Sam will be vacating immediately."

"I . . ." I cut off Sam by holding up my hand and my look of fury kept his tongue in check.

"I bet I could find some cool cartoons," I said walking over to the TV and punched the power button. The TV was turned to a pay-per-view channel featuring scantily-clad women. I glared at Sam who, I was gratified to notice, turned red and shrugged his shoulders. I walked to the coffee table and grabbed the remote and punched in three digits for the children's programming. I flipped through a couple of channels.

"Dora. Dora." I stopped channel surfing and Joey climbed onto the couch. I cleared her immediate area of dirty socks and backed Sam into my bedroom, shutting the door behind me.

I pulled my trusty digital camera from my coat pocket and snapped Sam's photo and then quickly turned and snapped more of the disarray in my room.

"I suggest you gather your stuff. You're out of here."

I turned, left the room and continued to snap photos of the filthy kitchen and the containers littering the coffee table. Sam came out of the bedroom within a few minutes, a duffle in his hand.

"Say goodbye to Sam, Joey." Joey half turned and waved, her vision never leaving the big screen of my TV. I walked to the door and opened it. Sam made a quick tour around the apartment, stuffing his belongings into the duffle and meeting me at the door.

"If you ever enter here again without my invitation, you'll be facing charges and I don't care who you work for."

"I want your camera chip." Sam's voice was steely and he was glaring at me.

"No."

"Don't make me take it from you." His reply seemed infantile but the cold steel in his eyes did make me pause. I didn't want to get in a brawl I was sure to lose. I didn't break eye contact as I considered my options. I was unwilling to give up any leverage I had, especially with the many charges I expected to incur from my unwanted visitor.

Joey pulled on my arm asking to be lifted, breaking the stare down and the tenseness in the moment. I realized Sam was unwilling to do anything with Joey in my arms. It may have been cowardly but it wasn't my idea either. Joey turned, looping her arms around my neck and pushing herself around so she was between the two of us. She wrapped her legs around my waist and put her arms under my jacket and made a big show of giving me a huge hug.

For a moment I wondered if she was saying goodbye before Sam pummeled me to death. I returned the embrace and with my head I motioned Sam to leave. He reluctantly stepped out the door. I slammed it shut with my foot and locked it, realizing that would be futile since he obviously had been getting in and out for more than a week, judging by the amount of mess.

Joey was wiggling in my arms and I set her down. I wondered if she realized what she had done. She returned to the couch and fiddled with her hat before placing it on her head, losing herself in the TV show. I shook my head. I needed to use the restroom myself.

I walked in and wanted to gag. My stainless steel faucets were peppered with white spots and my tub and shower were equally gross. I pulled my camera from my pocket and powered it up. I went to take a photo then realized the screen said. "No card."

No card? I had been taking photos with it only a few moments ago. What had happened to it? I played the last couple of minutes in my mind and the only one who had touched me had been Joey and her hug. I looked at her calmly watching TV. Had she removed the photo card?

I went over and sat on the couch. Dora was finishing and I grabbed the remote and silenced the TV. Joey looked up.

I showed Joey my camera and to my amazement she put it up to her eye and tried to take a photo. When it didn't work she turned it over in her hand and looked at it. She looked up at me and I shrugged my shoulders.

Joey pulled off her hat and dug in the band around the inside. She pulled out a card and after a single try, popped it into my camera and took my photo. "Let me see," she demanded.

I took the camera and turned the switch to view and showed her the photo of me with a stunned expression on my face. "How did you know how to do that?"

"Mommy liked to take pictures. She showed me." I took the camera back and decided to see if the ones of the disaster of my apartment showed the detail.

Instead of my apartment I saw someone else's living room. A lamp was casting light in a pool next to an easy chair. I didn't recognize whose room it was. The next shot was a movie and I played it. The room was the same but the shadows were longer. A rough sounding voice that was vaguely familiar spoke off camera.

"I want your photos. You had no business on my property and I want them back."

I saw a woman move forward from the left. She was pretty in a plain sort of way and she looked familiar. Her hands were on her hips and she was all about attitude.

"I don't know what you are talking about. Please leave. You're not welcome here."

"Lady, you don't know what you are messing with. Give me the photos and no one will get hurt. You don't want to see that child of yours have an accident, do you?"

"Aieeeeeee."

Chapter 27

I nearly dropped the camera at the anguished cry from Joey. I had been so intent on the image wondering where it came from. Joey was holding her hands over her eyes and emitting the strangest keening noises.

"Noooo. Stoooooopppp." I turned the camera off and pushed it into my pocket. Joey grabbed hold of me and buried her head into my jacket. I could hear small cries but I couldn't see her face. I patted her back to try and console her. Her arms snaked around my waist. I sat rooted to the spot unable to make sense of the strange turn of events.

I was on information overload. What had happened? I wanted to get back to the pictures on the card. It hit me what the tape contained. The vaguely familiar woman had to be Joey's mother.

What an idiot I was! No wonder Joey freaked out. Who wouldn't? I was about to replay her mother's death captured on camera, but by whom? Before my mind could wrap around that thought, another entered. It was Joey who held the key all along. She hid the card. No wonder she always took the cap with her. It was all she had left of her mother. She'd lost her teddy bear at the other murder scene.

Whose voice was so menacing on the tape? Could it be Buck's?

Whoever was on the tape didn't know he was on tape. That was obvious. I was itching to watch the rest of the tape to get the answers, but knew I couldn't watch it with Joey on my lap. I couldn't make my young friend relive her worst nightmare. I needed to closet myself somewhere and see the tape. I was a reporter. I had to know.

Joey quieted as I rubbed her back. She eventually went limp and I knew she was asleep. I gently rearranged Joey, extricating her from the folds of my jacket and took small steps not to jostle and awaken her until I was on the edge of the couch with only a single cheek. I was about to make my escape when Joey rolled over.

My little rescuer had turned from a happy kid into a frightened baby with a flip of my camera's switch. Joey turned her head in my direction. I saw her face wet with tears and silently cursed my stupidity again. I was new to this sensitivity stuff. Her arm reached out and grabbed my leather jacket pulling me back down to her. I squeezed her in an awkward hug.

"So sorry, Sport. So sorry."

I brushed my lips across her forehead and her eyes opened.

"I love you, Uncle Mitch."

"I love you too, Sport." She took a hiccup of a breath and then another. I watched her eyes flutter shut. I held her close for several more minutes until I realized she had dropped off to sleep again. I slowly slid her from my lap to the couch and placed a throw pillow under her head. I rose and retrieved a blanket from the linen closet next to the bathroom, then returned to Joey laying it over her sleeping form.

I went into the bathroom and shut the door, grimacing in disgust. Sam had left toothpaste blobs on the mirror and shaving stubble in the sink. Damp towels lurked in the corners and the toilet looked as if he did jumping jacks when he peed. I'm not a neat freak, but I could barely stand in the room without gagging. There was no way I'd have let Joey in, had I known.

I pulled the tub and tile cleaner from under the sink and sprayed it liberally over every surface. I wished I had rubber gloves. I should have known he would be a slob. This is a guy who doesn't leave suspects alive or worries about a little girl's life.

After I cleaned the tub, I turned on the shower rinsing the walls. I shut the curtain and pulled out my cell phone.

Without waiting for the preliminaries of even hello, I launched in. "I've got a short movie of Joey's mother's death. I started watching it, but Joey freaked out and I had to turn it off."

I was sure Dennis's loud expletive would wake Joey, but she hadn't moved when I peeked out the door. He fired questions that had my ears ringing and I couldn't answer until I finished the rest of the tape.

"I can't play it here and I want to download it. I'm at my apartment but I need to get Joey distracted. She really lost it when it was at the beginning. I think she did the photography."

"How, where?"

I cut Dennis off, my mind scrambling to fit the pieces together. "I figured out why she was so attached to that Tiger's cap." I told him about the trip to my apartment. My voice trailed off as I began to scrub the sink. "Oh, who is the best locksmith you know?"

"Harrison, off Division and Ninth Street, why?"

"Seems Sam, the FBI man, has been using my crib while I was in hiding at the hotel. I need to lock it up tight. I'm not letting pig pen get back in."

"Want to press charges?"

"No. I have a better idea." I said knowing having something on a Fed might come in handy.

"Roger that in double time. Just a sec."

I heard a muffled conversation and then Dennis's voice. "Mitch, how about meeting me at my house and we'll go to the station. We can make copies, logging it for evidence. I don't want this tape bounced out of court on a technicality. Wait, better yet, bring Joey to the station and we will get some video of her and her Tigers cap. I will have Colleen meet us and she can take the kids for ice cream or something while we examine the tape."

"Great. See you in about a half hour?" I disconnected, turned off the shower to what was now a humid room. I finished cleaning the sink, toilet and even sprayed down the tile floor with disinfectant a second time for good measure.

I opened the door, pleased with the results until I looked at the living room. It would only take us a couple of minutes to get to the station. Time enough to get rid of the smelly cartons. I walked over and picked up Joey's hat.

I was looking it over and flipped down the inside lining. Sewn neatly into the band were three little pockets that an X-D camera card could slide into. I refolded the lining and looked. You couldn't tell they were there until you flipped the lining down. Ingenious – and there were two more chips. One had to be mine but I couldn't wait to view the other two in their entirety.

I placed the hat where Joey had left it and got a garbage bag. Within minutes, the coffee table, kitchen table and counters were cleared of garbage. I moved to the refrigerator to grab a beer to steady my nerves before heading to the station.

"Good God." My refrigerator reeked of spoiled milk, and other containers that I couldn't guess their contents. Again I wished for rubber gloves or better yet one of those bio hazard suits.

I shut the refrigerator door and closed up the filled garbage bag. I saw Joey's head pop up from the sofa. "Hey sleepyhead, want to go meet the Flaherty's and get some ice cream?"

She jumped up to her feet, took one bounce on my cushion and vaulted over the couch heading for the door.

"Whoa, slow down. I need to make one call and we need to give them time to get ready. I want to finish getting this trash out too."

I walked into the bedroom and started stripping the bed. I felt violated. I saw something glint as the nightstand rocked with the force of my anger. I picked it up and smiled to myself as I saw Samuel L. Sloan printed in gold letters along the bottom of an American Express card. Hmmm, I could only hope this was his company card and the charges would need to be explained. I'd call the cable company and have my bill paid by a charge this month. It also should work to get my locks changed. I looked up the telephone number for Harrison, the locksmith, and dialed.

"I need new locks for my door and I want state of the art, money is no object. Any chance you could do it immediately?"

"Sure, Mack. I've got the Deadbolt 3000 that not only requires the correct key but the key must contain the right coding similar to a bar code, makes the lock unpickable."

"That sounds perfect. Can you have it done in a couple of hours and drop the keys off at the downtown police station?"

After his grunt of approval, I gave him the credit card number and name on the card, telling him the FBI owed me the new lock and to leave the receipt on my counter. I threw the sheets in the washer and cleaned the nightstands looking for anything else Sam had left. I found nothing but trash. I figured he reclined on the bed and ordered all his take-out, forgetting to put the card back in his wallet. So sorry, Sam. Not! A satisfied smile curled each side of my mouth.

☙☙☙

We arrived at the police station and sat on the front steps. We were watching the clouds drift by putting shapes to their cumulous outlines. "That one's a tiger, Uncle Mitch."

I laughed and pulled the lid of her baseball cap over her face. She laughed and I wished we didn't have to go inside. I was about to suggest it as Dennis pulled up in Colleen's minivan. Joey ran to meet Sean and Kelly and they started talking excitedly about ice cream and what flavors they wanted.

"Hey guys, I thought we were going to do a tour of my work place?" Dennis said. The kids quieted.

"I'll race you." All three took off and ran up the fifteen faux marble steps to the front entrance. I hung back.

"The department's child psychologist will meet Joey and videotape it in their special children's room," Dennis said as we started to climb. I was glad the specialist had returned from her vacation.

Dennis showed the children around and ended up on the second floor. He opened the door and I was surprised to see a room that didn't reflect anything of a police station's drab walls. It was decorated in bright colors and the ceiling even contained clouds and a sun. The kids ran to the mini slide and climbing unit near one corner. In the center were pint-sized chairs, a small table and a box of crayons and white paper on it. The kids continued to explore as a woman in a Hawaiian print dress entered the room. She had orange flip-flops and all three stopped in their tracks to watch her shuffle in.

The woman nodded to us and sat at the table to color. Colleen, Dennis and I stood awkwardly waiting near the door. After only a minute, the kids huddled around Emily. She asked them their names and told them hers. Dennis had briefed me on the procedure. We were to leave all three children with Emily after we told them we were going. She would do the rest.

I went to Joey. "I'm going to go with Dennis for a couple of minutes, but if you need me, ask Emily, okay?" She nodded her head unconcerned.

We filed out and entered the room next door. A technician

manned the controls while we watched via hidden cameras, microphones and a throw back to less modern times, a one-way mirror. Emily continued to color while the kids explored. Emily asked Joey if she wanted to color. She shook her head.

"Why do you have orange shoes?" Joey asked.

"I like bright colors. Why do you have a Tiger baseball cap?"

"My Daddy gave it to me before he went away." But the reply was stilted. Joey took a step backwards and grabbed the cap protectively.

"He did, did he? My daddy used to give me things and they always had hidden surprises. Does yours have any surprises?"

Joey shook her head vehemently and took another step backwards. I started to leave the room to return to Joey when Dennis grabbed my arm. "Wait." I didn't miss the steel command in his voice.

"Your Uncle Mitch said you did a pretty good magic trick with it. He said you took the chip out of his camera and made it disappear."

A smile spread across Joey's face. "Yup. I can do that."

"Can you show me?" Emily pulled a camera similar to mine out of her flowered pocket and set it on the table.

Joey stopped and looked at her for a minute and then the camera. She walked over and Emily pulled the seat out so she could sit down.

"Mommy said the key to magic was making you look somewhere else. Look," she added, pointing across the room. Emily looked. We followed Emily's gaze but Dennis poked me and motioned toward the camera. Quicker than seemed possible, the chip was gone, out of the camera and in Joey's hand.

Emily turned back and Joey smiled and pulled off her hat. "Do you want me to try now?" We watched Joey slip the camera chip into her hat under the table, while Emily looked at the camera on the table.

Dennis and I looked at each other and chuckled. Joey was good. How had she gotten so much practice to pull it off with such ease and why?

"Sure go ahead," Emily said.

Joey took the camera, opened it and showed Emily it was empty. Emily looked at her and then broke into a light, lilting laughter.

"You minx. You're good. Can you tell me where you learned that?"

"My mommy takes lots of pictures. I used to get mad and take her chips. Then she could play with me. Mommy made the pockets so I wouldn't hurt or lose the chips and she could get them back later. After we played first." She used the stubborn tone I knew so well, that usually had me giving in to demands for doughnuts or pizza.

"Your mommy was smart. Where is she?"

"I don't know." Joey's voice was higher in pitch. Her head went down on her arms on the table, her shoulders shaking. Emily was quiet, waiting. After a few minutes, Joey's tears were spent. She raised her head, eyes locked onto Emily, waiting too, but you could see the unease in her carriage. Sean and Kelly also were quiet, seemingly intent on their play but watching, too.

"Joey, you are a brave girl. Will you tell me about the last time you saw your mom?" The air suddenly seemed to be charged with electricity. I saw pain flash in Joey's eyes. She hiccupped as she drew in a deep breath. The camera angle was nearly too much zoomed into her face. Her pain, up close and personal in high definition.

"I was outside playing when I saw the big black car drive in. Mommy called me in and told me to stay out of sight. She didn't like the people in the car. I wasn't supposed to watch but I did. She set up her camera on the bookshelves. She saw me watching and not hiding."

"What did she say?"

"Mommy said she was going to make the bad men go away. My job was to practice my disappearing trick and not come out until she said the magic words."

"Did you see who came?"

Joey nodded.

"Can you tell me what they looked like?"

"The scary man with the red raspberry ring. He hit my Mommy." Joey's thumb went in her mouth.

Tears started down her cheeks again. Emily kept silent and waited. "I must have made a noise and the man saw me. I ran and hid." Joey pulled her thumb out long enough to talk, then put it back.

Emily let Joey tell the story in her own time as events occurred to her.

"I heard someone follow me but they couldn't find me. They kept yelling. 'Come here kid. We won't hurt your mommy.' They fibbed."

A world of emotion was in those two words. It was accusation, it was anger, it was determination. I wanted to protect Joey. I wanted to make it all better for her. I wanted to stop her from remembering, from telling the story but I knew I couldn't. She had kept so much bottled up. No matter what happened, she needed to get it out. For her sake and for her mother's. I didn't know if she had confided in Patrenka or not. From the way the story unfolded, I guessed not. I thought back to the times I would return from an errand or the pair would return from the pool. I would have noticed if Joey was as upset as she was now, wouldn't I? I specialized in details and it was a big one to miss.

"What do you remember next?"

"I heard Mommy scream. There was a loud noise." More tears. I wasn't sure how long I could watch her pain. I knew it was necessary, but I couldn't stand it. An arm encircled my shoulder, gave a quick squeeze and was gone as fast. I thought I'd imagined it until I caught Dennis's concerned look. I looked in a monitor that wasn't on and saw my reflection. My look was fierce and totally alien to me. I returned my attention to Joey.

"I wanted to go help my Mommy. I couldn't move." Silence echoed the statement. The only sound was the dull hum of the recording equipment.

"I was so scared." Joey had her hat in her hand, squeezing it under the table.

Emily reached out touching her cheek with two fingers lightly tilting her face up.

"Honey, you did the right thing. You did what your Mommy wanted. I'm sure she is proud of you."

"I didn't help her." The voice was small and full of recriminations.

"Sometimes, honey, you can't help the way you want. It's a Mommy's job to keep her children safe. I'm sure she is proud of you for following her wishes."

"Where is my Mommy now?"

"I don't know."

"Will she come back?"

"I don't know that either, honey."

That slight contact from Dennis moments ago, released a dam of emotion in me. I wanted to sob like I had never sobbed in my life. I vowed to my dying breath to bring to justice to whoever caused Joey this pain. My stories on these bastards would have the biggest headline. There wouldn't be any place they could hide. I lost my objectivity. I was not an unbiased reporter writing about the facts. I was fast becoming a vigilante. I looked back in the room.

Joey looked at Emily and nodded her head. She slid off the small chair and joined Sean and Kelly. Emily sat there for a moment longer, a faraway look in her eye and then began to color.

Dennis clapped me on the back and I glared at him. "I told you she was good." His tone wasn't cocky but subdued. The session had bothered him too. "She'll continue in a couple more minutes."

I nodded and wandered around the room noting nothing in particular. In a few minutes she called Sean and Kelly over to critique her coloring, Joey's curiosity overcame her and she followed. They all colored with Emily making small talk about this and that.

"Can we talk some more?" Emily asked Joey. "Your friends can stay and you can keep coloring."

"About what?"

"Can you tell me what happened when you came out of your hiding place? Where was it?"

"It was a cubby under the kitchen sink. Mommy said it used to be a pump house outside. Only I was small enough to slide behind the pipes and move into it."

"Sounds like your little clubhouse. Would you show me it sometime?"

Joey shrugged her shoulders.

"Tell me what happened when you came out."

"It was dark. I couldn't see." Joey stopped and Emily kept coloring.

"The kitchen was a mess. Mommy's stuff was spilled where she made her pictures. Somebody's going to get in big trouble for that." A few snickers were heard around me. Emily nodded trying not to show any emotion.

"What did you do?"

"I looked around for Mommy. She wasn't anywhere. I went to the bookshelf and took down her magic black box."

"What was that?"

"She used it in the woods to get photos of animals." I assumed it was a waterproof box set up on a timer or triggered by movement or someone remotely so animals wouldn't pick up a human scent and flee.

"I found the box and took the chip. I started calling for my Mom. I heard something."

Emily continued coloring, stopping to look up and then resumed.

"I was trying to hide back in the roof cellar when Sam grabbed me. He scared me." Joey made me smile again with her accusatory tone.

"What did you do with the chip?"

"I hid it in my hat. Mommy had given me another chip when the bad men drove in too."

"What happened?"

"Sam said we had to leave before the bad men came back. He told me he would take me to my Mommy. He fibbed."

Another black mark on Sam. I couldn't run up his charge card fast enough. I vowed never to promise Joey anything I couldn't produce. I wanted to find her mother but was afraid when I did it wouldn't help, only hurt. That was, if I was lucky enough to find her. I didn't even know where to look.

Chances were it was a shallow grave in the woods she liked to photograph so much.

Chapter 28

Dennis motioned me to follow him. I didn't want to leave the observation room but I wanted to see what was on the chips. The room across the hall was filled with monitors, computers, keyboards, reel-to-reel tapes, some moving and some still.

Dennis gave the two chips to another technician. "We need copies and preserve the originals, Bud."

Bud was sitting in an office chair in front of a panel of monitors. Surrounding the monitors was equipment and gauges that I could only guess at their use.

"Sure thing, Detective. Give me about ten minutes and you can see what's on them."

Dennis pulled me back. I had been leaning over Bud examining his monitors so I could describe the mechanics for my story. I sheepishly stepped back to let Bud do his thing.

As Bud worked his magic, I shuffled back and forth and inched my way closer. After a few minutes, Bud turned and looked at us. "Look in this screen and I'll pop up what's on the Fuji chip."

Dennis and I leaned in close.

"There appears to be only one file on this chip. It's a video clip." He clicked something on his computer and moved the mouse, clicking again, then looked at the screen.

The screen went dark and then we could see movement. Within seconds the light became balanced, but dark. Camouflaged men were moving around and many of them were carrying some type of assault weapons. It could have been a news clip of the training of Iraqi soldiers without the desert.

How could Joey's mom have taped something like this? What was this and why was it so important that Joey's mother disappeared because of it? She wasn't a news correspondent. The tape was about ten minutes long. The photography was excellent but I was still mystified. The scenery was heavily wooded and shaded and none of the men looked foreign. This had to be somewhere close by. What had she stumbled upon?

Occasionally the camera panned upwards to the canopy in the trees. The sky wasn't visible but was hazier. During the drills, the camera panned around the area.

We watched the tape several times. The camera would zoom in occasionally on trees with a unique branch structure or flaws in the bark, then pan back to the men. I could recognize the area by the trees, I thought, after watching it for the fifth time. Joey's mom was smart and a darned good photographer seeing both the big picture and the small detail. Several faces were zoomed in on and then the tape panned out again. The camera also zoomed in on vegetation and out. A creek or small river was in the background. One man was clearly in charge, barking orders and directing the men. He seemed familiar in his camouflage gear, but I couldn't place him.

When the screen went dark, I turned to Dennis. "What do you make of that?"

"I don't know. Some kind of training, but what?"

"What do you make of the guy in charge? Ruthless or what?"

"Scary. Let's look at the other one and see if we can find something that will tie it together," Dennis said, sliding a chair toward me and grabbing another. We each flanked the technician.

As the technician did a few things, I remembered what Sam had said when Joey had nearly ripped his pants down.

"Dennis, Sam let slip that Patrenka was working to uncover a terrorist plot. Do you think it could be their training that Joey's mother ran across?"

"Maybe, but we don't have any proof. It could be the garden club for all we know."

Then the other chip started to tell its tale. I saw the interior from earlier.

"This is the one that Joey freaked on."

A living room came into focus that looked comfy in a country way. Large, overstuffed couch. Lots of plants.

The rough sounding voice belied the comfort. "I want your memory card. You had no business on my property. Where is it?"

A woman moved forward from the left. I was pretty sure this time she must be Joey's mother and a chill went up my spine.

"I don't know what you are talking about. Please leave. You are not welcome here." Her resolve and strength were beginning to crack.

"Lady, you don't know what you are messing with. Give me the photos and no one will get hurt. You don't want to see that kid of yours have an accident, do you?"

At that statement the lady was visibly shaken. I still couldn't see who the man was clearly, but he only needed to move a little more out of the shadows to be in the picture's frame.

"I don't know what you are talking about," she stammered but with little bravado from before.

"Lady, we saw you leaving our property with your camera. I want your photos and I want them now."

My blood turned cold when I saw Joey appear and run to her mother who picked her up and made a show of comforting the little girl. From the camera angle you could see her whisper in her ear and Joey hugged her mom even tighter. The mother whispered something else but was interrupted.

"Lady, we don't want to hurt the kid. Give me the card."

The mother whispered again. Joey nodded imperceptibly. The mother made a show of turning and Joey leaped from her arms and disappeared from the screen.

"Get the kid," the voice barked out the order as he stepped into the light. I stopped dead at the rage and lack of control on Buck Rockwell's face. Two others were scrambling around behind him trying to catch Joey but failing. Joey was one fast kid. My stomach dropped again when I got a look at one of their faces. It was my buddy from Denny's, Frank Stolnek. He and I were going to have another talk. He was going to tell me exactly what had happened to Joey's mother. My eyes returned to the action on the screen.

"Not a smart move," Buck hissed, advancing toward her, hand outstretched with the large raspberry stone on his finger. "We'll find the kid and you'll both pay. This could have been a simple exchange." It was eerie watching Buck go from out of control to serene in a matter of steps. This guy surely had a nut loose.

I had to give Joey's mother credit. She didn't cringe from the advancing bulk. She stood her ground and even raised her chin a bit in defiance. I saw a piece of Patrenka in the gesture.

Whack. Then a shriek.

The sound reverberated from the screen and all motion in the viewing room stopped in stunned silence. This is what Joey had described to us only moments earlier.

Buck had cuffed Joey's mother across the cheek. She crashed to the floor. I started up from my chair, a natural reaction to the violence, when Dennis' hands gripped me from behind. "Let's see the rest of it."

I tried to relax down into the seat and concentrate on the video, my nerves tight. I was ready to beat the crap out of whoever stood in my way.

Buck turned to Frank and said. "Kill her and her brat and put their bodies where they'll never be found."

"Yes, boss." Frank stepped toward Joey's mom and grabbed her arms to drag the semi-conscious woman.

"I don't want any screw ups." Buck buttoned his coat and turned to go as calmly as if he had finished dinner.

Before she moved out of the film's frame, she made a valiant effort to collect herself.

"The least you could do is tell me why? What are you doing with all those men? What are you planning?" Joey's mom called after Buck's retreating form in a weak voice.

I admired Joey's mother's strength trying to get as much information on the tape so her death wouldn't be in vain.

Buck moved back toward the woman and into the camera's range and knelt beside the crumbled woman on the floor.

"You know what you saw. They weren't training for a picnic. I'm making millions using my land as a training ground for those who don't believe Democracy is the way to do business. They'll be demonstrating that in a couple of weeks, but you won't be here to see it."

"I'd be saying my prayers that we make your death quick, although I wouldn't begrudge my men a little fun first." Buck patted her cheek, rose and walked away with a nonchalance that was eerie.

Once Buck was out of sight, a car started and then the engine noise faded away.

"Look for that kid. See if she made it outside," Frank ordered.

The tape went black.

"Let's see it again, Bud." Dennis said.

I stepped back from the monitor and powered up my cell. I punched in each number for that lying bastard, Frank. What had he done to Joey's mother? My blood pumped hotter as I watched the tape roll a second time. This time I knew what was coming, but it didn't make it any easier. Frank was Buck's little lackey doing whatever he was told. How he'd found the balls to leave, I would never know. The guy I had shared hamburger stories with was tough. The Frank in the tape was a sniveling coward.

The last words on the tape haunted me. "Frank, clean up this mess."

Chapter 29

Frank had a lot to answer for. I clutched the phone tighter and tighter with each ring.

"Hello," a female voice answered after the fifth ring.

"Is Frank there?" I ground out.

"May I ask who is calling?"

"Mitch Malone and I want to speak to him now."

I heard some rustling and then an echo as an extension banged against the receiver as it was picked up.

"Do you have Daisy out of there?" Worry laced the deep voice but didn't faze my anger. I heard a click as the other phone was hung up.

"No and it ain't going to happen. What happened to the woman at the cabin in the woods?"

"What are you talking about?"

"Jo-," then I stopped myself. I couldn't tell the man who had been charged with cleaning up the mess that I had another witness. I shifted gears trying to get myself under control and not reaching through the line to grab Frank by the neck. "I watched a tape of Buck at a cabin demanding photos from a woman and guess who had a supporting role in the drama?"

There was silence at the end of the line. "I can explain. I didn't know there was a tape. Gee, is Buck going to be livid when he learns that."

"You don't need to worry about Buck. You need to worry about me. What happened to the woman in the tape? Is she dead?" My heart stopped beating for a pause. Afraid of the answer, but I never backed down from asking the tough questions. I could hear breathing on the other end of the line. I could picture Frank hunched over the counter looking like an eighty-nine pound weakling. I knew murderers came in all sizes and shapes. Thing was, I'd liked Frank. Even worse, I liked Daisy and wanted to help them. They obviously cared about each other and were such a perfect match in a garish sort of way. But I couldn't help a murderer, especially not one that killed Joey's mother.

"I didn't kill her." The voice was a whisper.

"Is she dead?" I clenched the phone to my ear waiting. There was another long pause.

"No." The tone was sharp and quick.

"How do I know that?" I ground out, listening for telltale signs of pregnant pauses signaling a lie.

"You can't. You have to trust me. I've never killed anybody. How's Daisy? I haven't heard from her." His words kept coming, not letting me answer.

"Daisy's fine or at least she was. Buck's men were roughing her up a bit when I stopped after we talked the last time." I bit out making it sound worse.

"Is she hurt?"

"No. She's scared and in a tough spot. I'm not sure her joining you is a good thing. What are you going to do to her if she knows too much or if Buck tells you to clean up that mess?"

"I told you I didn't kill anyone." The voice was so low it was hard to make out the words over the connection.

"I only have your word for that." I growled into the phone.

"So you're not going to help Daisy get away?"

I paused to think. I didn't want him to know we're closing in on Buck because I still wasn't sure Frank wouldn't tip him off. What should I do about Daisy? Truth was I wanted to help her, but I wasn't sure I wanted her with Frank. She needed a break. I didn't think she'd ever had a break.

"I'm going to get Daisy. She's ready. The boys scared her good last time. I'm not sure I want to hook her up with you. I still have lots of questions about that."

"You bring Daisy to me and I'll answer all your questions. Got that? I didn't do anything. I'm the good guy here. How do I know I can trust you? You bring me Daisy and I will tell you what I know. If anything happens to Daisy . . ." He left the threat hanging in the air. I heard something in his voice, a hint of pleading. I knew he cared deeply for Daisy. I still didn't trust him completely, but I could work that out later. Daisy was an adult. Joey was a child. I needed to find out what happened to her mother and Frank was that link.

"If I get Daisy out, how do we connect?" This way I figured I could check it out ahead of time. "I need directions to where you are staying."

I was subtle alright. He would never figure out my ruse to get directions was so I could beat the crap out of him.

"The directions are a bit complicated," he said. "You might want to write them down." I pulled my ever present notebook and pen from my back pocket and jotted down the directions. I figured it was a good hour away in a rural area. For all I knew it could be in the middle of the National Forest.

"Don't go anywhere. I'll be in touch." I hung up and went back to the video room.

"Is that the only image?" said Dennis, a little frustration tingeing his voice.

"Yes," the technician replied.

"I wish there was something that showed what happen next. We'd at least know the why. I need to notify my captain. We'll need search warrants. That's going to take some time. I'm not sure we will find anything after this much time has gone by."

"Is it enough for an arrest warrant?" I asked.

"Not for the murder. We don't know there was one. We do need to get Homeland Security onto the terrorist plot though," Dennis added as an afterthought.

I watched the tape a couple more times and noted the mundane things like the home was neat and clean and decorated in earthy tones. Joey's mom was gutsy. I saw where Joey inherited her strength of character and intelligence.

I wondered how the search for Joey's father was going. Was he on his way back to claim his child? How would he react to his wife missing, presumed dead? When had Joey gotten the chip if she had run away when her mother told her to? I still had too many questions and wondered how Joey was doing with Emily.

I wandered out of the technician's domain and returned to the mirror observatory. Emily was gone and the children were playing, having a good time.

"How come everyone wants to talk to you?" Dennis's son, Sean, asked as they built a tower out of foam blocks.

"I dunno," Joey replied.

"Where are your parents?" the boy persisted.

"I dunno."

"Are they going to come back?"

"I dunno," and Joey's head dropped to her chest and she was struggling not to cry but trying to shield her face from Sean. Before I knew it, I was out of the room and in the next, grabbing the little girl who had faced so much without cracking and now was undone by another child's curiosity.

"It's okay, Sport. It's okay to cry. Let it out. You'll feel better." Her head buried itself in my neck and her shoulders shook with the force of her sobs. I felt helpless. This was the first time I had seen the depth of emotion and realized how much it cost the small mite to hold it in. I mentally cursed myself for allowing the shrink and even my own not-so-subtle questioning to chip away at her defenses.

I wondered how many adults would have held up as well as she had in the last few weeks with the uncertainty and loss of everything she knew, her home, her family. I hated the questions but knew we needed more. After watching the tape, I could imagine the trauma and guilt that must be plaguing her. How many times had she wished she hadn't run? I wanted to tell her how brave she was but I didn't know how. I wanted to walk out of the police station and never have Joey face it again, but I knew that wasn't possible. After watching the tape, we had to revisit it.

I came back from my own thoughts as Joey pushed back from my shoulder. I hadn't realized her sobs had quit as quickly as they had started. I looked down into eyes still shadowed by fear. Her cheeks were wet, reddened by the salty river. So was my shirt, but it didn't bother me. I looked around and saw Emily at the door and Sean and Kelly huddled in the corner.

"You okay, Sport?"

She nodded squirming in my arms so I set her down. "Are you up for more questions?"

"Will it help find my mother?" She ran the back of her hand under her nose, sniffed loudly and then wiped her hand on her shirt.

"It could," I didn't want to get her hopes up but we were getting closer. "What happened that night you saw your mother last? She told you to run and you did a great job of hiding because the bad men didn't find you. You were so brave. Tell me what you can remember."

"Mommy and I used to practice for tornadoes. I knew how to open the floor to get in and out. When we would have bad weather, Mommy and I would pretend we were spies."

"So you got in the cellar through the trap door?" Joey nodded. "How long were you in there?"

She shrugged her shoulders and I realized she didn't have any concept of time yet. "What happened next?"

"I don't know. I was really scared and cold. I found a blanket we used to sit on and wrapped up. I think I fell asleep. I was scared."

"I would be too. What did you do when you woke up?"

"I was hungry. I snuck out and was careful. I didn't want the bad men to find me. I made myself a sandwich. The kitchen was a lot worse than your house." I smiled at her comparison.

"That was good. You were smart to get yourself something to eat." She shook her head. "I was supposed to stay hidin'. Mommy said so."

She took a deep breath before continuing. "I was making my sandwich and he came up from behind."

"Who came up to you?" I was ready to fight any battle to protect her.

"Sam. He scared me. He grabbed me. I thought he was one of the bad men. Sam was mad. I thought he was going to hurt me." Her words started coming faster as I saw the terror return with her memories. I wanted to tell her to stop, but I couldn't. I wanted to hit something in anger at her fear and uncertainty. I decided the next time I saw Sam, I would make him pay. I didn't care if he was twice as tall.

"I had an accident." I almost missed Joey's whispered confession. I saw Joey cast a sideways glance at Sean and Kelly to see if they had heard and what reaction they had.

"Sam said some really bad words. He pulled me into my room and made me change my clothes." Joey made a face.

"What, Sport?"

"He made me wear those baby pajamas. They were blue. Yuck!" Her look was precious in anger. The blue pjs also explained her attire when we found her and why she would never put them on since even with the small wardrobe. It also explained why the few items she had in the box weren't very practical.

"He said a lot of bad words when I said I didn't know where my mom was."

Another blow was coming for that the insensitive jerk. "You didn't know Sam until then?"

Joey shook her head. "I was scared. I kicked him and tried to get away but he caught me."

"When did you get the chips?"

"Mommy gave me one when she saw the car of bad men come. She told me to hide. I took the other one when I was looking for my mom after coming out of hiding. She wouldn't want anyone to steal her photos."

"Where did Sam take you?"

"He asked me questions but I wasn't going to answer. We finally stopped at a house and there was a really nice lady."

I nodded to encourage her to continue. "She asked if I was hungry and gave me a peanut butter and jelly sandwich and a bath. Afterwards I was still hungry and she gave me Cheerios."

This line of questioning didn't seem to bother Joey at all. "She was really pretty and smelled good."

Joey stopped and looked at me. "What happened next?" I prodded.

"I woke up with you," she said simply. I flashed back to the woman in the red dress on the porch. I found myself saying a quick prayer of thanksgiving that Joey would not carry that memory too. It seemed everyone in Joey's life had either died or disappeared, except me. How long would it be before Joey pieced together that fact? I hoped she never would but I couldn't guarantee she hadn't. She just hadn't mentioned it aloud.

I thought of Patrenka. I missed her quiet presence, but was still angry for her leaving. I was adjusting to carrying for Joey twenty-four, seven. She was an FBI agent and had a job to do but when did the job stop and family duties begin? Damn it, she shouldn't have left. What was more important, Joey's psyche or finding out what happened? Both were important, but Joey was family. Joey had quit mentioning her, since she was gone. Did she do that with everyone in her life after they were gone? Not for the first time did I think how unfair it was for someone so young to have seen so much violence and despair.

"Well, Sport, I guess that was your lucky day, huh?" I tipped the Tigers cap up from the back so it fell over her face and eyes. She pushed in back into place and smiled.

My heart melted. This little girl and her simple smile in the face of such incredible violence and memories of loss had grabbed hold of my heart and she would leave a huge hole if she left.

I loved this brave little girl. I knew it was only a matter of time until Dennis would be forced to contact protective services and put her in the system or her dad would return to claim her. I didn't want that to happen. At least now she was as happy as she could be and she definitely wasn't a number. I wanted to keep taking care of her.

I had changed! I didn't want her to leave my life. I was no longer anxious for Joey to leave. No one had ever made me consider giving up my solitary existence. How had that little mite of a child done it? That was the question. Correction, that didn't matter, she had done it, I didn't have an explanation. I didn't want to be the Lone Ranger anymore. I was willing to make what ever changes necessary to make her happy. I was putting her first, which was the biggest change.

Could I go from being the Lone Ranger to acquiring a Tonto? It made me yearn for a family with Patrenka and Joey. It made me petrified. I stopped cold, then started to sweat with my next thought. Could I become her legal guardian?

"Are we going soon?" Joey asked.

"I think so. I'll leave you for a minute and see if we're ready."

I walked out of the room and tried to act normal but I was on shaky ground. Then I realized the shakes were me. I heard the door click behind me. I put my back against the wall and slowly slid down. I used my forearm to wipe my forehead. I was experiencing all the symptoms of shock. My thoughts scared me. I'd always been alone and liked it, but I really cared for her.

Dennis touched my shoulder. "You okay, man?"

I nodded still amazed by my own revelations, but wasn't ready to share them with anyone. "Joey's ready to leave, that okay?"

"Not yet. We're working on warrants. I need to talk to the prosecuting attorney and see if they will authorize arrest warrants yet. That may be shaky. We may have to serve the search warrants first. That could tip Rockwell off and have them rabbit. I'll know in a couple of hours how we're going to handle it. We have to call in some additional personnel to serve the warrants. The captain is on his way in. He wants to talk with Joey before it goes further."

I stood up. I didn't want Joey to go through any more trauma. My emotionless reporter professional, who can look at dead bodies without shedding a tear, cracked. Dennis's arm came out again grabbing my shoulder. "He'll be gentle. I've seen him do this before. He has a way with kids."

My disbelief must have shown.

"Trust me on this. He did some work before he made captain getting child abusers off the street including pedophiles. I saw him do an interview once. He was amazing getting the information without a tear. Trust me, man. I don't want Joey to go through any more than absolutely necessary."

Chapter 30

Dennis had no sooner uttered the praise then the man himself stepped out of the elevator at the end of the hall. The captain was dressed more casually in black sweat pants and a red t-shirt. His tennis shoes made me want to crack a joke. They looked like clown feet in red Converse high tops.

I stood off to the side while the captain and Dennis put their heads together for a few minutes. I was sure Dennis was briefing him on what had happened, the chips in Joey's hat and what was on them. They disappeared for a few minutes presumably to look at what was on the chips.

The captain returned without Dennis and I thought he was going to usher me out.

"Mitch. I need to talk to Joey. The sooner we can get the warrants the better off we'll be. I want to confirm some things. I will be gentle. I don't want to cause this little girl any more harm, but we need to get these guys off the street. I want make sure there are no loopholes, no slip ups."

I nodded.

"You can observe from the room," he said, which I knew was a huge concession for him. I was usually given the boot.

"I'll be watching." I sounded like a petulant two year old.

I was worried about Joey going over the same ground again. The captain would be the last one, I vowed as I entered the observation room.

The captain entered and headed to the table without as much as a hello to any of the three children. He started coloring like Emily had. After a minute, Dennis' daughter came over and watched him color.

"Aren't you my daddy's boss?"

"Yes, I am," he said.

"Why are you in here coloring? Don't you have something you should be doing so my daddy can take us for ice cream?"

I chuckled at her statement and turned to Dennis who was beet red. If the captain was surprised or irritated by the statement, he didn't show it. Instead he continued coloring.

"I have a job to do too."

"What's your job?" Sean asked.

"I have to catch bad guys like your dad. My job is to make sure they don't get away because we didn't follow the rules." I saw him glance at Joey who I knew was taking in the conversation but pretending to be busy.

That satisfied both of Dennis's kids and the captain continued to color. I was about to interrupt and take Joey because this was a waste of time. Nothing was happening. I didn't want him to irritate Joey but I didn't want to wait for an hour while watching the big man fidget on the child-size chair pretending an interest in Crayolas.

Before I reached the door, Joey came over and sat opposite him. "I want to go for ice cream."

"Me too," he replied. "But I have to ask you some questions first. Is that okay?"

Joey nodded.

"Did you see anyone hurt your mother?"

Joey shook her head, her eyes doubling in size and looked shiny.

"Did you go with your mother when she took pictures in the woods?"

Again she shook her head. "Do you know where it was?"

She shook her head then stopped. "Are you going to get the bad men?"

"I'm going to try but I need to know where to find them."

She thought for a minute. "Mommy said she couldn't believe

they were so close to us and we never heard them. She found them by accident. She was supposed to take pictures of owls for a magazine article."

"What kind of owls?" the captain asked.

Joey shrugged her shoulders in defeat. "I can't remember." She burst into tears. I launched myself out of the room and into the next before Dennis could hold me back.

"Enough," I said. "This interview is over."

Chapter 31

I was looking forward to packing up our belongings at the hotel and moving back into my place. I smiled to myself remembering the locks charged to Sam's account. On our way out of the police station, I picked up the new keys and hoped Sam the Slime would try again. Then I thought of his height and training and thought, maybe not.

I grabbed Joey's hand naturally as we entered the hotel and followed the familiar nondescript path to our room. I reached in my pocket and handed the cardkey to Joey who liked to open the door. I didn't see any reason not to.

After the electronic lock light turned green, I reached forward, turned the handle and pushed the door open allowing Joey to enter first.

Something was wrong. I didn't know what it was, my senses jumped to alert. I reached forward and grabbed Joey by the back of her shirt and hauled her back out the door. She looked up at me indignantly. I put my finger to my lips to signal silence. Joey's eyes grew round and worried. I hoped I was wrong about my caution. You couldn't ignore your sixth sense.

I motioned Joey to stay by the wall outside the door. I entered slowly looking first back behind the door. The room only had the light between the beds on and I know I didn't leave it on. As I surveyed the room, I noted the bathroom light was on and the door was closed. I heard scuffling of feet and a scent that haunted my dreams.

I knew our guest and had been anxiously awaiting her return.

I returned to the door and motioned Joey inside. She gave me a quizzical look and I said only one word. It was the word of my hopes, dreams, frustrations, and disappointment.

"Patrenka."

Joey's face brightened and she ran to the bathroom door and knocked.

"Auntie Patrenka, I have so much to tell you."

The door opened. She was in the jade satin cocktail dress that had my fingers itching to travel her frame. It was the dress she wore with Buck at the Roadhouse and my stomach had butterflies. My words stuck in my mouth and I had to clear my throat to get any moisture at all in the parched interior. I croaked, "Hello."

I didn't know what else to say. I wanted to strangle her. I wanted to ask how Buck was in bed. I wanted to ask what the hell she thought she was doing.

Then Joey launched herself at her. Patrenka picked her up and hugged her, whispered I knew not what in her ear. There was so much I wanted to say and none of it would be appropriate in front of my young charge. Another thought hit, making my heart hurt. Would she take Joey and go now?

Would she now take charge of Joey? Did I want that? Surprising myself, I felt a heaviness in the pit of my stomach. I wasn't sure what it was at first but then it hit me. It was fear, loneliness. I wanted some answers to some tough questions from that woman. I was not about to abdicate my role as caregiver under any circumstances. I couldn't trust her to stay with Joey. She could get another hair-brained scheme and be gone. How reliable were FBI agents anyway? Look at Sam. He was a major lowlife. Could Patrenka be the same type of slime? They worked closely together. Has she been in my bed with Sam? I barely controlled the urge to leap on her and beat the answers from her.

I watched her snuggle Joey, again muttering things I couldn't hear. Patrenka looked up and our eyes met. I saw concern, gratitude and a pleading look that I had never seen.

Joey pushed away from the embrace and turned to look at me. I attempted to smile, but I don't think I succeeded. We had come here to grab our things and move to my apartment. Would I be moving there alone? I stopped midstride. That was not going to happen. Joey was staying with me. I knew that could not last forever, or could it? Could I take on the responsibility of raising a small child as my own? That, of course, was if Joey's mother was gone. The longer I spent with Joey, the more I felt she was, or she would have returned. She wouldn't have willingly abandoned her child. Dennis had no luck locating Joey's father through the American Red Cross either.

My legs felt weak with the responsibility I wanted. I was terrified. Scared that I would get Joey and horrified that I wouldn't. What was involved in making the arrangement more permanent? Patrenka could fight me and she was a relative, but I would be a fierce opponent. I lusted after Patrenka like I had no other woman before, but that wasn't going to impede my responsibility toward Joey.

Responsibility? So many thoughts were crashing through my brain and many were foreign to me. I, the king of the crime beat and reporter extraordinaire, never had any responsibilities for anyone. Now I was ready to fight to take on the responsibility of a small child.

My reverie was broken by a tone I had never heard in Joey's voice. "Why'd you leave?" I wanted to cheer Joey's directness. Maybe she would get the answers I wanted.

Patrenka looked down at Joey and then bent at the knees to bring them face to face. "I had work to do."

"What work? Where did you go?" I admired Joey's questions, which were demands in a fierce voice. I thought with pride that Joey had a future as an ace reporter.

"Honey . . ." Patrenka started to say softening her voice to pure seduction that made my knees go weak with wanting. Joey wasn't buying any of her patronizing tone though. Joey's hands went on her hips and her stance stiffened. I couldn't see her face but I was sure her lips were set and her eyes blazing.

Patrenka stopped and then looked up at me. I could see she wasn't sure what she should do. It was about time somebody upended her world and I was disappointed it hadn't been me.

I wanted Joey to continue grilling Patrenka to get answers but realized some of it might not be fit for a small child's ears. Joey had had enough for one day. I surprised myself by even thinking like a parent.

"Joey," I said softly and she turned. I saw remains of defiance fading fast into tears. I'm not sure how I knew it, but I did. I walked over and grabbed her up. "We have a change in location to make and it's late. How about if we sort this all out in the morning?"

I saw gratitude in Patrenka's eyes that I wanted to collect on, but knew I couldn't then. Joey and I were changing locations. I walked behind the entrance door and pulled out the suitcase.

"Joey, go get all your stuff and put it in here."

Patrenka looked at me.

"We came here to pack up our stuff and move back to my apartment." I couldn't help the anger that crept into my voice. "Your buddy Sam commandeered it for himself and trashed the place, all the while telling me it would be safer to stay here. His con is now over."

Patrenka didn't look surprised by the news and I realized she knew. I killed her with a look and jerked the dresser drawer open, taking my irritation out on the furniture instead of the beauty who drove me to consider violence. I grabbed up the contents with a single swoop and walked to the suitcase and dumped them unceremoniously. Joey did the same thing. Bless her, she had the same nuance of anger in her posture. I wanted to laugh at her great imitation, but I knew it wasn't any laughing matter.

"Joey can stay here with me." Patrenka said sounding like a demand but her voice cracked at the end.

It couldn't have hurt worse if she had kicked me in the groin. I couldn't get any air, I couldn't breathe. I knew this was bound to happen but I still wasn't prepared. I don't know where the alien idea of my wanting to keep a small child had come from. How I thought it was possible. The violence I never thought was part of my character wanted to do something brutal, but I was immobile.

"No." It sounded like it came from a petulant two year old. I had to look to make sure that voice belonged to the mini adult that I was willing to give up my bachelor status for. Leave it to a small child to decide the fate of mere mortals in total logic. Just when I thought I was protecting Joey and being the adult, the tables turned.

"I want to go to with Uncle Mitch to his apartment. I don't want to stay here anymore."

I couldn't have summoned a better argument and apparently neither could Patrenka. I enjoyed watching her uncertainty about

Joey's feelings and where her accommodations were going to be. I wasn't sure I wanted her under my roof.

That was a lie. I not only wanted her under my roof but I wanted her under my body as well. I also wanted answers out of her and my apartment walls were a lot more soundproof then the hotel room. I fantasized about stripping away the jade and encouraging noises about my sexual prowess erupting from Patrenka.

I realized I had to make some gesture of invitation but for a wordsmith, I was suddenly unable to come up with anything. Again, Joey, my preschool companion, solved my dilemma like we were on the same wavelength.

"You can come, too. Can't she, Uncle Mitch?" but Joey's voice didn't sound all that welcoming. I nodded and Patrenka nodded.

"Let's get out of here," I said finally finding my voice and realizing I wasn't about to lose either of them. At least not tonight.

After packing up our meager belongings in the hotel and stopping at a grocery store for a full load of food, we carried everything to the apartment. It felt good coming home even if I would be having two roommates.

I settled Joey in the spare room on a futon I'd kept from my college dorm room. Patrenka had two choices, she could bunk with me on the California King or it was the couch in the living room for her. Joey already was fading fast at the grocery store so I fixed her a grilled cheese for dinner and tucked her in.

"I like your place, Uncle Mitch," she said giving me a hug. I said good night and flipped out the light. "Uncle Mitch?"

"Yes," I said pausing at the door, thinking she needed to use the bathroom or wanted a glass of water.

"Are you ever afraid?" I stopped and returned to perch on the edge bed hoping the dark masked my uncertainty. I was trying to figure out how to answer. I opted for another reporter technique of answering a question with a question.

"Why do you ask?" I could see her shrug her shoulders under the blanket and didn't want to let the question pass without seeing if she was hiding her fear. I could see she was thinking so I waited.

"My Mommy wasn't afraid of that guy when he first came and

he hurt her. You aren't afraid and I don't want you to go away." Her voice trailed off at the end and I knew she was putting Patrenka in the same thoughts. I leaned over and gathered the pint-sized waif in my arms.

"I'm scared, Joey, but the key is not to let that stop you. You have to do what is right. The bad man needs to pay for hurting people. I'm going to try hard not to get hurt and not to let him hurt you."

I felt her chest rise and she let out a deep breath. She stayed in my arms for a few minutes, then became quiet and her breathing evened out. I laid her back gently onto the pillow and whispered: "Sweet dreams." I bent down and lightly kissed her forehead.

I stood and backed up a step or two, watching the outline of Joey's face, in awe of her cherubic features relaxed in sleep. I nearly collided with Patrenka who had been outside the door in the hall. I lifted my finger to my lips to signal silence and went into the living room. I turned on the stereo to a classical station I liked and then beckoned Patrenka to join me on the couch. I expected reluctance. Surprisingly, she sat at the opposite end and hugged a sofa pillow to her middle.

We started at each other for a few heartbeats, each trying to read the other's thoughts. I wasn't going to make it easy for her, but I wanted to pull her into my arms and make her hug me the way she held the pillow.

The orchestra was reaching a crescendo of a movement. The music matched my chaotic feelings of wanting to both comfort her and torment her for leaving us without a word. I was leaning more and more toward forcing my attentions when she finally spoke.

"I'm sorry, Mitch," she said. I waited for more but the curtain came down in her eyes, blocking out all emotion. I cracked.

"Sorry? You're sorry? Are you sorry for making Joey afraid? Sorry for leaving Joey like everyone else in her young life has? Sorry?" My voice was rising with each word, building in intensity with my righteous indignation. "You could have scarred her for life." I didn't mention that she also had broken my trust as well.

"I felt helpless sitting day after day in the hotel. I had to get out and try to find some kind of lead." The eye contact she had at the beginning dropped into her lap at the end.

"Did you find anything useful? You were pretty cozy with Buck and all." I sneered. Patrenka popped from the couch and went behind it.

"Yes. I know he is working with a sleeper cell of terrorists, plotting an attack within the next couple of weeks. They are training on Buck's property. After they leave, he'll begin his development. He uses the funds from the trainings to finance his infrastructure improvements. It's really rather ingenious."

I hated her admiring Buck when I knew what a mean bastard he was. I played it cool, rolling my eyes. "Tell me something I don't know."

She looked at me, surprise written all over her usually impassive face. Then it was gone and she circled around the coach and stopped in front of me. Patrenka stared hard at me willing me to expound. It was the strangest thing. It was almost as if she was hypnotizing me as I fell into the depths of her eyes. I was realizing why she was so good uncovering facts.

"If you had stayed, maybe we would have found the video with the terrorist on it sooner. We have proof of their activity, thanks to Joey."

"Joey?"

"Yes, the little dynamo that you left without a backward glance, without even a note to allay her feelings of continued abandonment. At least the last sound of you wasn't a scream like her mother."

"What happened to her mother?" She advanced on me, but I wasn't going to spill. I knew how to protect my sources. She owed me more.

"Not good enough."

"What do you mean, not good enough?" Her voice was going from smooth and sultry to high-pitched and staccato.

"You crushed that little girl's spirit. We had no idea where you went or even if you were okay. You didn't even call us. You took everything you owned like you never existed. We didn't know what to think." Patrenka stepped back as if I'd struck her.

"I get the picture. What do you want?" She said the words with venom. She was beautiful in her anger and I wanted to throw her to the couch and jump her.

Busted. My little diatribe went a bit too far. Especially her special inflection on "you." I needed to turn the tables and fast. I would lose everything if she found out how I really lusted after her. If she knew, I would never be able to resist the pull of her eyes and spill all my secrets. Not going to happen. Not now. Not ever. She was not going to take whatever I had and disappear. She was not going to stomp on my heart and she was not going to stomp on Joey's.

"Joey and I are a team. She knows when I'm going and when I'm coming back. I leave her with people that protect her and like her. I never run off. When you hurt her, you hurt me too. That's the we. Got it?"

She did. I was safe. Maybe when this was done, we could see. While she made me ache, I had a responsibility to Joey. I had a responsibility? That thought didn't make me want to run off and hide like I'd been running for the last decade. I was staying. I cared.

Patrenka had been talking and I missed her first salvo. ". . . never good at relationships or working as a team. That's why I'm so good at undercover work because I work well with minimal contact with my handler. I've had to survive on my own. All the domesticity in the hotel scared me. I needed a break."

"Domesticity? Give me a break. You wanted to grab the glory. That's what it's all about for you. You come in, snag the kudos and you're off to repeat it in another town, on another day."

"That's what I'm trying to tell you. This one scared me. So I completed the pattern. I'm sorry. I never came back before."

"So, how was Buck, the terrorist, in the sack?"

"Great, you Neanderthal." She moved around the couch placing it between us.

"So you did sleep with him to get the information?"

"Excuse me?"

"You didn't sleep with him?" I asked testily.

"No, you idiot."

I watched her throw her head back in righteous indignation. Her mane of hair rippling with the thrust looked like the thoroughbred horse she was named after.

"Only insecure males bring sex into everything. Whether I had sex or not is none of your damn business. I'd thought better of you. I was wrong. Professionals know how to get information without sex, you ignorant moron." I was mesmerized.

Before I realized what she was doing, she picked up the pillow she hugged earlier. Patrenka chucked the pillow at my head and stalked from the room. I was feeling pleased with myself to have held my own for only a fraction of second. Then, I realized she retreated to my room. I heard the lock click with finality.

"Damn." I'd lost not only my fantasy night coming true, but had only the tossed pillow and the lumpy couch to sleep on.

Chapter 32

I reached to quell my alarm's bleating tone only to fall a foot to the floor, belatedly realizing I was on my couch and not a bed. The ringing was not my alarm but my cell phone. Sleep eluded me for hours the night before, but I wasn't sure if it was because of my accusations at Patrenka, my newfound responsibility or the lumps in the couch.

"Mitch Malone," I croaked.

"Up and at 'em. We've got dragons to slay, m'boy."

"Dragon slaying? Dennis, I don't have my eyes open yet. Could you be a bit more specific?"

"I want to slay dragons," Joey's voice hailed from the kitchen. She had a bowl of cereal and was already dressed. Patrenka pulled her head out of the refrigerator. It was a cozy little domestic scene and everyone was ready for the day except me. I glanced down. I was in the same clothes as yesterday only a lot more wrinkled.

"You there, Mitch?" Dennis asked.

"Yes, but a little worse for wear. What's this about dragons?" I swung my feet to the floor, stretching, trying to work the kinks out of my back.

"We got our warrants. Want to be there?"

"You bet," but then I stopped and looked back at the household routine in the kitchen. I could ditch them, but then I'd be like Patrenka. "I've got extra baggage."

"Colleen said to drop off Joey. The kids really miss her." Dennis chuckled.

"Great," I said, sounding less than enthusiastic.

"I can't believe you don't want to be in on this," Dennis said, exasperated by my hesitation.

"I have a houseguest." I said it quietly because I didn't want Patrenka to know I was talking about her or the information Joey's hat uncovered. I was still mad about the night on my own coach. If she wasn't going to share, neither was I.

"You want to bring a houseguest?" Dennis yelled.

"You said she had great interview skills." I said defensively, not wanting to let Dennis know my real reason for not showing my excitement.

"Patrenka's back? Did she find anything out?"

"Yes. Terrorists are training on Buck's land for a mission, but she doesn't know what it is. You can bet her fellow agents are on it."

"Great. Just great. They ordered me off one case, but I'm not sitting on the sidelines for this one. We're coordinating with Homeland Security. Period. They can coordinate with the damn FBI."

"Sounds like a great plan. See you in a half hour." I hung up before I could listen to him bitch about the FBI.

Patrenka heard and understood more of my conversation with Dennis than I wanted. I planned to leave Joey with her. Again, luck was against me. By the time I walked out from my two-minute shower, the ladies were dressed and waiting expectantly.

We looked like the perfect family off for a picnic when we left the apartment. Joey bounced off the walls not even thinking about what Patrenka and I were doing, excited to play with her new friends. She wasn't aware that neither adult was speaking to the other.

"What are we doing, Uncle Mitch?"

"How about a day playing with Sean and Kelly?"

"Yeah!" The bundle hurled herself at me giving me only a second to ready for impact.

We pulled into Dennis's drive and Joey was out before the engine stopped. She was running and yelling for Sean and Kelly at the top of her voice. "I'm here. I'm here."

Colleen opened the front door and Joey was gone. Dennis appeared behind Colleen, giving her a kiss. Colleen waved to us as Dennis walked to his car. I backed out of the yard and waited to follow Dennis to the police station.

I parked in my normal spot and thought how ironic that life came full circle. This case started when Patrenka and I took off for the double murder. Now we were returning to help solve it. She wasn't a lowly intern but an incredible-looking FBI agent who could collect family secrets from a mute.

We followed Dennis into the building and for some reason I was feeling self conscious. I was the caboose in this train and I didn't like it. I never followed anyone, especially not a woman. Something had shifted in the last week. What would we find today? Then it hit me. Daisy. I promised to get Daisy out before anything went down. I hustled to catch up to the parade, trying to figure out a plan. Women. They complicated everything!

We trooped into the war room. Basically, it was the daily shift briefing room but the white boards were covered with large aerial shots, black Xs marking exits and arrows marking entry points.

The captain was front and center in his element. The officers were talking about what points were best to enter and strategies for locking down the compound with the least bloodshed. The pros and cons of several were discussed. I watched the captain, impressed with his logical comments to each of the other officer's suggestions. I wondered if he'd stay so calm and rational when he noticed he had two extra guests along for the ride.

As if the captain had read my mind, he turned in our direction and scowled. He turned his back to the tactics and marched in our direction his jaw clinched, ready to do battle.

"Sergeant Flaherty, what's the meaning of this?"

Before Dennis or I could get a word in, Patrenka slipped between us brandishing her FBI shield, which I had never seen before. I wondered briefly where she kept it for easy access. That may bear further investigation at another time.

"Captain, I'm Patrenka Peterson with the FBI, currently assigned to the counter terrorism unit. I have done extensive reconnaissance at the Rockwell premises." While she talked, she moved toward the aerials. We followed the new ringmaster.

"If I could suggest, sir," she said pausing briefly. The captain nodded. "Only a small contingent should be at the front with the warrants. The majority of Rockwell's men will be located here and here," she said pointing to two small outbuildings that weren't part of the major plan.

"These are the living quarters for Rockwell's enforcers. There'll only be a half dozen men in the main house. Each of the buildings will have at least twenty men. Secure those first before knocking on the front door.

"The security is primarily focused on the main house and perimeter. I can disarm the perimeter security and Buck will not know what is coming. He has been having some problems with the system and won't become immediately alarmed when it goes off line. That will give your men time to secure the outbuildings and still be able to surprise Mr. Rockwell."

I looked at the captain and he was nodding his head, agreeing to Patrenka's plan.

He barked out orders to the men who quickly dispersed to get the needed firearms from the armory. This was going to require more than the standard police-issued pistol. Shotguns and assault rifles were distributed.

"I don't want any heroes. We do this by the book. You stay behind cover until your next position is secure." The captain said, making eye contact with his officers, antsy to get to the action. The captain spotted me and pulled up to his full height.

"No civilians."

I was about to launch into all the reasons I should be allowed, including the fact I was the one who provide the crucial piece leading to the search warrants.

"Captain. Mitch Malone is working with the FBI on this one. I will vouch for his conduct and restraint." My mouth hit the floor. She was going to bat for me? When had that happened before? I wanted to kiss her right there, but kept my expression stony.

The captain stared at Patrenka for a full minute and she didn't flinch or waiver. He nodded. "Your responsibility and liability."

Patrenka nodded.

I wanted to hug her, but knew that would be unprofessional. Suddenly her disappearance wasn't such a bad thing. She'd only been doing her job.

Then Sam Sloan walked into the room.

Chapter 33

"Captain," Sloan said walking to the front of the room. I glanced at Patrenka and saw an emotion, she quickly hid behind her icy façade. She wasn't happy he was here either. "Sam Sloan, special agent in charge. Brief me on the plan." He flipped open his wallet and showed the captain his ID.

The captain wasn't pleased, but complied with his request. I looked at Dennis who seemed as bewildered as I was. The pair talked for a few minutes and disappeared. I looked at my watch. It was after nine. According to the timeline, ten was when "Operation Blockade" went into motion.

I was edgy. I needed to get Daisy out and wasn't sure when that would happen. Would she need to leave if Buck and his gang were rounded up? I couldn't guarantee that they wouldn't think Daisy was the leak. I needed to help her. I should go now but didn't want to miss anything at Buck Rockwell's estate. I wanted to be there to get every detail of his capture and arrest. Not only for closure for Joey but for my readers as well. I wanted to get to Frank and beat out of him what happened to Joey's mother.

I wasn't sure why all of sudden I felt that something was off. That we wouldn't be successful in nabbing Buck and Joey would never be safe. Maybe it was Sam showing up. I had no respect for him. Patrenka's anger at his arrival added to my unease.

Before I could ponder those thoughts, the captain returned without Sam and gave the orders to move out. "Operation Blockade" was mobilizing.

Both marked and unmarked cars pulled out of the lot. Patrenka returned to mine and we joined the parade. All too soon we pulled into the Wal-Mart parking lot that was the staging area. The Roadhouse was only a half mile away but I figured it was too early for Daisy to be working. I watched the unmarked cars peel off to get in position behind the estate. Finally it was the marked cars and us.

We pulled along the walled fortress out of sight of the gates. It was show time. Patrenka slipped out of the Jeep and I watched her walk to a hundred yards from the gate near a small box a foot off the ground. She opened the cover, pulled some wires out and quickly slit them with a small knife that materialized in her hand.

Where did she hide her tools of the trade? She was in black pants that hugged her curves and a gray fitted blouse and a black blazer completing the ensemble. I didn't see a holster for her gun or any extra bulges from her bulletproof vest. I'd never notice her carry a purse.

The gate was already unlocked and the troops were ready. More than ready. Guns were drawn and officers were dancing on the balls of their feet waiting for the signal.

"Stay here. Don't move. I don't care who gave you permission to be here," the captain ordered before taking point on the frontal assault.

Waiting outside Buck's compound until the scene was secured was fine with me. My adrenaline was rushing but I wasn't fond of guns. The other vehicles were loaded and sped through the gates. I stayed with a patrol sergeant who wasn't exactly combat ready unless it was in a doughnut eating contest. I was antsy as well. I couldn't sit in the car with my escort. I got out and paced up and down the road. I even walked in front of the gate but was unable to see anything through the manicured foliage.

Since the cars had taken off through the gate, it had been unnaturally silent. It seemed even the birds were holding their breath. I was starting to relax when a shot rang out followed by a burst of fire. The sun's heat intensified to a boiling point, drying my mouth and forcing the sweat out every pore in my body. Was

Patrenka hit? I started for the gate.

"Hey, get back here. The scene is not secure," the doughnut king yelled.

I looked at him and realized I could be in before he could lift his bulk off the seat. So I slid through the gate and followed the one-hundred-year oaks up the side of the drive, always keeping a tree between me and the house for protection. I forgot to ask for a bulletproof vest.

Another volley of shots rang out along with a couple of shouts, but I couldn't make out the words. I didn't know who was winning the battle. I was breathing heavily and realized at some point I need to start a work out plan to get in shape. I slowed, breathing heavily. Ahead two unmarked cars blocked the drive. No one was visible. All was quiet again.

I was uncertain how much further I wanted to go. I wasn't sure where any officers were and what was going on. I hadn't heard any more shots but it had only been a couple minutes. I saw movement off to my right in a thicket of trees on the other side of the drive.

I didn't know what I expected but I certainly didn't expect to see Buck sneaking along the marked and unmarked police cars littering the drive like pick up sticks. Buck looked around and didn't see me behind a tree. He raced to a dark unmarked police car and jumped in. Buck turned the engine over, popped it into gear and squealed toward the gate.

Someone should go after him, but no one did. I sprinted to the other car and followed him. Realizing what a stupid move it was, I negotiated the last curve before the gate. I didn't have any experience chasing down criminals, but I wasn't going to let Buck get loose. Joey would never be safe again.

The radio crackled and I grabbed the mike. I had listened to hours of police scanners in the newsroom every day but I couldn't think of what to say. So I said the first thing that came to me. "Buck Rockwell is escaping his estate in an unmarked police car and I'm following him."

Suddenly the radio was alive with voices. "Would the officer who just transmitted repeat your twenty."

"I'm not an officer. I'm following Buck Rockwell headed north from his compound."

I passed my chaperone, and honked and waved. Had the

situation not been so serious, I would have laughed at his expression. At least he had the presence of mind to get the make, model and license plate of the car Buck stole.

The radio sputtered to life. "This is one delta fifteen at 5000 River Valley Lane. Suspect wanted for questioning is traveling north on River Valley Lane in a navy Crown Vic, license number AZA 4359. Please advise units that the suspect is mobile."

"Roger one delta fifteen, standby."

I heard more chatter but was unable to make it out. I concentrated on keeping the car Buck took off in, in sight.

"One delta fifteen, what is your location?" I heard a siren in stereo – both from behind me and through the radio. I looked back and saw the sergeant pulling up fast. I could see the other car in front of me. The sergeant flew by me like I was standing still and I hit the gas, staying on his bumper.

"One delta fifteen. I have the suspect in sight. On River Valley Lane approaching River Hollow. Suspect turning, heading west on River Hollow."

"Roger, one delta fifteen."

This time I heard the tones followed by the broadcast. "All units. Pursuit in progress on River Hollow Drive west of River Valley Lane. Man is believed to be armed. Wanted for questioning."

I listened to other units sound off their position and the coordination of the net ensued. I knew I should back off but I couldn't let Buck get away. I wanted to be there to face down a man who had such little disregard for a woman and her small child. We were heading into a highly populated area. He turned on Sherman Street – the busiest commercial street in the city with two lanes of cars in either direction. It was harder to see around the black and white and keep the nondescript car in sight. Buck wove in and out of traffic and appeared to be pulling away. If he pulled into a super grocery store and parked, we'd lose him for sure.

Suddenly up ahead I saw other lights. Police cars were coming at us as well as up behind us. At the next intersection, two red and blue flashing bars blocked the intersection. All the way back to us, brake lights were coming on like dominos as everyone was rapidly slowing to maneuver around the cars.

Buck careened to the left and around three cars and then pulled over in front of another. I couldn't believe my eyes. He cranked the wheel hard left again and then spun, doing a one-eighty in the left turn lane. The engine gunned and he shot toward me, playing chicken with the cars in the center lane.

I had been to many a fatality in my years but never had seen one happen. If Buck didn't stop, I was sure I was going to. Buck swerved around my chaperone. I spun the wheel and hit the gas. I wasn't fast enough to block Buck's escape but I did clip his car's back quarter panel.

"Damn." I didn't get him. I slammed on the brakes and slid, nearly hitting a semi. I thumped my palm on the steering wheel and looked around. The magnitude hit me. I could have killed myself or other innocent bystanders. What was I doing? I rested my forehead on my hands still clutching the steering wheel. I closed my eyes and tried deep breaths to still my racing heart. I jumped at a rap on the window. I looked up and only saw a giant mass of khaki jelly barely held in check with brown buttons. I followed it up to see my chaperone.

"You okay?"

I nodded and attempted to find the door handle.

"Where'd you learn to drive like that?" he asked.

"What do you mean?" I was confused.

"That move of hitting the car. He jumped the curb and spun away from the traffic. It was amazing."

I looked up the street and saw Buck's head being pushed none too gently into the back of a police car while another officer was reading him his Miranda rights from a card.

"I did that?"

"You didn't plan it? Hell of a move."

I stood and had to grab the car's roof for support as my legs gave out under me. I surveyed the road in both directions and it was literally a parking lot. This would take some time to get the bumper-to-bumper traffic moving again, but then, it didn't really matter. I decided to sit back down in the driver's seat.

"Any word yet on what happened at Buck's compound? Was anyone hurt?"

"No. There was an exchange of gunfire and a couple of hostiles were wounded, but nothing life threatening."

I watched the car containing Buck pull across the five lanes of stopped cars and disappear back the way we had come along the shoulder of the road.

"Is the car drivable? Can we move it to get traffic rolling again?"

Staring ahead I took a deep breath and avoid looking at the jam I had created. Slowly, I nodded and slid my legs under the wheel, surprised to find the engine still running. I backed into the left turn lane and then pulled forward facing the right way. Other than a little shimmy, the car responded well. I did not respond so well. I was shimmying too. I pulled into the nearest parking lot. I cranked the air conditioning to high, turned up the radio and calmed myself to a little Blood, Sweat and Tears from an Oldies station. After a half dozen tunes, I pulled into traffic, remembering I had another mission to fulfill.

Within minutes I pulled into the Roadhouse. I was tired, hot and hungry. I wasn't sure what the protocol was for returning a commandeered police car but figured they wouldn't notice if I parked it. The search of Buck's compound would take several hours. I had a promise to keep. I walked in with a jaunty step, elated that Buck would be behind bars. I waved at Daisy behind the bar. She spun on her heel and disappeared in the kitchen. I felt my lighthearted mood and happiness to be alive plummet. I sat on my regular stool and glanced around not looking for anything in particular. I stopped cold. The well-dressed man who'd been with Buck on my first visit was here, and so were Mutt and Jeff, the pair who had abused Daisy.

This wasn't over yet. Not everyone was rounded up. What should I do? My cell phone chirped.

I prepared to answer it but realized I had garnered more attention than I wanted. "Hello," I stammered falling into my drunk routine for lack of anything else. I hadn't recognized the number that came on the caller ID.

"Mitch?" Patrenka's voice purred over the line. Every time I heard her voice, I wanted to melt. There was no time for that now. I needed to call in the troops to round up the Neanderthals. I glanced in the mirror and found my eyes meeting those of the well-dressed gentleman. They eyes were cold and suspicious. I had to get him to think I was harmless.

"Hey baby. I'm here waiting for you at the Roadhouse. Where are you, love?"

"Love? Mitch, Are you in trouble?"

"Yes, I can't wait for you to get here. You're bringing friends? I thought it was going to be us? No, I haven't been drinking." I pulled the phone from my ear and snapped it shut disconnecting the call in disgust. "Damn women. Ain't able to make 'em happy." I looked around and seemed to have lost the attention of the suit. Unfortunately, I had garnered some from Mutt who stepped up beside me.

"Hey, don't I know you from somewhere?"

"Maybe. Hey, you went to Central High School? I went there." I said putting my arm around him like he was best buddy hoping to make him uncomfortable so he would leave me alone. He wasn't so easily dissuaded.

"No. But you look familiar."

"I get, I get around. I spend a lot of time on a barstool at Jack's, Jack's down the street. Ever go in there?"

"Ya, maybe that was it."

Daisy came out the doors carrying two platters and set them down at Mutt and Jeff's table and Mutt wandered back. I sighed in relief.

She wheeled and left again. About a minute later she re-entered and pulled a draft and set it in front of me with a napkin.

Written in small letters in the corner were two words. "I'm ready." I looked up and made eye contact. "I'm not quite ready to order yet. Can you give me a few minutes?"

"Let me know when you're ready." And she disappeared back into the kitchen.

I looked in the mirror on the wall behind the bar and watched the well dressed man check his watch and glance around. He tapped his tumbler in impatience. I quickly shifted my gaze to the frosty mug in front of me.

A shaft of sunlight bathed the area in brightness as the door opened. A large shadow filled the door frame. Dennis was in an untucked faded blue denim shirt and jeans. I got off my barstool and stumbled over. "Dennis," I slurred loudly. "You came to buy me a drink." I hugged him clumsily and whispered in his ear. "Two at nine o'clock and one at eleven o'clock."

I felt Dennis push me back on my feet and snort.

"Hey buddy, how about you let me drive you home? There's a woman who's not too happy with you right now."

"I can't leave yet," I slurred, willing him to get my message but sure he didn't.

"Why not? We can have a party at your place. Let's go."

"Nope, I haven't finished my drink yet," I said in my loudest belligerent drunk drawl I could come up with twirling away from his and swaying back to the bar.

"Suit yourself, buddy. I don't need you puking again in my wheels. Adios."

Dennis retreated to the door and opened it.

"Last chance, buddy," he said while holding it open. I thought I saw shadows cross the threshold, but couldn't be sure with the sunlight hurting my eyes.

Mutt turned and growled. "Close the door."

The door shut. I waited a few minutes for my eyes to adjust to the dark, then stumbled back to the bar.

A few minutes later the door opened again. Patrenka walked in and her blazer was gone and her blouse was unbuttoned nearly to her navel. I wanted to throw myself at her and cover her from view. I raised my eyes to her face and saw a warning there. I forced my eyes from her cleavage turning back to my beer. In the mirror I watched Patrenka walk along the booths. Mutt and Jeff stopped eating to ogle Patrenka. They started to rise, then recognized her as Buck's woman and backed off before they were standing. She continued along the booths like a gazelle until reaching the well-dressed man in the last booth. Her gait changed imperceptibly. Her face quickly shifted from the man to directly in front of her. It seemed like her back straightened and she tightened her hold on her purse.

Something was wrong. She continued down the hall and entered the restroom.

I wasn't sure what was going on, but something had spooked Patrenka.

Who was he? He was tan with perfect black hair that looked like he had come straight from a barber. Realization dawned. Could he be a terrorist? He screamed wealth from the gold crest ring to the excellent cut of his suit. He kept looking at his watch and I wondered if he was expecting Buck to join him.

I didn't know if they had collected all the terrorist trainees in the woods but this guy didn't look like a trainee. He looked like a man in control of his destiny. I wish I had paid more attention to the talk about the terrorist cell. The names were Greek to me. It wouldn't help me even if I did know his name. My beer was fast disappearing and I realized I'd better slow down or I would be intoxicated. I didn't have time to eat when Dennis called only a few hours ago.

Patrenka came out of the restroom and slid into the booth with the suit. Daisy returned from the kitchen and took Patrenka's order for a scotch, neat. I watched as Patrenka flipped her hair over her shoulder and stared at the man. I knew this trick and wondered if he would spill his guts like every other red blooded American.

If he wasn't American, would her endless eyes work? I saw the man nod and say something I couldn't hear.

Daisy returned to the table and set the glass down with a napkin under it then continued. As she passed Mutt and Jeff, Jeff reached out to detain her. "Hey, you got any ketchup for my fries?" he said chuckling. I didn't like the chuckle and knew he was not being flirtatious.

"Let me go and I will get you some," Daisy said trying to jerk her arm free.

"I think you will tell us what we want to know first. We know you've been talking to Frank and we want to know where he is."

"Frank? Who's Frank?"

"Don't get funny with us," and he twisted her arm behind her. Daisy gritted her teeth.

"I don't know where he is," Daisy rasped a higher pitch than I'd ever heard from such a low voice.

"Hey, I need a beer here," I said coming to feet without knowing what I was doing.

"You stay out of this, drunk. We've got business with the bartender."

"I told you I don't know where he is," Daisy rasped again but even in a higher pitch. I could see the color fade and knew her arm was close to breaking.

Frank may be involved in Joey's mother's disappearance, but Daisy was innocent and didn't need these goons hurting her. I had to do something.

I continued my drunken act and weaved my way toward the altercation. "Hey man, I don't want any trouble," I slurred. "I want another beer. Is that too much to ask?"

By this time I was abreast of their table and beside Daisy. Mutt started to rise but I invaded his space as I weaved closer and he backed off. I needed to get Jeff to break his grip and not make it any worse for Daisy.

I pretended to trip, catching myself by dropping both hands on the table's edge. In catching myself, I pushed the table into Jeff's midsection. His breath gushed out from impact and he dropped Daisy's arm. I stepped around the table between Jeff and Daisy. It didn't take a second for her to disappear behind the bar.

I turned my back on the table, stumbling to my stool like nothing had happened. Before I was able to take a couple steps, Mutt said: "I remember you. You were here the last time we were trying to get information out of the old bat. Maybe we can get the information out of you." He stood and advanced. I took a step back and collided with a wall – a human wall. One glance over my shoulder and I saw the crested ring gripping my shoulder. I followed the hand higher and looked into the coldest, blackest eyes I'd ever seen.

Fear gripped me. I knew this man would show no mercy and I didn't have any skills in self defense, nor could I do much under the intense pressure on my shoulder.

Mutt and Jeff were in front of me. These two were with him. The slightly accented English voice repeated Jeff's question. "I think you do know where Frank is. Tell us or a broken arm won't be your only injury."

I wanted to pee my pants. Before I could, pandemonium broke out. The grip on my shoulder lessened and I turned to see Patrenka applying pressure to the muscular cords of the head goon's neck. His eyes rolled back in his head. Silver flashed from her other hand and she had one in handcuffs before he hit the floor.

I turned to Mutt and Jeff. I wanted to laugh. Daisy was charging with a baseball bat from the end of the bar. She got one crack on Mutt who was heading in my direction with murder on his mind. Before Daisy could do any damage, she was then scooped up by a man who materialized like magic from the darkness near the door. Another man dressed all in black grabbed Jeff and cuffed him.

"Let go of me. I haven't done anything," Daisy threatened in a low tone that would have caused most people to quake. Her captor repositioned his grip to keep her from kicking his shins.

Another approached me. "You alright?"

I nodded still too stunned to speak. Daisy continued to struggle. I finally recovered my wits.

"Quite struggling, Daisy. You're going to get hurt. This is the Calvary."

Neither Daisy, her captor nor I moved for a moment. She finally nodded and was quickly lowered to the floor. As if on signal, the doors opened bathing the room in sunlight and more people flooded into the interior. More confusion followed. I tried to keep Patrenka in sight. I wanted to find out what was going on. I wanted to take Daisy and get to Frank. He had answers I needed. Answers Joey needed.

Cops and FBI agents flowed into the room, guns drawn, ready to secure the scene.

Patrenka walked over and nodded to the man in black who led Jeff out.

"You okay?" Patrenka asked looking at both me and Daisy. I nodded and she turned her back.

Another group of officers pushed their way in our direction. I was pushed over the back of a table, my arms pulled behind me.

"Patrenka." She turned.

"Not him. He's with me." I went weak in the knees. Patrenka said I was with her. That had to be an improvement in my status. Maybe we could get together yet.

"Who's the chick in the fancy duds?" Daisy asked nodding her head toward Patrenka Her hands were still cuffed behind her.

"This is FBI agent Patrenka Peterson," I introduced. "Patrenka, I would like you to meet Daisy." I paused. I never did get her last name. It never seemed important. I was really slipping as a newsman who needed first, last and middle initial for every source in a story.

"Gomez," she said holding out elbow as if to shake her hand.

Patrenka, nodded turned and was gone.

While I was disappointed she didn't stay and chat, I took advantage of the opportunity to have a private word with Daisy.

"You said you were ready to go? Is that still true even if you don't have to go now with all the riff raff in jail?"

"Yes, I think so," she said a sheepish smile spreading over her face. She was a beautiful person when she smiled which I suspected wasn't often. "I want to be with Frank."

"Okay. How about we make plans then?" I flipped open my phone and punched in the number.

"Dennis, any sign of Joey's mother?"

"Sorry, no. We've only started searching though and it will take us hours to scour the grounds, Joey's house, the woods and then put the reports together. I'm going to be tied up most of the day."

"Found anything to corroborate the info from Joey's photo cards?"

"No, we haven't apprehended either of the two men with Buck on the tape. We'll find them."

"I don't think you will." I wanted to call back the words I didn't mean to say aloud. It must be the beer loosening my tongue.

"What aren't you telling me, Mitch? Tell me where he is and we'll pick him up."

"No, I've got it covered."

"Mitch, don't even think about tracking him down. Don't even think about taking justice into your own hands."

"What was that, I didn't hear you? I'm losing my signal." I closed the phone and then reopened it dialing Dennis' home.

"Hi Colleen. How's Joey?"

"Good. The kids are having a great time." I could hear shouts and whoops in the background.

"Would you mind if Joey stayed overnight?"

"Sure that's fine. Is everything alright?"

"Yes, a bunch of loose ends to finish. I want to do a story and figured it would be faster if I wrote it before I picked her up. Can I talk to her?"

"Sure."

"Hi," came Joey's voice a little unsure.

"Hey Sport, having fun?"

"Uncle Mitch, we are sliding and swinging."

"That's great. What would you think about staying overnight, a sleepover while I tie up a few loose ends?

"Yeah." There was a long pause and Joey continued. "You are coming back, aren't you, Uncle Mitch?" The tone in her voice broke my heart.

"Sure, Sport, but there is a lot of paperwork involved in rounding up the bad guys and I have to write my story for the newspaper. I'll see you in the morning, okay?" I hated lying to her but wanted to give her closure.

"Okay." The reply lacked any emotion. The one word made me feel horrible.

"Tell you what, Sport. I'll stop by and see you for a few minutes before I write my story."

I hung up and hoped there wouldn't be any problem keeping my promise to Joey. Too many people had disappeared in her life and it didn't look like anyone would find her mother in the near future. My last lead was Frank. I planned to beat him to a pulp unless he told me where Joey's mother was, even if it was only where he buried the body.

I dialed another number. A woman answered again and I asked for Frank. Immediately, he was on the line.

"What's happening? What's taking so long. My Daisy okay?"

"She's fine and with me now. She's all set to go. How about some directions on where you're at?" I thought I knew where he was from my research, but I wanted to confirm it. A reporter always gets a second source.

"I'll meet you the same place we met last." The rough voice said.

"No." I wasn't going to go somewhere public. I wanted blood.

"What do you mean, no?"

"We need someplace private, not public."

"Why?" I could hear caution in his voice.

"I need to get quotes for my story and I don't want anyone to overhear us. You are going to give me my story?"

The silenced stretched and I could see him, scratching his head in thought. "That'll be okay, I guess. There is something I want to talk to you about."

Frank gave me directions to the cabin.

I made my last phone call.

"Ken, Mitch. Any chance you could send a photographer out to shoot some photos for a story?" I gave him Buck's address and gave him a summary of what had happened so far, promising him an exclusive soon that would send the state and national media into a frenzy.

Chapter 34

Daisy and I went through the kitchen, grabbed her suitcase from the Roadhouse's pantry and exited out the back door. No one challenged us and then I realized I didn't have a car. My mode of transportation had been a police car that had one too many accidents.

"Wait here, I have to get keys," I said turning to Daisy.

I re-entered the Roadhouse from the front and searched out Patrenka. She sat in a booth with the dark haired gentleman asking him questions. It didn't look like he was answering them. As I neared, Patrenka nodded to an agent standing at the end of the booth. She rose and met me a couple feet from the table.

"What, Mitch?" She seemed frustrated

"I need your keys. I came in a patrol car," I said nonchalantly.

"Where are you going?"

I was still a bit piqued by her disappearance.

"I need to get Joey and write my article," I lied.

"Oh," I could see she was taken totally off guard, distracted. I admit I liked her like this.

"What's his story?" I asked.

"He's the ringleader of the terrorists but we're going to have to let him go if I can't get some evidence that says he was doing anything but having dinner here."

"His assault to my shoulder doesn't matter?" I was pissed.

"He says he was coming to the aid of the two men you assaulted, which they corroborate." She pushed her hand over her forehead lifting her hair up and a telltale sign of perspiration lined her scalp. "Without proof, he's spouting diplomatic immunity. I can't get him to talk." He must be one tough nut if Patrenka couldn't work her magic. I was thinking about how I knew him. Maybe I could get Patrenka on her backside with a little insider information.

"How about a witness or two that saw him meeting with Buck in the same booth not two days ago?"

"That would work. Know anyone who could testify?" A smile graced her features and I wanted to melt.

"Sure do, but they need a vehicle right now so they can get things done."

Patrenka wrapped her arms around me and the world stopped moving. Before I could meld my body to hers, she moved back and handed me the keys. "Dark blue Buick parked in the handicapped spot," she said. "Don't leave town. You're my witness now." She purred seductively.

I was a little miffed by her territorial attitude toward me. The only time I got a cheap feel was when I was valuable to her, but it left me wanting so much more.

I returned to the parking lot, found the car and was on the Interstate heading north within ten minutes with Daisy beside me. She stared straight ahead and wrung her hands.

My cell phone sounded and I answered it without thinking.

"Where the hell are you and what are you up to?"

"Dennis, I never knew you cared."

"I talked to Colleen. What's up?"

"I'm on my way to your house right now. I'll pick up Joey." I lied.

"You're not going after the guy on the photo card." Dennis left that statement hanging in the air. "Yes I heard you accuse him on the phone. Don't try and pull a fast one, Mitch. This isn't some parlor trick for a headline."

"I have a debt to pay." I couldn't keep the defensive note from my voice.

"You're going after the other guy in the video? Don't hold back on me. This could be dangerous. You need back up." I could hear the concern in his voice and a little of his common sense sank in.

"Okay. I'm heading north to a cabin in the National Forest at 4053 Five Mile Road, in Bromley. Feel free to back us up if you're not too busy."

"We, who do you got with you? Patrenka?"

"No. A promise I need to keep."

"Quit being so damned cryptic. I'm not looking to steal your story," Dennis fumed.

"Gotta go," I said, hanging up.

I took the next exit and wound my way through a couple subdivisions and stopped out in front of Dennis's home. Joey was nearly at my car before I could tell Daisy to stay put.

"Uncle Mitch, who's the woman?"

"A friend." I jumped out of the car and walked over to Joey and picked her up. "Joey, we got the bad guy. The man from the TV, he's in jail. You're safe now."

"And my mom?" The voice was a whisper, afraid of the answer.

"I'm going to see a man who can tell me. I don't know yet, Sport, but I will. As soon as I do, you will. I promise. Now go on back and have fun. I'll be back before you know it."

Joey took off at a run and did a little hip hop step along the way. I watched her run to Colleen who wrapped her arms around her small body. I was happy Joey was with someone who could comfort her.

Just then, a small blood-curdling cry erupted from the back yard. Colleen set Joey down and rushed to the back yard. I followed and Daisy exited the car as well. Daisy and I stopped at the fence. Colleen was on her hands and knees in front of Kelly, running her hands up and down her leg focusing on her ankle. We watched her bend low, kiss the ankle. Kelly popped up and ran for the slide.

"Kids, they certainly heal quickly," I said, but wondered if Joey would heal as quickly if we couldn't find her mother. I pushed the thought away as we climbed back in the car.

All was silent for a few minutes until traffic thinned.

"Why did you tell that guy on the phone where we're going?" Daisy turned in her seat to face me .

I was hoping she would have forgotten. I should have known better.

"There is a little bit of information I need to tell you before we get there. I'm trusting you with this information. You have a good heart, Daisy. That little girl I hugged? Her mother disappeared because of Buck Rockwell. We have a short video showing him threatening the mother. The last thing on the tape is Buck ordering Frank to take care of her and the little girl. The girl was able to escape and hide. She was taken to a safe house that wasn't really safe, but that's another story."

"What happened to the mother?" Daisy asked.

"We don't know. She hasn't been seen or heard from since. We need to get answers out of Frank. I have to find out what happened to that little girl's mother. If he hurt her in any way, he will come to justice. I promise you that."

"Frank couldn't hurt anyone," Daisy declared. "He's as gentle as they come. If you're going to hurt him, you can stop right now and let me out. I don't want any part of it. My Frank is a saint."

"Daisy, I know you have a kind heart. I trust you to help me find the truth. I hope you're right and he didn't hurt the mother. He has to take us to her and I don't want him knowing the child is still alive. I don't want to do anything to put that child in danger. Understand?"

"Yes, but you're wrong."

"I hope so."

We fell silent as I got off the highway and had to concentrate on the directions to find the place. The cabin was more remote than I anticipated. The road to it was five miles of gravel and few houses. The drive back to the cabin was another mile of two track with waist high weeds between the tracks. I wasn't worried about pings and scrapes the weeds made on the undercarriage. It was a government vehicle after all. I was worried we were traveling down the wrong road.

I glanced at Daisy when the drive allowed. Her teeth clenched, staring ahead, unfazed by the bumps and jolts.

I wanted to comfort her, but couldn't. Until we found Joey's mother, no one was going to get any slack. The adults could stand the unknown. Kids couldn't. The primary goal was to find Evelyn Smith.

Odd. I always had been story-motivated before. I was always writing the story in my head as the events unfold, mentally revising it as events warranted until I got to my cubicle. Now, I was involved in the biggest story of my life. It had murder, terrorists, a beautiful FBI agent and a human interest angle. Those did not come along every day, but all I could think about was Joey's face and my promise.

Yes, something had changed and it was me. When had I started caring? Was it when I saw Joey's sleeping form in the cubby hole? When she and I were left alone while Patrenka interviewed Buck? When she woke me to tell me Patrenka was gone? I couldn't say for sure, but my world changed when Joey entered my life. Joey was more important than my dream woman. I had seen faults in Patrenka, though I was still interested in developing that relationship, but Joey came first.

I smiled thinking about how smart Joey was. How she hid the evidence, how she cried to make people talk. How Joey would be a good reporter. We could be a great team. I pictured us in matching leather bomber jackets and her with her own notebook and pen ...

The car bounced. Thinking about my team resulted in a mental lapse in my driving and we left the drive momentarily. I jerked the wheel back and didn't look at Daisy.

I wanted Joey on my team. Mitch Malone was not a team player but was willing to add a half-pint as if it was the most natural thing on the earth.

I hit the brakes to negotiate a ninety degree turn when the log cabin came into view, nestled among giant maples, oaks and towering pines. Smoke rose from the stone chimney and the lawn was neatly cut near the cabin. Frank stood on the porch leaning against a roof support. A shotgun leaned on the railing beside him. Not a good omen.

"Remember what I said about finding the kid's mother," I hissed to Daisy.

Daisy nodded as she opened the door and I scrambled out too. We walked to the porch stopping about five feet from the single step.

"You okay?" Frank asked Daisy.

Daisy nodded.

"You can hit the road, now," Frank said.

"No, I can't. You have some questions to answer. You promised me my story."

"You don't even have a pad to write the answers, what's this all about?" He was right. I had forgotten my notebook.

"Frank, answer his questions," Daisy whispered.

I wasn't sure if she whispered because she was afraid of the answers or she didn't want me to hear. Either way, she got Frank's attention and his belligerence shrank a little.

"Shoot," he said and then chuckled to himself looking down at the shotgun.

I swallowed with difficulty, wondering if he would be shooting me next.

"We saw a tape of Buck ordering you to get rid of a woman who took photos she wasn't supposed to. What happened to her?"

"I ain't killed nobody if that is what you're asking."

"Where is she?"

"She's safe. Is Buck in custody?"

"Yes, at least when we started this journey. He had been arrested for firing on police officers and fleeing and eluding. I believe more charges are pending depending on the results of a search of his estate."

"Do you think you got all his goons and the men training in the woods?"

"I believe so but don't know what the headcount is. The ringleader was also arrested and detained by the FBI."

"The FBI is involved?" Frank asked incredulously.

"Homeland Security will be pursuing federal offenses. With those charges there are stiffer penalties and less likelihood of bail. You're quite safe but will need to answer some questions and take responsibility for your part."

"There isn't a chance they could get off?"

"I don't think so, but nothing is ever a hundred percent. The cops have quite a bit of physical evidence and with your testimony corroborating what was planned, Buck could be gone for a long time. Where is the woman in the tape?"

"I know where the woman is but she needs your help." Frank stepped back toward the cabin and opened the front door. He spoke to the person inside. "It's all clear."

A woman stepped out. I recognized her immediately. It was the woman on the tape. I was speechless.

"I couldn't kill her. I hid her here. Before Buck figured it out, I disappeared too. That was why he was so desperate to find me. I have the key evidence against Buck." Frank turned pointing to the woman. "Here she is. Evelyn, Mr. Malone, will help us."

"Mr. Malone, we need you to find my daughter. No one has seen or heard from her since the night on the tape." The woman broke into sobs and Frank reached over to comfort her, one hand remaining on the shotgun. "I was knocked out by Buck and didn't regain consciousness until Frank had me here."

"You didn't have a choice, Evelyn. You couldn't have gone back or you would be dead now. Mitch Malone will find her."

I stood, staring, unable to move. Joey's mother was alive. I was happy for Joey but desolate for myself. My dreams of us being a team were disappearing fast. I watched her struggle for composure.

"Can you help me? I've been frantic. We scanned the papers, called children's services about an abandoned child, but nothing. I tried to contact my step-sister in the FBI but she's undercover and unreachable. You have to help. You are our only hope. She could be dead or hurt somewhere."

I could see the pain and worry etched on Evelyn's face. Her clothes hung on a body that had lost weight. Shadows outlined her eyes and the hollowness of her checks. I knew she'd been mentally beating herself up since she was safe here and her child was still missing.

"Please," she implored.

Daisy turned toward me with a look that said get on with it.

"I can help." The relief in the faces was palatable. "In fact I can personally assure you that Joey is fine and currently enjoying a sleepover with two new friends. We can pick her up in the morning. She is quite something, your little girl."

"You found her?" her mother said incredulously.

At that point a pint-size tornado hurtled herself into her mother's arms.

"Joey, is it you?"

"Mommy."

I stared at Joey. She should have been safe at the Flaherty's.

Evelyn held Joey away from her and gave her a good look from top to bottom. "How, why?" She again gripped her in a fierce hug. "Oh, honey. I'm so glad you're safe. How did you get here?" She looked up at me and Joey hid her face in her mother's shoulder. I started laughing. I couldn't help it.

"I've been teaching my two new friends magic tricks," Joey beamed. "Kelly fell off from the swing so I could hide in the car. Sorry, Uncle Mitch."

"Freeze. Put your hands in the air. You on the porch, step out into the yard away from the gun."

I looked around and saw brown uniforms materialize out of the woods with guns drawn. "Which one of you is Mitch Malone?"

"I am." I raised my hand.

"You okay?" the officer in charge asked.

"I'm fine. Everything here is fine. What are you doing here?"

"A Detective Sergeant Dennis Flaherty asked for our assistance. We have a warrant for a Frank Stolnek on suspicion of murder."

"Why, you dirty double crosser," Frank sputtered.

"Officer, could I see that warrant?" I stepped toward the officer who appeared to be in charge.

I read and started laughing. All eyes looked at me like I was insane. "Officer, this can be cleared up easily and quickly. Frank, you are being charged with the murder of Evelyn Lippistan Smith."

"I'm Evelyn Smith and I'm alive and well."

The silence was priceless. "Don't that beat all?" Daisy said dryly, breaking the ice.

"Officer, if you will allow me to call Detective Flaherty, I can clear this up."

He nodded and I pulled on my cell. "Dennis. Thanks for the back up, but it wasn't necessary."

"Do they have Frank Stolnek in custody?"

"Well, yes, but the warrant will never fly. Joey's mom, Evelyn has been hiding out with Frank. She is alive and well."

"That will get me out of hot water with Colleen for not personally smashing Frank's face with the butt of my gun. Sean and Kelly confessed their part in helping Joey stow away in your car. I'm assuming you've discovered her?"

"Yes, she's with her mother now."

"Frank could help lock the case against Buck."

"Will he testify?"

"I think you could get Frank's cooperation a lot easier if we didn't arrest him now. Something could happen to him in jail. Remind me never to get on the wrong side of your wife."

"Good point, especially about my wife. I'm with the prosecuting attorney, just a minute." I heard a muffled conversation. "Okay. Here's the deal. Frank and Evelyn must testify and they can stay where they are. We'll get statements from them tomorrow. Frank must testify against everyone arrested at the compound."

"They'll agree to that. How confident are you that you have everyone in connection with Buck and the terrorists?"

"A couple may have slipped through but they are long gone. Most of Buck's men are singing for a reduced sentence. There isn't much love lost between Buck and his men. I think it's pretty safe. We also have the terrorist and the king pin thanks to the FBI. A pretty good joint operation, if you ask me."

I chuckled at Dennis's irony then noticed the officer in charge frowning. I handed him the phone. Dennis made quick work of the terms and I was given the phone back.

"Stand down," the officer said and guns were holstered and stances became relaxed. The officers left and the five of us went into the cabin as daylight was beginning to fade. Joey was unwilling to let go of her mother and I felt bereft.

Frank scrounged up an old notebook and I went to work. I had a story to get. "Joey, why don't you run and get my camera from my jacket pocket." Joey raced out of the home.

"You have quite the little lady there." I said, meaning every word but I was heart broken. "Joey was rescued from a safe house thanks to your step-sister, Patrenka, isn't it?" At the women's nod, I continued. "Joey was found in a home where two former agents were killed execution style."

Joey's mother gasped and looked ready to collapse. Realizing my mistake, I quickly added. "Don't worry. The woman hid Joey from the gunman. She has no recollection of what happened. She slept through it. She does, however, have nightmares about the night Buck came to your house. I'm sure those will disappear now that she is reunited with you. She is quite something. She kept the tape you made hidden and helped the police capture Buck."

"Thank God she's alright. Frank kept saying that even Buck wouldn't kill an innocent child, if he could find her, but I wasn't sure. She was always so good at hiding I knew Buck would never find her. Unfortunately, Frank couldn't find her either. How did Patrenka get involved?"

"Patrenka's supervisor, Sam Sloan, got your message and found

Joey. He placed her at the safe house until Patrenka could finish her current job. It was because of her that we found Joey in the home, alive and well, sleeping in a hidden nook. She has been with me and Patrenka since, helping us."

Joey returned, dropping the camera in my lap, then raced back to her mother. Evelyn pulled the little girl into her lap and looked unwilling to give her up. I snapped a photo.

Evelyn told her story in detail as I took notes. Frank added tidbits but mostly grinned at Daisy who seemed out of sorts. After an hour, Frank pulled out the grill and fried up some burgers that were to die for. Maybe he did have a good chance of succeeding with his burger joint. We all ate heartily, laughing and joking like old friends.

After dinner I pulled Daisy aside. "Are you sure you want to stay?" When she didn't answer I continued. "You could return with me. Now that Buck's men are rounded up you could return to your job."

I was concerned because Daisy had never shrunk from anything in the short time I knew her. She glanced at Frank who was looking at us with murder in his gaze. Not a gentle look for the woman he professed to love.

"What's going on here?" he asked roughly looking at me as he crossed the room to us.

"Daisy will be returning with me," I said.

"You trying to move in on my woman?" Frank said a challenge in his voice.

"No."

"Frank, I'm not sure I fit in here," Daisy said quietly.

"What do you mean? I like having you here."

"I'm not a country girl. I've always been in the city."

"We don't have to stay here. I've got this building I've been looking at. It's the perfect location for the restaurant we've talked about. It's in a small city about an hour north of here. You'll love it. We can find a place you'll like. You can pick it out."

She still seemed hesitant.

"Maybe she needs time," I tried to mediate.

"No. I love you, you can't leave. We are going to be married."

At the mention of marriage, everything on Daisy's face changed. "I thought you forgot about the wedding stuff, Frank Stolnek. I ain't no loose woman and I ain't staying with you unless we get hitched."

"No problem. I went to the clerk's office and got the license. It's good for thirty days. You say when, pumpkin, and it's done."

Daisy flew into his arms. "You want to marry me!" She kissed him soundly on the mouth.

Don't that beat all, I thought, in my best Kentucky drawl. She was a lady through and through. But what a woman, I thought, remembering Daisy ready to take a swing with a baseball bat.

"You take good care of her, Frank, or you will have to answer to me," I said. "Now, I have a story that needs to get written." I didn't want any long goodbyes. Joey and her mother would stay with Frank and Daisy for a few days just in case. Before I could leave, Joey had one request I couldn't refuse.

"Can you tuck me into bed, Uncle Mitch?"

"Uncle Mitch," she said as I tucked the sheet under her chin.

"Yes, Sport?"

"I love you."

"I love you too, Sport." I kissed her on the check. "Get a good night's sleep and I'll visit in a few days."

I walked back to the living room. My heart was aching and I didn't know what to do about it. I didn't think there was anything I could do.

Daisy walked me to the sedan.

"Thank you for everything Mr. Malone. I wouldn't have made a move if it hadn't been for you." And she kissed my cheek.

"Name's Mitch and I want to give the bride away."

Chapter 35

My drive back was filled with story ideas. I had the main story, a couple of sidebars. As I neared the city limits, I thought about Joey. I tried to keep it simple. How was I going to handle her? Was I going to mention her at all? I took the exit nearest to Dennis' house. I pulled over along the side. A tear slid down my cheek. I had found Joey's mother. I had reunited the two. I was happy for them both. Then why were tears sliding down my face? I had to face it. Joey had wormed her way into my heart. We had spent a week together. Me, the guy who never had time for a girlfriend, was bawling his head off at the thought of losing his three-foot roommate.

What was I going to do? Joey was with her mother and I would return to my empty shallow life. Joey had brought something into my life that I didn't even know was missing.

The pain. I had never felt such pain. She had cracked my heart. Another single tear rolled down my check followed by a waterfall. I never cried when my parents were killed. I never felt. I bottled it all up and now it was draining out. I sat there for ten to fifteen minutes trying to get myself under control. I wiped my eyes on the bottom of my shirt making sure no trace of moisture remained. I took a deep shuddering breath, then let it out slowly and shakily, hiccupping a little. I was a mess. Mitch Malone was never a mess.

Blood, guts, murder, mayhem. Nothing bothered me. I covered it all. I had a story to write. This was no time for sentimentality. I turned from my thoughts of Joey and went to the newspaper. I parked the unmarked sedan at the police department and hiked down the hill to the newspaper, slipping in the side door.

No one noticed my arrival. I slid into my cubicle and powered up my computer. Sitting down to write the story seemed anti-climatic after the last few hours.

I started typing. It poured out. The terrorist, Buck Rockwell and his land-leasing scheme, Frank's quotes on Buck ordering him to kill Joey's parents. It all came out in black and white. I decided against giving Joey a supporting role. She was the star in real life. Without her evidence of the threat, there would have been no search warrant, no cooperation with the Feds and a huge terrorist incident planned for Chicago. Joey's role, however, would remain a police secret to keep her safe until after the trial.

I finished the story and then reread it carefully. It was by far the best thing I had ever written. Funny, I didn't care about the awards it might lead to. I felt empty. I should have felt exhilarated for a job well done. The hollowness, the despair was almost too much. I had a sudden urge to cry again. How can a man who hasn't cried in years, want to cry twice in one night? I didn't need a preschooler dogging my trail. This story was going to make me a household name, maybe even spots on *Good Morning America* or the *Today Show*.

I took a deep breath, trying to command my heaving emotions when an exotic scent permeated my consciousness. I froze. I was shaky and not sure I could take more mental swordplay. I turned. She was standing two feet behind me at the entrance to my cubicle. She nodded at me and I nodded back. Seems we were back to the old communication style of no communication. I reached up and put my hands behind my head and looked at her. I drank in the sight and smell of her.

Patrenka had captivated me from the moment she walked into the newsroom. Then she lied, deceived, ran away, cheated and returned without an explanation. Her shine had worn off but she still pulled at me. This time she was not going to get the better of me. I had lost too much today. I was not going to lose any more of my dignity, at least not at the hands of a Fed.

I smiled at Patrenka and waited. She cocked her head as if

trying to decide something. Then, she smiled back at me.

"Story finished?" she asked.

"Yes."

"May I?" She stepped further into the cubicle and leaned over me to read the screen. The scent was even stronger. When I cocked my head up toward her I feasted on my view of the V of her red sweater. I felt a grin cross my face for the first time in a long while, an easy relaxed feeling of contentment. I had a great view, the stress was draining away as other parts of my libido were awakening. This job did have its perks. I would enjoy it for as long as I could and it was an in-depth story. I breathed deeply and examined my view more fully.

"Hungry?" Patrenka asked. She smiled and I wanted to jump her right there. I could see that she read my thoughts clearly. "I was thinking doughnuts."

"Sure," I replied shrinking at that prospect and liking my other one much better. I didn't have a pint-sized roommate anymore and I did have a California king-sized bed for enjoyment. For the short term, I would have to settle for comfort food and Donna's doughnuts were the best.

Chapter 36

The woman of mystery sat across from me. As her teeth sunk into a six-inch diameter glazed cinnamon pinwheel doughnut, I saw her eyes close as the lightness of the doughnut mingled with the sweetness of the glaze and melted into one in her mouth. A hint of glaze outlined her upper lip and I ached to cup her face and wipe it off with my thumb. Actually I wanted to leap across the table and use my tongue instead, but I sat frozen in the booth.

I angrily launched into my bear claw, hoping for something to distract my thoughts. The sweet apple taste didn't assuage my lust, but it did give me something to concentrate on beside Patrenka's full lips. We ate in silence and for once I was determined to break hers. I needed to win this major battle to recapture my self esteem. Patrenka always seemed to carry it away while I watched the cute sway of her hips. Not this time! I was not going to be outmaneuvered by any FBI agent no matter how they filled out the soft curves of the red cashmere stretched across two mounds of incredibly enticing

I mentally slapped myself and moved my gaze back to her eyes to wait her out. I didn't like the sparkle I found, stiffening my resolve to win this exchange and get more information for a follow up for tomorrow. After all, a reporter was only as good as his next story. It was time for me to stop acting like a hormonal teenager on his first date. I was a reporter. It was time to attack.

"How long have you been in the FBI?"

"About eight years."

"Do you enjoy your work?"

"I like getting the bad guys and matching wits with them. They think they are so smart but in the end, they spill and the case is closed."

"Do you ever think you would stay in one place?"

Patrenka shook her head slowly. "Mitch, I'm not built that way. I get bored way too easy. I have a job to do and I never know where I am going to be from one case to the next. I can't stay in any one place after a job is done. Undercover assignments don't work that way. I need to be anonymous."

I got the message. There is no us, there was no us, there would never be any us.

"How about we go back to your place and get more comfortable."

There it was. The answer to my dreams. A night of hot sweaty bodies locked together. I could picture it all including waking to find Patrenka gone at the end. No. The interview would end on my terms. I ignored her innuendo. "Tell me how you knew this case was something the FBI would be involved in?" I pulled a new notebook out of my back pocket that I had grabbed on my way out.

She looked me in the eyes for several moments before answering. I wanted to break contact but couldn't let her see how her words had crushed my hopes and libido. She dipped her head slowly down. She never resumed eye contact as she gave me my follow up story.

When she'd left Joey and me without a word at the hotel, she was headed toward Buck's house. She told me how she had seen Buck and a man wanted for a bombing in Europe come out of the bar as she drove by, but couldn't prove they'd been together. She knew Buck had spotted her and had to do something quickly. She gave herself a flat tire. Buck, the ever-chivalrous man, offered to buy her a drink, while his chauffeur changed it for her. That's when I had seen her enter the Roadhouse.

"I knew if Buck was meeting with a man like him, this was more than a local issue. My step-sister had told me about lots of campouts in the woods and what Buck was involved in was starting to take shape."

"I had to notify my superiors. Sam wasn't returning my phone calls and I could only surmise that he was here investigating a suspected terrorist link. I contacted my SAC, er, that's special agent in charge. That set the ball rolling. I was briefed on what they suspected and my information and what you were giving Dennis wrapped up everything all nice and tight."

"So the FBI was already here investigating?"

"Yes. It was the terrorist who killed the couple in the safe house. We executed a search warrant on the cars in the parking lot of the Roadhouse. In the trunk of a rental we traced to the terrorist was the wallet and purse of the dead agents. I can't prove it yet, but I will. It fits his MO. I don't know what Sam was thinking, putting Joey in their safe keeping. They were in the middle of an undercover investigation. We believe Sam was followed from Evelyn's farm to Mark and Ashley Smith's home where he deposited Joey," Patrenka paused in her story.

"Sam has been suspended pending a review of his actions and his carelessness."

"It couldn't happen to a nicer guy," I said under my breath.

"Ashley gave her life to protect Joey. When we left the police station and we ended up at their house, I was scared. This was the first time any of my undercover assignments was personal. I was so afraid Joey was dead too. When you found her in the hidden cupboard, I wanted to kiss you senseless. I had to pull myself together. I knew I needed to keep Joey safe and you were my best option. That's why I didn't say much."

Her voice held an apology of sorts but I was still reeling from the kissing me senseless comment. "Why did you leave the hotel without a word? That nearly killed Joey. She had already lost so much."

"I knew you would be there for her. You weren't comfortable with her at first but you learned. I had to find out what happened to Evelyn and couldn't follow up on that and put Joey at risk. She was safe and in good hands."

Patrenka paused as if deciding something. "I didn't know you could protect and care for a child and solve the mystery at the same time. I had demanded to be paired with you because of your reputation as a good reporter. Who knew you would come up with the one piece of the puzzle I most cared about and couldn't find myself. Joey had the proof all along and it was under my nose. You'd make a hell of an FBI agent, Mitch."

I looked up from my notes and realized she was offering me a possible future. Then I realized it had killed me too when she left and I couldn't watch her do that again even if I was able to join her as an FBI agent. My place was firmly as a reporter. I looked up and shook my head, trying to let her down gently. "I'm a reporter. Always have been. Always will be."

I flipped my notebook shut and started to stand. Patrenka followed.

"Thanks, Mitch, for everything." She leaned across to kiss me and I turned my head. Her lips landed on my cheek. My hands fisted at my side.

"You're welcome." I turned and left Donna's, never looking back.

I walked down the dark street breathing in the stale city air. I watched the trucks start to haul the day's edition out of the paper's parking lot. The Mitch Malone exclusive took up most of the front page. In addition, my name was cleared and I was free to return to work. I didn't want to think what would come next. There would be a big hole in my life and I could only hope that the next story would fill it. I was Mitch Malone and I was back on the police beat.

About the Author

W.S. Gager has lived in West Michigan for most of her life except for stints early in her career as a newspaper reporter and editor. Now she enjoys creating villains instead of crossing police lines to get the story. She teaches English at a local college and is a soccer chauffeur for her children. During her driving time she spins webs of intrigue for Mitch Malone's next crime-solving adventure.